About Pippa

GH00865542

Pippa Franks grew up in Whitby, a pretty s〉 Yorkshire. It's famous for its connections wi〈 ⸗ptain Cook and Bram Stoker's Dracula, not to mention the best fish and chips! She now lives in Warwickshire with her husband and their rescue dog, Bailey. He can be seen on the front cover of Pippa's debut novel, 'The OMG Test.' Pippa is proud to support Dogs Trust. A percentage of author royalties from the sale of that book will be donated.

Pippa is delighted to bring to you her second novel and hope you enjoy reading it as much as she enjoyed writing it!

Pippa would love to hear from readers, through any of the following contacts:
http://pippafranks.blogspot.co.uk
Email: pippa.franks@hotmail.co.uk
Twitter: @PippaCheryl
Facebook: Pippa Franks Writer

To

My 2nd Book

Audrey
Love
Cheryl

The Seventh Day of May

By

Pippa Franks

My mum's nickname was 'pip' and her maiden name was franks. Hence:- pippa franks!

iii

First print: 2015

ISBN-13: 978-1508849261

ISBN-10: 1508849269

Acknowledgements

I'd like to thank the following people from the bottom of my heart:

Every single person who has supported me in publishing my debut novel, 'The OMG Test.' Whether you've bought the book, reviewed it, shared posts, retweeted links, featured me on your blogs, or sent words of encouragement, I cannot thank you enough. I love you all!

Joanne Clancy for being a constant support and fab friend. Although you're busy with your own writing, Joanne, you never fail to do everything you can to help me. You're amazing.

Cindy Davis, my wonderful editor. Thank you for loving the book. See you soon for book three!

Paul Beeley of 'Create Imaginations,' for working so hard on the covers. Nothing is too much trouble and you work so quickly too. I'm looking forward to working on the next book cover with you.

My gorgeous three bridesmaids:
My sister Karen Peacock
My daughter Gemma Louise Barlow
My step-daughter Anna Mae Henderson
Thank you all for your love and support. I don't know what I'd do without you and love you to bits. Family is everything…and I have the best!

Last but by no means least, my wonderful husband, Dean. I love you more each day. Thank you for believing in me and supporting me the way you do. It means everything to me. I'm so lucky to have you.

A massive thank you to everyone who buys this book. I hope you enjoy it. Writing stories for people to enjoy is all I've ever wanted to do.

There's no stopping me now. Book three will be out by the end of the year. Thank you all so much for your support.
Love Pippa x

Dedication

Karen

My beautiful sister and best friend.

There is a Pot of Gold at the End of the Rainbow
When the soul learns all lessons and acquires full control over the seven virtues, the consciousness does not need to incarnate in the physical world anymore, becoming completely free from the chains of the physical existence. The pot of gold symbolizes the golden spirit that emerges from the experience through the seven colours of the rainbow.

Love you always

Peril
xxxx

Chapter One

'Oh, for God's sake! You're mega stressing me, Ellie. What do you think you're doing?' Jenna Croft tapped the light switch four times, as she stood in the doorway to the living room. It wasn't indecision whether to have lights on or off that compelled Jenna to do this. Rather, the cold hard plastic underneath her fingertips was a comfort.

Keep calm, Jenna. Deep breaths.

She surveyed the scene before her. Her best friend and lodger was in the process of heaving the settee to the other side of the room. It was, as far as Jenna could see, the last item of furniture to be moved — to the wrong place.

'Hi, Jenna, don't worry, I'm nearly finished.' Ellie beamed. 'You'll be able to sit down in a few minutes. Good day at work?'

'I've been up to my eyes in shit all day, the last thing I need is to come home to the proverbial shit here. What the hell's going on?'

1

'There's no need to be like that. Calm down, darling. Getting worked up isn't good for you.'

'Calm down? Ellie, you're seriously doing my head in.' Jenna clasped a hand to her forehead.

'You know, Jenna, your yin and yang is out of balance at the moment. But not to worry, we'll soon have it restored. That's why I'm doing feng shui in here, the qi flow isn't right.'

'Come again? What the hell's qi flow when it's at home? My home, to be precise.'

Don't mess with this house please, Ellie. Anything but the house.

Ellie cast her eyes around the room. 'It's a flow of energy, and if it doesn't flow correctly your life will be unbalanced.'

'If you ask me, it's you who's unbalanced, Ellie.'

'It feels much better in here now, Jenna. Each corner of the room represents an area of your life. The energy couldn't flow properly the way you had the room arranged. It was affecting my energy too you know.'

'Oh, really? Sorry, how inconsiderate of me. What on earth was I thinking? Get it all moved back. Now.' A wave of panic surged through Jenna's body. The chaos in the room echoed that in her mind. Her hand strayed back to the light switch, and she tapped it four more times.

'But, Jenna —'

'I want to be able to watch TV properly, not have to try and guess what's happening behind my back. If I can't do that by the time I've had a bath, the energy will definitely be flowing around the room. It won't be called qi though. It'll be called plate or cup and flowing in your direction.'

Ellie shook her head. 'If you don't mind me saying so, you've been on a much shorter fuse lately. I blame that job of yours. Use some of my marjoram oil in the bath. It's good for tension and stress.'

2

'The job's fine,' said Jenna. 'But you're right, I have been stressed lately. For about the past three months actually, since you moved in. Strange that, isn't it?'

'Sorry, Jenna, I'll find somewhere else soon,' said Ellie. 'But in the meantime, I'm only trying to help.'

'I know, but I like everything to be in its normal place. You don't have to move out though, Ellie. Take your time.'

I hope 'time' passes quickly!

Jenna poured a liberal amount of scented oil under the tap, and sank into the bubbles. She scrubbed her entire body until it was covered in broken skin and abrasions. It hurt like hell but was deserved. Being angry with herself had been second nature for years. A big sigh escaped from her with a whoosh.

Was she being too hard on Ellie? After going through such a tough time, she needed support, not Jenna laying into her. The trouble was, Ellie was doing her head in with all this self-help mumbo jumbo.

To be fair, Ellie had always shown an interest in the magical and mystical. Jenna just hadn't realised how much before. She zoned out when Ellie went into great detail about her latest whim. It was never long before something else came along to grab her interest.

Ellie moved in with Jenna when her marriage of two years broke down. It came as a huge shock when her husband had announced over his dinner of sausage and mash that he loved her, but was no longer *in* love with her. What amazed Jenna upon hearing this, was the fact that he'd eaten his

3

sausages with apparent enjoyment first. And even asked if there was any more. How callous was that? Especially given the fact that being a vegetarian, Ellie found it difficult to manhandle sausages, never mind cook them. They continued to live under the same roof for a further two months, until Ellie could no longer take the strain. She'd found the 'bad karma' intolerable.

Jenna thought he had a cheek not moving out, but he'd been in no rush to leave.

In hindsight, Jenna had rushed too quickly saying Ellie could move in. But how could she not have offered? Ellie had been there for her and now it was Jenna's turn to help. Anyway, she'd been struggling with the bills and mortgage, and wrongly thought the arrangement would be of benefit to them both.

Ellie had given up her job in a mind, body and spirit centre to live with Jenna, as she lived twenty miles away, and understandably wanted to make a fresh start.

The fresh start included Ellie finding a job, finding herself and finding her soulmate, but not necessarily in that order. In Jenna's opinion Ellie was so far lost that she would need a map and search party to find herself. It was possible, no probable, that Jenna had just assumed Ellie intended to get a job. It hadn't been said in words.

Ellie had signed on at the local job centre just after moving in, and was put on jobseeker's allowance. It hadn't been a good start when the first interview they wanted to send her to was in a butcher's shop. She'd refused point-blank to go. "The thought of being surrounded by all those dead carcasses swinging about above my head, staring at me accusingly. It goes against my human rights, Jenna." Even Jenna acknowledged that Ellie had a fair point. The next interview had been with an estate agent. Apparently Ellie had got confrontational about their stance on affordable housing, which was supposedly government legislation. She'd then gone on to explain her issues with tenants' rights, which had been the final nail in that particular coffin.

The most recent interview had been for a receptionist job in a doctor's surgery. Ellie had deemed it necessary to inform them that she could improve their reputation for being known to treat patients as if they were a nuisance for actually wanting to *see* a doctor. Needless to say, a job offer wasn't forthcoming.

Jenna dreaded the upcoming interview and what Ellie would come out with. It was getting to the point where Jenna couldn't bear to listen to any more on the subject of Ellie's 'principles,' and that she had to stay true to herself, whether people liked it or not. Which they obviously didn't.

She stepped gingerly from the bath, wincing as the towel rubbed against her inflamed skin. Tying the belt of her fleecy robe she tried, but failed, to ignore the crumbling plaster and peeling paint. Unfortunately they were not confined to the bathroom; the whole house seemed to be falling apart. Just like her life had been doing for the past five years.

Jenna blinked hard as tears gathered. Suddenly, the hairs on the back of her neck stood on end. The air around her felt different. Heavy. With the distinct impression someone was watching her she spun round, but nobody was there. Giving herself a mental shake she padded back downstairs, taking deep breaths before entering the room. It was time to make a determined effort to be nice to Ellie.

'You're really taking the piss, Ellie. What do you think you're doing now?' Okay, maybe 'being nice' was too optimistic a phrase. She was only human, after all.

Ellie sat crossed legged on the floor, a huge sheet of cardboard in front of her. She was in the process of drawing a picture, while consulting a book.

Ellie glanced up. 'I'm putting together a profile of my ideal man, my soul-mate. Look, what do you think?'

'My God, Ellie, if you want someone off the scale in ugliness, he's your man.' A grotesque face stared up at her; she shuddered.

'I'm learning how to read faces, so I'll be able to put together a picture of the kind of person I'm looking for. For instance, I've drawn the eyes wide apart, which means these people are easygoing, which is a must for me.' She threw Jenna a sideways glance.

'You can't seriously think you can create your ideal man from something a book says. That's ridiculous even by your standards, Ellie.'

'It's interesting. I need someone with cheekbones that aren't too high. That indicates intolerance.'

'I'm worried you're on the rebound, and about to jump into something with somebody unsuitable.'

'I'm preparing myself now, to avoid that happening. Listen to this: Somebody who is a great listener generally would have long ears. The same can be said for lips. If you have long lips you tend to be friendly, and can talk to anyone. Mind you, medium lips aren't bad. They can communicate well. I'll put a question mark next to them for now.'

'I'm going to bed. Sort this room out.' Jenna moved towards the door. 'You know I love you but I hate all this upheaval. I want it back to how it was by morning. Goodnight.'

Approaching the light switch, Jenna tried to hold her hand back. But it was no use. As she ran her hands over it four times, it became clear her OCD was getting out of control again. In fact, it had been worse than ever since Ellie moved in. Something had to change, but what?

She couldn't kick her out. Ellie had been a good friend over the years and being a bit more tolerant was a small price to pay.

She needs someone to whisk her off her feet…and out of this house. So…I need to find a man with wide-set eyes, cheekbones that are not too high, long ears and medium to long lips. Nothing too specific then. Oh, bugger! Frankenstein lookalike, where oh where can I find you?

Chapter Two

Jenna trudged down the path of the residential care home where she worked relieved the shift was finally over. Jenna understood why a lot of people could only do this work for so long. It was rewarding, but also demanding. Many of the clients took out their frustrations on her. Being dependant on someone to assist in all your basic needs, which many of the clients did, was no fun for anybody. It was easy to understand why they vented their anger at Jenna and the other staff. For a moment she thought of what she should have been doing with her life, but dismissed it from her mind. There was nothing to be gained by dwelling on the past any more than absolutely necessary.

As she approached home, taking care to walk in a straight line over the cracks in the pavement, her elderly neighbour, Mabel, waved from the window. Jenna decided to pop in to see her as she often did when passing.

'Come in, dear. Sit down.' Mabel's normally sad eyes lit up when Jenna walked into the room. 'You look a bit peaky. Take the weight off your feet. You work far too many hours.'

'I have to do as many extra shifts as I can. The trouble is, on my wage I'll never be able to keep on top of all the jobs that need doing in the house.' Jenna thought of the kitchen drawer stuffed with unpaid bills and closed her eyes in an attempt to eliminate this picture from her mind. 'I'll make us a cup of tea, shall I? How are you feeling? Is your new medication helping with the pain?'

Mabel suffered from arthritis. In the two years since she'd moved into the sheltered accommodation next door, they'd become close.

'Yes, I'm fine. I'll make the tea.' Mabel hobbled to the kitchen, with Jenna hot on her heels. 'Is your lodger still driving you mad?'

'Yes.' Jenna nodded. 'But I feel guilty for saying that. I don't know what to do, Mabel.'

'She's a nice girl. It's good of her to come with you to visit me sometimes. You two girls are such opposites, yet you've been friends for a long time, haven't you?'

'We've known each other for over twelve years, since secondary school,' said Jenna. 'Ellie's more than just a friend, she's like family. Especially over the past five years.'

'You mean since you lost your parents?'

'Yes. She saw me through it, listened if I needed to talk, even in the middle of the night. Then there was all the practical stuff to sort out. I was in no fit state to deal with it all.' Jenna wiped her eyes. 'I love her to bits. She's been like a sister to me.'

'Even sisters have disagreements, dear. You need to tell her how bad things are with the house and your finances…and your other problem.'

Jenna's gaze dropped to the floor. 'Other problem?'

Mabel took Jenna's hand. 'Your hands are red raw. They look like they've been scrubbed with bleach.'

'Oh, I was cleaning and didn't have any rubber gloves.' Jenna snatched her hand away.

Mabel dropped the subject, much to Jenna's relief. Her 'secret' obviously wasn't as secret as she'd thought. Although Ellie knew about her OCD to a point, she didn't know the extent of it. Jenna carried the tray of tea into the sitting room setting it down on the table by the window, where Mabel liked to sit and watch the world go by.

'Talking of cleaning, can you just give the room a quick polish please, Jenna? Would you mind? It gets so dusty in here.'

Mabel was house-proud, even though visitors mainly consisted of home care-workers who popped in twice a day to check on her.

She and her husband had been unable to have children. No medical reason was found. Mabel was philosophical, but Jenna thought how lonely life must be since her husband died. She often wondered why Mabel moved the few miles from where she'd lived for most of her life, leaving behind everything familiar. But maybe that was the reason: familiar was too hard to cope with. All the reminders of what was no longer there. Jenna had tried to broach the subject, but it was clearly not a topic Mabel wished to elaborate on. It was probably too painful and Jenna could sympathise with that.

Jenna held the can of polish between her knees while moving ornaments along the mantelpiece.

'It's a long time since I've had a bit of sparkle between *my* legs.' Mabel chuckled.

'You're so naughty.' Jenna turned and grinned. 'I bet you were a right one, when you were young.'

'I had my moments. I only had eyes for my Bert though, from the minute I met him.'

'How long were you married?'

'Fifty years. We'd just celebrated our Golden Wedding anniversary before he died. At least he lived to see that.' Mabel's eyes misted over. 'How's your young man, Jenna?'

'He's fine. We're going to his grandparents' golden wedding party tonight as it happens.' Jenna sighed. 'I don't mean to sound unkind, but Jake's mother can be a bit of a nightmare.'

The nightmare had lasted two years so far, and the thought of an evening in her company filled Jenna with dread.

'Oh dear,' said Mabel. 'I was lucky. My Bert's family was lovely.'

'His mother's a pain. Her name suits her, it's fitting.'

'What's she called?'

'Officially, Mona. Unofficially, as in by me 'The Mona.' Every time she opens her mouth, an urge to clamp it shut with tape overwhelms me. I know it sounds awful, but she never stops whining.'

Mabel chortled. 'You've got your work cut out then. If you feel like that now, it can only get worse.'

'Thanks for that, Mabel. On that cheery note I'd better get moving. I'll see you soon. Be good.'

'I'll try. Enjoy the party.' Mabel laughed. 'See you soon, dear.'

As Jenna went out onto the street, she turned to wave to Mabel. For a split second the sadness in her face and eyes was as visible as if it was illuminated by a neon sign. Mabel quickly changed her expression into a cheery smile. Jenna wished there was something she could say or do to take the sadness away. But there was nothing. Other than be there.

'What do you think?' Ellie indicated some crystals tied with ribbon, hanging from the curtain pole. 'Aren't they pretty?'

'Yeah, beautiful,' said Jenna. Out of the corner of her eye she saw what looked like a face staring at her from one of the crystals. She blinked and looked again but of course nothing was there. A good night's sleep was what she needed. One without nightmares preferably. 'It's the party tonight, Ellie. I'd better get ready, I suppose.'

'Oh, yes. Party time with Jake's mum.' Ellie grimaced.

'She's not that bad.' Jenna shook her head. 'Well, okay she is, actually.'

'Don't let her spoil your evening,' said Ellie. 'I'm going out later, too. There's a spiritual event on. I'm meeting a girl I used to work with.'

'It'll do you good to get out,' said Jenna. 'You will remember to turn everything off before you leave, won't you?'

'Yes,' said Ellie. 'Relax, there's nothing to worry about.'

I'm only twenty-six and my life has turned into nothing but worry. I can't cry though. If I do I'll never stop!

The moment she and Jake entered the social club function room, something hit Jenna with the force of a sledgehammer. The Mona was clearly on the warpath, and it was leading her in their direction.

'The caterers should be sacked! Ladders are required to get to the filling in the vol-a- vents, and you'll need a magnifying glass to see the cheese on the cocktail sticks.'

12

Jake placed a placating arm around Mona's shoulder. 'I'm sure it's fine, Mum. Everybody seems to be having a good time.'

'And the band! Call themselves musicians! I've never heard such a din, it's bringing on one of my migraines.' Mona rubbed her forehead with as much drama as a Shakespearean play.

Someone shoot me now!

Jake headed for the bar and Jenna went to find a table. Her heart sank as Mona pulled out a chair next to her.

'The decorations are lovely.' Jenna admired the red balloons and streamers all around the room. 'You've been busy, Mona.'

'Yes, well, I could've done with some help.' Mona sniffed. 'But neither you nor Jake offered.'

'We've been busy at work.' Jenna sighed. 'I did a fourteen- hour shift yesterday and was back early this morning to do another ten hours. Jake's putting in a lot of hours at the moment too, isn't he?'

'Yes.' Mona's eyes narrowed as she looked at Jenna. 'If he wants to be a partner in the firm one day, he has no choice but to put in the hours now. He's got ambition, my boy does.'

Nothing she could say or do would ever be good enough for Mona, despite trying so hard to win her over, only too aware of the importance of family. But it was abundantly clear she'd never be good enough for Mona's precious only son. Since Jake's dad died when Jake was young, Mona had clung to Jake for support and companionship. This was understandable to a certain extent, but as far as Jenna was concerned it wasn't healthy. She should've made more of an effort to get involved with people her own age, instead of holding Jake back and interfering in his life. But he never challenged Mona. Hating confrontation, it was obviously easier to go along with everything she said, much to Jenna's frustration.

The only time Jake had shown any anger towards his mother was when he and Jenna first met, and Jake had told her about a previous relationship he'd been in. It lasted four years, until the girl, Amber, ended it. She was going to be a nanny in Italy. Apparently she really loved Jake, but couldn't see it working, mainly because Mona didn't like her. Jenna clearly remembered the look of pain in his eyes as he spoke about Amber. Jenna wondered how often she crossed his mind and whether he regretted letting her go so easily. What Jake didn't know was how often Mona mentioned Amber to Jenna, as if they'd been the best of friends. The conversations were a deliberate attempt to make Jenna feel second best, and it had worked. She felt a stab of jealousy each time Amber was mentioned, yet she also felt sympathy towards her. How could she not? The thought of escaping to another country to get as far from Mona as possible was more than appealing. She loved him, but the relationship felt comfortable and safe. Was that enough? Especially when a force of evil was busy plotting to undermine her at every opportunity. She couldn't imagine a life with The Mona featuring in it so prominently. A sudden shiver ran through her.

As Jake placed the drinks on the table his hands shook. Jenna glanced up and saw beads of sweat gathering on his forehead. 'Are you okay, Jake?'

'I'm fine,' said Jake, not very convincingly.

'My boy's just tired, aren't you, Jakey? And no wonder!' Mona threw an accusing look in Jenna's direction. 'All that DIY he's been doing at your house, after a hard day at work.'

'Jenna didn't ask me to, Mum. I'm doing it because I want to.' Jake gave Jenna an apologetic look before downing his pint in record time. Jenna's jaw dropped. Something was bothering him, but what?

'Can I have your attention please?' the lead singer of the band suddenly boomed into the microphone, and then waited until the room fell silent before continuing. 'Jake has something he would like to say. Come up here, Jake.'

Jake made his way slowly to the stage. So this was why he'd not seemed himself. Jenna knew how difficult it would be for Jake to stand in front of a roomful of people and make a speech. Why hadn't he mentioned doing this for his grandparents?

'Erm,' Jake mumbled into the microphone as he turned his gaze towards Jenna. 'I love you, Jenna.' He cleared his throat.

What's he doing? I don't understand!

'So, would you do me the honour of becoming my wife?'

Jenna gaped at him. Everything blurred in front of her — the stage, his face and the band who she saw hitting their palms together in a clapping motion. All she could hear though was the blood pounding in her ears, and the gasp of 'No! Jakey no!' coming from her left where Mona sat. Everything seemed to be happening in slow motion.

The fog in her brain cleared enough for her to do as the singer asked, and as she stumbled towards the stage and Jake, a thought crossed through her mind.

I wouldn't have to sell the house! That's not a good enough reason to marry him though. I do love him…but do I love him enough? Yes! No! I don't know!

It was like looking in on somebody else's life as Jake slid a ring onto her finger. A huge cheer echoed around the room. Had she actually said yes? If so had she hadn't been aware of it. But one look at Jake's face wreathed in smiles gave her the answer.

Jake led her down from the stage and towards his grandparents, who were beckoning. Her clothes felt damp against her body as she was embraced by Jake's grandmother.

'I'm so happy for you both,' she said. 'This is the best gift we could have wished for, isn't it, Stan?'

'It certainly is.' Jake's grandfather nodded. 'I hope your marriage will be as happy as ours. We've never had a cross word, have we, Jean?'

'No, we haven't.'

Jenna studied both their faces. They gave no indication as to what they were really thinking. Maybe they were speaking the truth, but to Jenna this wasn't a good sign. Fifty years of marriage and not a cross word? If this was the case surely resentments had been brewing under the surface. Had they spent their life together walking on eggshells? She didn't see how it was possible to live with someone all that time and agree on absolutely everything. Before she had time to consider this further, Mona stalked up to them.

'Well...this has come as a shock, Jakey!' Her eyes glinted and mouth tightened. 'So, when's the big day? I expect you'll have a long engagement?'

This was clearly wishful thinking on Mona's part, but for once Jenna agreed with her.

'Obviously we haven't had time to discuss it yet, Mum,' said Jake. 'But I don't see the point in waiting too long.'

Mona swayed to the side, causing Jenna to stumble. 'Jakey, I don't feel well. Can you take me home please?'

Say no, Jake. It's obvious she's putting it on.

Jake's brow furrowed. 'Of course. I should've driven but it's better to be safe than sorry around alcohol. We'll get a taxi and drop you off on the way, Jenna. I'll see you back at your house once Mum's settled.'

16

He's so weak! That's not a nice thing to think about your future husband, Jenna. Maybe not — but it's true! Isn't it? Oh, I don't know. I wish I could switch my brain off sometimes.

Suddenly Jenna wanted to be alone. She needed space to think. It felt as though everything was closing in on her.

'Stay with your mum, Jake. I'll see you tomorrow, I'm exhausted. It must be all the excitement. Anyway, I need to tell Ellie the good news.'

'If you're sure?'

Yes, Jake. That's the only thing I am sure about.

'I'm sure.'

'Okay, I'll see you tomorrow night. We can discuss the wedding then.' He smiled. 'I have an early start in the morning, so I'd best go get some sleep.'

Although he said it as if an early start was unusual, the truth was that Jake was in the office at the crack of dawn most days. He was a solicitor in a family firm and had set his sights on becoming a partner in the business. This meant proving himself by often doing a sixteen hour day. Just lately he'd started going in over the weekends too.

With Jenna herself working long hours, quality time between them was becoming more and more infrequent. They were either working or exhausted. Still, Jenna had a fleeting sense of doom: neither of them could make more effort this evening, when they'd been engaged for all of an hour, what did that say about their future together?

Jenna was relieved to find a note from Ellie to say she'd gone to bed. Her head felt fuzzy, and the large glass of wine she

17

poured would only succeed in making it fuzzier, but continued anyway. One of her neighbours made it and kept Jenna well-stocked. Anything named Elderflower should be innocent enough, yet Jenna knew to her cost how misleading this could be.

Kicking off her shoes she curled up on the sofa, taking a large gulp of wine. Thank goodness Ellie had moved the furniture back into place. But for how long? She held out her arm, watching the diamond in her ring sparkle. It was small and dainty, so why then did it feel as if she had the weight of a rock on her finger?

'Congratulations,' said a nearby voice.

'Thanks.' Jenna sighed, and then froze. She must be hearing things. It must be the wine.

'You're making a mistake,' came the voice again, this time louder.

Jenna opened her mouth to shout for Ellie, but the words wouldn't come. She curled into a tight ball, too paralysed by fear to make a run for it.

'Don't be frightened, I'm not here to hurt you.'

'Who are you? What do you want?' Jenna swallowed. Her eyes widened as a figure of a girl around the same age appeared slowly before her and promptly fell in a heap onto the floor. To all intents and purposes there was nothing unusual about her appearance — except the faint glow around her. Despite Jenna's shock she couldn't help but notice that the girl was stunning. A thick curtain of marmite-coloured hair with curls that bobbed and bounced around with every movement framed her face perfectly. The colour was in deep contrast to the paleness of her smooth skin. But the eyes that had Jenna mesmerised. Was she hallucinating? They reminded her of the Mediterranean Sea. Jenna remembered being enthralled by the vivid colours — shades of blue and green that seemed to change colour the more you looked at them. Her one and only holiday abroad, celebrating her twenty-first birthday and an exciting future ahead of her. Was it really five years since that holiday? If only she'd had inkling then of what was to follow just a few weeks later, she could've stopped it from happening. But she hadn't had any warning that her life was about to be torn apart.

Jenna came to with a start as the girl got clumsily to her feet.

'Oops, sorry about that, I'm not very good at this! My name's Alesha,' she said. 'I don't know whether I'm coming or going at the moment. A bit of both I think.'

'What?'

'Well, the energy in here's changed a lot since your lodger moved in.'

'Energy?' Jenna whispered.

'Yeah, it affects how easy it is for me to show myself. It's all to do with electro-magnetic fields. But never mind that. I'm here to help you, I need your help too.'

'You do? Why me?' Jenna was certain it was a dream. She wanted to wake up, but couldn't. The girl was still there.

'All in good time. Let's get to know each other first.' The girl pointed to Jenna's dress. 'I like your dress, it suits you. It matches the colour of your eyes.'

I hope she means the brown and not the yellow!

'Do you think so?' said Jenna. 'I wasn't sure if it made my bum look big.'

'It does a bit.'

Cheeky cow! She's not supposed to agree! Hang on, Jenna, she's not real.

'It's supposed to. That's the style, to create extra curves,' the girl, Alesha, continued with a grin. 'I used to wear them all the time. When I was alive, obviously.'

'Alliive?'

'Yeah, there's no point dressing up now. Nobody can see me except you.'

This cannot be happening! I've fantasised about talking to a ghost...but the conversations were never about the size of my arse!

Chapter Three

With reluctant necessity Jenna's eyes opened to sweep the room checking everything looked normal. Whatever normal was.

She rubbed the back of her neck. Although comfortable to sit on, the sofa wasn't the best place to sleep.

The events of the previous night came to mind, and she fiddled with the ring that now adorned the third finger of her left hand. The engagement didn't seem real. Neither did the ridiculous notion of holding a conversation, albeit short, with the apparition of a girl called Alesha. It must've been a dream, yet she'd only been in the house five minutes and realistically not had time to fall asleep.

So that thought is less realistic than seeing a ghost is it, Jenna? It's crazy, but it seemed so real!

Whatever it was that had happened, it had been cut short by Ellie going into the bathroom upstairs. As soon as the floorboards had creaked the girl had disappeared. Or Jenna had woken from her dream.

One thing was certain: there were more important things to worry about, such as the height of the pile of bills which would rival Mount Everest. And the prospect of having Mona Mansfield as her mother-in-law.

She hadn't seen that one coming. Although she and Jake got together at least four times a week and had been together for two years, the idea of them being together for the rest of their lives hadn't really entered her head. But then, Jenna found it almost impossible to see beyond next week, never mind forever.

She was torn from her thoughts when Ellie entered the room.

'Hi, Jenna, you're up early. It's your day off, isn't it? Why are you still wearing that dress?'

'I fell asleep down here. I've got something to tell you, but let me get coffee first.'

As Jenna placed the coffeepot onto the table Ellie shrieked. 'OH MY GOD! Is that an engagement ring?'

'Yeah.' Jenna held out her hand to show Ellie. 'Do you like it?'

'It's lovely, but you're not exactly jumping for joy.' Ellie stood, hands on hips and her forehead creased. 'It's more a shuffle of sorrow. I've seen happier expressions in soap opera weddings. And that's saying something.'

Jenna studied the ring and sighed. 'The truth is I was caught off guard. I can't even remember saying yes, and there was a roomful of people watching me, Ellie. It was mega cringey!'

'Your boyfriend declares how much he loves you and it was mega cringey?' Ellie leaned forward. 'If you're not sure, Jenna, you can't possibly go through with it.'

'But he's a good man. I know he'll look after me, I feel safe with him,' said Jenna. 'And I'll spend the rest of my life making him happy in return.'

'I felt safe with Adam, and look where that got me.' Ellie shrugged. 'But he's done me a favour. Yes, it hurt, but it wasn't meant to be. Anyway, there's more to life than 'safe.''

Is there? That's all I want from life. To feel safe. Yes, but that wasn't always the case, was it?

Jenna wondered whether Ellie actually believed what she was saying. She and Adam had been childhood sweethearts and although they'd married young, nobody had predicted them splitting up. Maybe Adam was having a mid-life crisis...about twenty years too early.

'Do you think you'll get back together?' Jenna asked.

'No! I wouldn't want to now, even if he did. I don't want to be with somebody who has doubts about me.' Ellie threw Jenna a pointed look. 'And I wouldn't do the same to anybody else, I'd be honest and end it.'

Jenna was saved from any further comment when her phone rang and Mona's name flashed up in warning. She hesitated before answering. 'Hi, Mona, I hope you've err, recovered?'

'Yes, I'm fine now. Jake mentioned it's your day off. Let's meet up for coffee, say about two, at that 'Nostros' place in town. They do a delicious cream scone. Mind you, they skimp a bit on the jam.'

'Erm, okay.' Jenna frowned. Mona had never asked to meet her before. But she could guess the reason: she wanted to stop the wedding going ahead and was about to make her feelings perfectly clear.

'See you then, don't be late.' Before Jenna could reply Mona hung up.

Ellie edged along the sofa and wrapped her arms around Jenna. 'Another reason to think carefully, Jenna. Do you really want the rest of your life to be dictated by The Mona?'

Hmm…let me think for a second. No!

Ellie continued. 'You're worth so much more than that.'

'Am I?'

'Yes! And let's be honest here, you've never had a real spark in your eyes when you talk about Jake. There's something missing and you know it.'

Jenna buried her face in the comforting folds of Ellie's cardigan. 'There *is* something missing, you're right. The part of me that died along with my parents.'

Jenna walked the short route into the centre of York, pulling up the collar of her coat and thrusting her hands deeper into the pockets. Despite the onset of spring there was a chill in the air. But this wasn't the only reason she shivered. This used to be her favourite season. The first sight of daffodils signalled the promise of warmer days and lighter nights ahead, and new adventures waiting to be experienced. But that was then and this was now. Five years on she could still only see dark days ahead, and even darker nights filled with nightmares. Was this how the rest of her life was meant to be? She longed not just to be able to see the daffodils, but to *feel* them again too.

'Over here, Jenna.' Mona waved a bony arm in the air.

Jenna edged her way through the tightly packed tables and pulled out a chair opposite Mona. She reminded Jenna of Basil Fawlty, but with a bit more hair and slightly less moustache.

She inhaled the aroma of the freshly brewed coffee, and eyed with satisfaction the plates of scones piled high with jam and whipped cream. The conversation was about to get heavy, but she was starving and may as well have some enjoyment first.

'I've ordered already,' said Mona, stating the obvious. 'I'll play Mother and pour the coffee.'

The emphasis Mona placed on the word mother wasn't lost on Jenna. Feeling a prickle of unease she glanced at Mona. Something wasn't right. The woman was smiling.

'Erm, this is nice,' said Jenna, cutting through the scone. The cream oozed out and although tempted to scoop it up with her finger, she refrained. At a guess this course of action wouldn't be deemed appropriate by any future daughter-in-law of Mona's.

'It is.' Mona agreed. 'Now, tell me, how does it feel to be engaged to my Jakey?'

'Well…I haven't got used to the idea yet.'

Here it comes. She's about to tell me not to bother trying.

'No, I don't suppose you can believe your luck, dear.' Mona took a delicate sip of coffee. 'I've brought you here to discuss the wedding. I'm going to help you plan it.'

What? And did she just call me dear?

'It's a bit soon —'

'Nonsense, dear. There's so much to organise.' Mona reached to the floor and pulled a notebook and pen out of her bag. 'I've started a list, but I've not got very far yet.'

25

Jenna looked at the 'list' in horror. There was enough paper to cover her bedroom walls. Twice over.

'Mona,' began Jenna, 'I don't think —'

'I've got a few things jotted down:

Venue

Caterers

Flowers

Photographer

Table decorations

Cake

Rings

Favours

Invitations

Transport

As I say, I've not got very far, but between us it won't be a problem.'

The expression on Mona's face had Jenna flummoxed. She'd never seen her look so animated. Or happy.

Trying to keep up with her flow of excited chatter, Jenna became aware of movement directly behind Mona's chair. She swallowed and blinked hard as Alesha materialised, peering over Mona's shoulder at the list. She grimaced then looked across at Jenna and waved, mouthing 'Hi.'

The hand halfway to her mouth, holding the scone began to tremble and the cream landed in her eye with a splat.

Jenna gasped and fumbled for a napkin as Alesha let out a roar of laughter.

Mona still scribbled in the notebook, clearly oblivious to what was going on.

Everybody in the room remained engrossed in conversation. Nobody paid any attention to the table where Jenna sat, head in hands, wondering if she was having some kind of breakdown. Alesha must surely be a figment of her imagination — a clear indication that the men in white coats would be escorting her away sometime soon. And she didn't mean the dinner jacket variety.

Peeping through her fingers with reluctance, Jenna realised two things: Alesha was still there, and even worse than that, Mona was in the process of licking a tissue and reaching over the table with the clear intent of wiping Jenna's face. Her mum used to do that when Jenna was a child, and she'd hated it. Although Jenna would give anything for her mum to be in front of her now, tissue in hand. No way was anyone else getting near her with a tissue full of saliva.

'Jenna, you're covered in cream! Here, let me see.'

A surge of bile rose in Jenna's throat. With clammy hands she lunged for her bag with the same level of urgency as a dog heading for a lamppost. She held up a packet of antibacterial wet wipes in triumphant relief. 'Thank you, but I've got these.'

Mona gave a brief nod then proceeded to take another sheet of paper from her bag. She salivated like a rabid dog then unfolded it and smoothed out the creases with the palm of her hand, before thrusting it over the table. 'I've printed this from the interweb. It took me ages to do but I think this dress will be perfect for you.'

Jenna stared at the smiling face of the model wearing the monstrosity. She must've been desperate for the money when agreeing to pose in that creation for public viewing.

So, The Mona has a vision of me getting married in fancy dress. She sees me as a snowman. But on the plus side all I'll need is a carrot nose-mould and a pipe. Voila! Outfit complete!

Alesha stuck two fingers down her throat and pulled a face. Jenna tried to ignore this, but she was learning fast that whoever or whatever Alesha was, she was intent on making her presence felt.

'What do you think?' Mona clasped her hands together.

That there's more chance of me walking down the aisle naked to the words of 'Love Stinks' by J Geils Band.

'Erm, well, it's lovely, Mona. But I think it's a bit fussy for me. Something simple but classy, maybe?'

'Yes, well, I'll keep looking.' Mona huffed. 'But I suppose anything will be an improvement on your usual attire.' She looked Jenna up and down obviously not impressed with the frayed jeans and 'Hip Hop Baby' T-shirt she was wearing.

Jenna closed her eyes and took a deep breath. 'Can I ask you something, Mona? I've had the impression you didn't like me much, and last night you didn't seem too keen on the idea of me marrying Jake. Why the sudden change of heart?'

Mona studied the table before meeting Jenna's gaze. 'It's not that I don't like you, Jenna, but I'll be honest, I wasn't convinced you were right for Jake.' She sighed. 'I know how hard it's been for you since losing your parents the way you did. My fear is that you see Jake as a security blanket, someone to look after you.'

Is that how I see him? Maybe, but I do love him…don't I?

Mona continued. 'And the engagement came as a shock. However, I've come to the conclusion that if you're his choice I must learn to accept it. I didn't sleep much last night, worrying about it all. I've grown to realise that I'm not losing a son, but gaining a daughter. And,' she tapped her nose with her forefinger, 'I have an idea. A surprise. But I won't tell you yet until I work it all out.'

Something about Mona's words bothered Jenna. She wasn't sure why, yet a sense of foreboding washed over her. What did Mona mean? Whatever the surprise was, she felt certain it wasn't going to fill her with joy. Needing air, she scraped back her chair and stood up. 'Sorry, Mona, but I have to go. I'm meeting Ellie and I lost track of the time.' Jenna hated lying but had to get away from Mona as quickly as possible. 'I'll see you soon and erm, thank you for your help with the lists and stuff.'

Mona pursed her lips then moved her mouth in what Jenna supposed to be a smile. 'Goodbye, I'll call you soon.'

Jenna made a beeline for the door. Outside she breathed in a lungful of air and steadied herself against the wall, gasping when Alesha appeared next to her. She'd almost forgotten about her, what with the unnerving exchange with Mona.

'Look, what do you want?' she snapped. 'Go away and leave me alone.'

'That's not very nice.' Alesha tutted. 'Are you always this rude?'

'You literally crash into my life, making me think I'm going crazy and expect me to be welcoming?' Jenna shot back. 'I'm having a bad day and the last thing I need is you appearing uninvited.'

'*You're* having a bad day?' said Alesha. 'Mine's not exactly brimming with glad tidings.'

Jenna was immediately contrite. Of course Alesha was having a worse day than her. She *was* dead, after all. 'Sorry.' She sighed. 'But surely you can understand that I'm a teensy bit upset and confused as to why I'm seeing and hearing you? I don't know if I'm talking to a ghost or hearing imaginary voices in my head. Do you see my problem?'

'Yes, love, I see your problem.' An elderly lady took Jenna's arm. 'Where do you live, dear? Do they know you're out on your own?'

A red-hot heat travelled through her body. Glancing round in trepidation, horror pierced through Jenna at the sight of a crowd of people gathering, all throwing sympathetic glances in her direction.

'Erm, I'm an actress. I have to learn my lines for a play.' Relief washed over her as the crowd nodded and smiled. Her relief was short-lived when they all began clapping and chanting, 'More.'

I should've brought a hat. They might have thrown me some coins.

'I have to go. Sorry.' Jenna curtsied to the crowd before sprinting in the opposite direction, Alesha by her side.

'Quite a performance.' Alesha giggled. 'Quick thinking.'

'It's all your fault,' Jenna hissed. 'Just get lost, will you?'

'I am lost,' said Alesha in a small voice. 'Only you can help me get to where I need to be, but we've a lot of work to do first.'

'What the hell are you talking about?'

'Nobody else can help me, Jenna.'

'I wish you'd tell me why you're here and what it is I'm supposed to be helping you with.' Jenna marched ahead, concentrating on walking in a straight line along the pavement cracks. 'Maybe then we can get on with it and you'll disappear,' she threw over her shoulder.

Alesha fell into step next to Jenna. 'Why are you walking like that? Is it to do with the OCD?'

Jenna halted mid-step and looked at Alesha. 'What do you know about that?'

'I know that all the weird things you do are a way to feel in control. Your life is a mess and instead of doing something about it you choose to wallow in self-pity and refuse to face facts.'

Pools of liquid welled up in Jenna's eyes and trickled down her cheeks. 'How dare you! You know nothing about me or my life.'

'I do,' Alesha whispered. 'It wasn't your fault. You have to quit blaming yourself. It was an accident pure and simple.'

Jenna staggered over to a bench and fell onto it with a bump. A sob escaped from her throat and she buried her head in her hands. Alesha sat next to her and squeezed Jenna's arm. It felt odd. Although she felt the pressure, it was more of a tingling sensation rather than a heavy grip.

Alesha continued, 'I'm sorry if it sounds harsh but patting you on the back and saying "there, there," isn't going to help. The last thing your parents want is for you to waste your life on regret. You must know that. All they've ever wanted is for you to be happy, Jenna.'

'How do you know?' Jenna wrenched her arm from Alesha. 'Don't you dare try to tell me what my parents would or wouldn't want.'

'Trust me, I do know,' said Alesha. 'As I told you to start with, I'm here to help you as much as myself.'

'How?'

'Okay, here's the deal. I died in an accident the same day your parents were killed. Obviously that's coincidence. I was run over by a car.'

'That's terrible!' Jenna gasped. 'You really are here, aren't you? I mean in a dead kind of way, obviously.'

Alesha nodded. 'The accident was my fault. I wasn't paying attention and stepped out in front of a car. The driver had no time to react.'

'Oh My God. Were you in a rush to be somewhere?'

'I spotted someone I knew on the other side of the road and without thinking ran to catch him up.' Alesha sighed. 'I have no recollection of actually being hit. The next thing I remember is looking down at my lifeless body.'

'And then what?'

'I knew in that instant I was dead. Sounds crazy, huh? I remember thinking, what a bummer. But I also felt calm. I mean it was freaky. Surreal, and at the same time kind of *okay*.'

Jenna couldn't for the life of her see how knowing you were dead would be okay. She could think of a lot of things to describe how it must feel, but okay wasn't up there as being the most obvious. She turned to Alesha. 'If you've been dead for nearly five years why are you here now? Why not sooner? I don't get it.'

'I hear what you're saying but time isn't the same when you've died. We don't think in minutes, days, months and years. Although, having said that, dates and anniversaries are still important. But the main reason I couldn't come before is because you wouldn't have accepted me then. It was too soon. And also, more to the point neither would the other people concerned.'

'What other people?'

'Look, that day five years ago tore so many lives apart. Too many people are either living with guilt and regret, or are unable to move on until everybody connected to the two accidents find inner peace and accept that life goes on.' Alesha took Jenna's hand in her own icy one. 'You're the key to it all, Jenna. The sooner you acknowledge both me and what I'm telling you, the sooner this can happen.'

'I guess I do believe in you now. I have no choice, have I?' Jenna shrugged and smiled. 'You're not about to leave me in peace anytime soon, are you?'

'Nope.' Alesha grinned. 'You're stuck with me for the foreseeable, so accept it and we can have some fun along the way. It's definitely lacking in your life — and fun hasn't been high on the agenda in my death either. At least so far.'

'You still haven't told me what it is you want.' Jenna furrowed her brow.

'Let's take it one step at a time and start with the issue of your recent engagement.'

'What about it?'

'If you marry Jake you'll be making the biggest mistake of your life. He's not right for you.'

'Yes he is! He's a good man and he loves me.'

'You didn't say you love him too.'

'Of course I do!'

'Do you? I mean really love him with a passion?'

'Life's about more than passion, Alesha. Anyway, that can't last forever in any relationship.'

Yes, but I've never felt that with Jake, even at the beginning.

'Maybe, maybe not, but strong attraction is supposed to last, surely?'

'Jake and I are fine. I know it won't always be easy, especially with his mother. But we'll get through it all together.'

In the house.

'The very essence of you was always spontaneity, Jenna. You knew what you wanted in life and weren't afraid to go and get it. It's understandable that you've changed, but Jake, nice as he may be, is too predictable for you. You may think now this is what you want but it isn't. Not deep down. I bet when he's coming he says: "Gosh, Jenna, I'm arriving!"'

'Alesha!' A bubble of laughter rose inside her. She tried to swallow it down but it erupted like a volcano. 'That's a horrible thing to say.' She gasped. 'You've got him wrong.'

'Hmm.' Alesha grinned. 'We'll see.'

As Jenna's breath returned to normal a knot of anxiety twisted in her stomach. Maybe in the past she'd wanted excitement and adventure, but her priorities had changed and she wasn't about to let a ghost girl tell her otherwise. Who did she think she was, following her about, *haunting* her and making fun of her fiancé? Well, she was having none of it. It seemed she would be sticking around and Jenna couldn't do much about that, but she wouldn't let her interfere in her relationship with Jake. That was a step too far.

'I'm marrying Jake whether you like it or not.' Jenna rose from the bench. 'It's got absolutely nothing to do with you, and if you really do intend to pester me you'd better get used to the idea. Okay?'

Alesha held up her hands. 'Hey, take a chill-pill! Don't be so uptight. Anyway, you laughed at my joke, what's the big deal?'

A familiar stab of guilt penetrated her — this time for allowing herself to be amused at Jake's expense. She was vile. Horrible. The nail of her right middle finger dug into her palm, scraping back and forth until the burning soreness came. Only then did calmness resume. It was the only way to feel better.

As she neared home, Alesha stepped out in front of Jenna, causing her to stop in her tracks.

'Please talk to me. I didn't mean to upset you.' Alesha sighed. 'Friends?'

'I may have overreacted,' conceded Jenna. 'Okay, friends.' She held up her forefinger and pointed it at Alesha. 'Hang on though. We need to have some rules. You cannot just barge in and out of my life when it suits you. I need warning first.'

'Hmm,' said Alesha. 'I get that. Here's what we'll do: If you hear me calling for you and it's alright for me to appear, then just call my name.'

Jenna nodded. 'Fine.'

'And dance an Irish jig.'

'What? You're crazy! Why would I make a fool of myself so you can appear? I didn't ask you to come in the first place.'

'It will work vice versa too. If you need me call my name and do the dance.'

'Whatever! Like I'll be sad and lonely enough to call my ghost friend for company.' Jenna scoffed. 'You'll be waiting for eternity.'

'So what? I've got eternity to spare. No rush.' Alesha grinned. 'But back to what you just said. You did ask me to come in the first place, actually.' She held up her hand when Jenna opened her mouth to speak. 'Okay, obviously you didn't ask me directly. But you called for somebody to come and here I am.'

'I didn't!'

'Subconsciously you did. And as I'm here now anyway, I've been left in charge of sorting out much more than I'd bargained for. I could've done with some back-up to be honest, but it's just the two of us. We need to get cracking.'

'On what?' Jenna rolled her eyes.

'Absolving everyone concerned of guilt over the accidents. Including yourself. To put it another way…I'm here to show you your true destiny. You can then choose to be guided into following the right path or ignore it and make your own way.'

'This is crazy. And I thought my life was bad before.'

'It can improve. Sooner rather than later.'

'How's that then? Do you know the winning lottery numbers?'

'No, but I do know how you can improve your finances.'

'How?'

'Well,' said Alesha. 'One of the main reasons for me being here is because I'm worried about my boyfriend. Or should I say ex-boyfriend. Ben is still blaming himself for my death and is determined to self-destruct.'

'Why's he blaming himself?'

'Because we'd had an argument and I left the house in a temper. It was over something silly, not important at all. He thinks I wasn't concentrating on the road for that reason.'

'That's a shame, but I don't see what it has to do with me.'

'You know I said I need your help, right?'

Jenna nodded and unlocked her door. 'What do you want me to do?'

Alesha took a deep breath. 'I want you to move him into here as a lodger. Think of the rent money. You can keep an eye on him and in the process convince him it wasn't his fault.'

Oh, is that all? And there was me thinking it was going to be something important.

Chapter Four

Jenna let out a deep breath and leaned against the door. Thank goodness Alesha hadn't followed her inside. She was not going to entertain the ridiculous notion of saving this Ben. How the hell was she supposed to do that anyway? And the very idea of having a complete stranger moving in caused her heart to bang inside her chest. It was bad enough Ellie being here. She could hear her in the kitchen and went down the hallway.

'Hi, Jenna. How did it go with Mona? Has she warned you off?' Ellie took a bottle of wine from the fridge. 'You look like you could do with a drink.'

'You're not wrong there.' Jenna reached for two glasses. 'Let's go through to the other room. Bring the bottle.'

Ellie poured two generous glasses and Jenna had a large gulp before she even sat down.

'Blimey.' Ellie grinned. 'I take it Mona was her usual charming self?'

'Actually she's in full wedding mode,' said Jenna. 'To be honest I preferred it when she was hostile. At least I knew where I was with her and knew what to expect.'

'Hmm, are you seeing Jake tonight?'

'Yeah, he's coming round later.' Jenna wasn't sure if she wanted to see him or not. Her mind was replaying Alesha's words over and over. She couldn't think straight. 'Ellie, you believe in ghosts, don't you?'

'Where'd that come from?' Ellie leaned forward in her chair.

'I'm just curious, that's all.'

'Well yes, I believe in life after death. It's fascinating. There's so much evidence to support it and that's aside from my own experiences.'

'You mean you've seen a ghost before?'

'I'm sure I've tried to tell you this in the past and you didn't want to know. But yes, a few times. The latest was a bit rude to be honest.' Ellie's brow furrowed. 'I couldn't believe what she said.'

'Really? It's obviously affected you, if you remember it so clearly.'

'I should remember…it was only last week.'

Jenna gasped. 'Last week? You mean here?'

Ellie nodded. 'Cheeky mare, she was.'

'What did she say?'

'Get a job!' Ellie banged her glass down onto the table.

Alesha! I'm starting to like her more and more!

Jenna attempted to supress the giggle fighting to explode from her. She turned it into a cough. 'What did she look like?'

'Totally gorgeous to be honest. Like a model. Not what you'd envision a spirit to look like.'

Jenna knew without a doubt it was Alesha. Maybe Ellie should know. Jenna could no longer cling to the hope that she was simply going crazy. If only it was that straightforward. Yet Alesha had promised to only appear if Jenna said it was okay. And danced an Irish jig. A whoosh of relief swept through her. There was more chance of England winning the world cup than there was of that happening. The best option was to keep quiet and hope Alesha would give up and leave her in peace.

'Why do you think ghosts appear to certain people, Ellie?'

I'm not sure I want to hear the answer to this.

'I think it's if they can't rest for whatever reason; maybe to get an important message across, or to help somebody. Maybe they need help with something.'

Yep…wish I hadn't asked.

'I always imagined ghosts to be like the ghosts you see on TV. You know, white and scary.'

'People talk of full-body apparitions, ghostly voices, orbs and shadow figures. I'm not sure what the significance with the black shadow figures is; possibly evil forces, or a residual haunting.'

'Residual?'

'Yeah. Apparently that's what a lot of so called hauntings are. It's a moment from the past that gets played over and over, like a tape recording.'

'Weird.'

'For instance: years into the future the building where X Factor is filmed could be a house. The residents may witness the spectre of Simon Cowell saying "That's possibly the worst audition I've ever seen," over and over again.'

'That really is scary.' Jenna grinned. 'So that type of haunting means the ghost isn't aware you exist?'

'Exactly! Whereas ghosts who can communicate with you are called intelligent hauntings. Not that our ghost here can be called intelligent! She should get her facts straight before throwing accusations.'

'You haven't got a job, have you?'

'Kind of. I've started my new career.' Ellie beamed.

'Really? What is it?'

'I'm writing a book,' said Ellie. 'Shall I read it to you?'

'Okay.' Jenna sat forward in her chair. 'How far have you got?'

'The first paragraph.'

Right.

Ellie opened her laptop and read: "Elizabeth flung out her hand to turn off the alarm clock, still half asleep. As her hand groped for the button she recoiled in horror."

Jenna waited for Ellie to continue then realised that was it. 'Erm…'

'What do you think, Jen?'

'Well…' Jenna paused. 'It's hard to tell just yet. But, well, I'm not sure turning off an alarm clock is the right way to start a book. Not that I'm an expert.'

'Ah, but why did she recoil in horror?'

'I dunno. Why did she?'

'I'm not sure yet.' Ellie shrugged. 'I'm working on it.'

I think the bailiffs will be a-knocking before she gets to page two.

'Good on you.' Jenna attempted an encouraging smile.

'Look, Jenna, I've been talking to Mabel. She's told me you're worried about the house.' Ellie reached over and stroked Jenna's arm. 'I'll get a job to tide us over until my writing career takes off. I know how much keeping the house means to you.'

'Thanks, Ellie. I'm really worried about it all, to be honest.' Jenna sighed. 'But at least when Jake and I are married it'll be easier. How did Mabel seem?'

'Not good. It's like she's given up on life. It's sad, but the only thing she seems interested in is what's going on in our lives.'

'I feel so sorry for her,' said Jenna. 'Oh, I think I hear Jake.'

Ellie opened her mouth to speak, but closed it again when Jake appeared in the doorway. Jenna noticed the dark circles around his eyes. He loosened his tie and flopped onto the sofa next to Jenna, kissing her cheek.

'How's my bride to be?' He winked and turned to Ellie. 'And how are you, Ellie? Any luck on the job front yet?'

Ellie's mouth tightened but she smiled. Jenna could see it was forced. 'I've started on my new career path. I'll let Jenna fill you in.' Ellie stood up and gathered her laptop and bag. 'I'll leave you two alone and go get on with it.'

As she left the room Jake turned to Jenna. 'What's she doing?'

'Writing a book.'

Jake's eyes widened. 'Is she? What kind of book?'

'Your guess is as good as mine.' Jenna shook her head. 'And hers! Do you want a drink?'

'Yes, but I've brought some decent stuff. What a day.' He unfastened his shoes and placed them neatly under the coffee table. 'So, let's have a proper look at your ring.'

Jenna held out her hand and Jake smiled. 'A perfect fit. How does it feel to be the future Mrs Mansfield?'

Hmm, Mrs Mansfield. Jenna hadn't had chance to consider their day to day life once they were married. Thoughts of what it would mean as far as keeping the house went, and being Mona's daughter-in-law had taken precedence.

'I haven't had much time to think about it,' said Jenna. 'What about you? Are you sure it's what you want?'

"Course I'm sure. I wouldn't have asked otherwise.' Jake ruffled her hair. 'I'm thirty-two now. It's time I settled down.'

Jenna wasn't sure this was the answer she'd been hoping for, but romance didn't figure on her wish list anyway. And she might be a lot of things but stupid wasn't one of them. If Jake wanted to climb the office ladder, he needed to show he was a family man. One of the requirements in his job description was to be respectable...and married. It suited his needs and it suited hers too.

'Jake, you will be moving in here after the wedding, won't you?'

'Yes, if you still want to stay here that's fine by me.' His eyes swept the room. 'We'll get it just the way we want it, back to its former glory.'

Everything was going to be fine. Jenna's heart lifted. Okay, this wasn't what she'd planned for her life, but neither was her parents getting killed on a motorway. She had to make the best of how things were now. And if that meant vowing to pick up Jake's dirty washing and ironing his shirts then so be it. Maybe now was the time to actually learn how to iron a shirt. She had a feeling it may take a while to perfect it; on that score Mona would be a hard act to follow.

Jake continued, 'I guess we should start thinking about dates soon. Mum's been asking. She's very keen on the idea you know, Jenna.'

Don't I just know it. Well I'm not dressing as a snowman. So there!

'Okay. I think next year though, Jake. We have a lot to organise. And I need to give Ellie time to sort out what she's going to do.'

Jake studied his wine glass. 'Yes, fine. But we still need to set a date. If we don't, things could drag on like this forever.'

42

Jenna nodded. 'What about Christmas next year then? You know how much I hate that time of year nowadays. It'll be cool to do it then.'

Jake gasped. 'But that's twenty months away, Jenna!'

'I know, but look how quickly time flies.' Jenna nudged his arm. 'Your mum will be in her element during the lead-up. If we do it too soon she won't have time to anticipate and plan.'

Jenna knew if anything would persuade him to wait this was it. Why she wanted to drag it out for so long wasn't clear. Maybe she just needed plenty of time to get her head round it all. And it would give her something to focus on and look forward to…wouldn't it?

'You mean you're putting it off as long as possible because you don't really want to do it!' said the unmistakeable voice of Alesha.

A rush of anger surged through her. 'Oh, leave me alone,' she spat. 'I've had just about enough of you.'

'Jenna?' Jake edged away from her, mouth agape.

Jenna's heart sank. 'Oh, sorry, Jake. I didn't mean you. It's erm, memories. I keep getting flashbacks in my mind.' That much was at least true.

Jake pulled her to him and wrapped his arms around her. She breathed in his musky scent. He smoothed the hair back from her face.

She waited for the familiar feeling of calm to wash over her at his words. This time it didn't come. With a jolt it hit her that not once had he asked her how she felt. What exactly had happened to her parents was never discussed. He knew the basics of course, but he had never delved deeper. Maybe he thought it would upset her more, yet there had been times where she had been desperate to talk. He'd changed the subject, clearly uncomfortable and unsure how to deal with the distraught and sobbing Jenna. Consequently she rarely mentioned anything relating to the subject; instead she covered up how she felt and painted on a smile.

'I'm okay.' She twisted out of his grasp. 'But maybe I'll never get over what happened, Jake. The memories of that day are always there.'

Jake winced. 'I know, but you must try to move on, Jenna. It's what they would want you to do, isn't it?'

'Don't you think I'm trying to move on?' She put her hands to her head. 'Do you think I enjoy feeling like this? I wish I could go back to being the person I used to be. But I can't.'

If I did, Jake wouldn't recognise me. Just as I don't recognise myself now.

'Maybe it would help for you to erm, talk to somebody.' Jake cleared his throat. 'A counsellor.'

'You know, you're right. Talking to somebody would help,' said Jenna. 'But the man I'm due to marry and spend the rest of my life with was more the one I had in mind. Stupid, eh?' Jenna wiped her eyes with the cuff of her jumper. 'I'm tired, Jake. I'm going to bed.'

'Jenna —'

'Night, Jake. Let yourself out.'

Jenna undressed. As she was about to climb into bed, he walked into the bedroom. His jaw dropped when he looked at her. He put his hand to his mouth, his pure horror only too evident.

'Oh, my God. What's happened to you? Your skin looks as if it's been dipped in acid. You need to see a doctor.' Jake gasped. 'You must be in agony.'

So I should be.

Jenna covered her torso with her arms. 'Oh, I've had an allergic reaction to some bath products,' she lied. 'It looks worse than it is.'

Jake pulled back the covers and ushered Jenna into bed. 'I won't stay over, you need to get some rest.' He pulled the duvet around her chin. 'I'll call you in the morning.'

As she drifted into a restless sleep a thought preyed on Jenna's mind: Why had Jake accepted her explanation so eagerly? The marks and broken skin on her body looked nothing like an allergic reaction to anything. But it was probably easier to believe what she said than to face the truth: that his future wife was losing the plot. Until recently she'd have been relieved to have fobbed him off with a flimsy excuse. So, why tonight was she unhappy that he hadn't forced the truth out of her? Was it too much to ask, to be treated as a person with feelings, and for him to be prepared to listen? Unless he really was that naïve to think she was being honest.

Blimey, don't say Jake's going to be the only man on the planet to believe every word his wife says. Does such a man exist? Surely they couldn't be that stupid. Especially not a solicitor who's trained to be sceptical about what clients tell him. He's always complaining that people talk a load of bollocks…but he probably wasn't expecting the worst offender to be his future wife.

Chapter Five

Jenna reached out her arm and groped in the vague direction of the alarm clock. She jabbed at the button to shut out the piercing whistle, blinking hard to gain focus.

As usual, her sleep had been disturbed by the sounds and visions she desperately wished could be erased from her mind. As if that wasn't enough to contend with, added to the mix now was the presence of Alesha and the doubts regarding Jake.

It was all Alesha's fault. Jenna wouldn't have confronted him last night had it not been for her interference. Who did she think she was to appear out of the blue, passing judgement on their forthcoming wedding? But deep down Jenna was forced to acknowledge she had a point. It had been easy to plod along, seeing him a few times a week and putting on a front. Spending the rest of their lives together though was a whole different ballgame.

For the first time since their engagement, Jenna imagined how it would be once they were married. A shudder ran the length of her body. They would continue to work long hours, often at different times to each other. Most of the free time they did have would be either spent talking about Jake's job, or trying to stay awake long enough to hold a proper conversation. And, most worrying of all, she would be living a life of pretence; there to support him but getting no support in return. Not emotional support at any rate. She'd be expected to put on a happy, smiling front, willing to fit in with him and his mother at all times. And also, to 'get over it.'

Jake wasn't a bad man, he loved her in his own way, and was kind and loyal. He was happy to do up the house for Jenna. That counted for a lot because he understood what it meant to her. Up until recently she'd have described them as being close. But that didn't necessarily mean seeing each other often. It meant knowing somebody well enough to know their fears, desires and less than perfect traits and loving them regardless. Did Jake really know her at all? And even if he didn't, she could hardly punish him for that. Not when *she* didn't even know who she was anymore.

Pulling on her uniform Jenna sighed. It was becoming harder to face the long shifts in a job she was growing to hate. Thank goodness it was just a morning shift today.

As she trudged to work, Alesha called her name. Jenna muttered that she'd talk to her later. It was the last thing she needed right now. Or ever. Although a brief truce between them had been called, that was before Alesha had announced her wish for Ben to move in. How ridiculous! Yet the house had three bedrooms, so even with Ellie there, a spare room stood empty and the extra money would be a godsend. Maybe she'd have to consider the possibility of letting out the room. Not to him, obviously, but the idea was something to think about. But not now. The very idea filled her with dread. Desperate times called for desperate measures though. Even if it meant that her life and home would feel more out of Jenna's control than ever.

Her mouth stretched open in a huge yawn. The alarm clock needed to be set earlier nowadays. It was taking longer and longer to get out of the house.

Jenna checked every plug socket, turning off ones that didn't need to be on. Then she'd go back round again to make sure. The only ones left untouched were the fridge and freezer. Getting as far as the door was becoming a major achievement, but it didn't end there. She locked the door and tried it, then unlocked it again, so that she could lock it a final time to be sure.

Pulling out a chair ready for the handover, Jenna cursed herself for telling Alesha she'd see her after work. Damn, she'd said it on impulse to get rid of her but was only succeeding in delaying the inevitable. She hadn't seen the last of her yet. Not by a long shot.

With a sigh she picked up her pen to take notes on the elderly clients. Half an hour later the eight members of staff set off in pairs to begin the task of getting all thirty residents washed and dressed. Today she'd be working with Kristen, which was a saving grace. She was blunt and to the point and that was what Jenna loved about her.

'You look knackered.' Kristen looked her up and down. 'Maybe it's you I should be washing and dressing this morning. You look more in need than any of the clients.'

Jenna grimaced. 'That bad, huh?'

'Worse!' Kristen grinned. 'Rough night?'

'Yeah, you could say that,' said Jenna. 'I'm not sure I'm doing the right thing by marrying Jake.'

Jenna could hardly believe she'd said the words out loud. It was one thing to think about it in private, but voicing doubts in public made it seem more real. Like she couldn't bury her head in the sand anymore.

'Well don't then! Simple! It's your choice and your life. Don't waste it. You know better than anyone how short it can be.'

'Maybe it's just wedding nerves. I don't want to hurt Jake.'

'You'll be hurting him more by marrying him and regretting it.' Kristen opened the bedroom door of the first client. 'Come on, crack a smile. It's hard enough doing this job without having to look at your sour-faced mug as well.'

'Oh, Whatever!' Jenna pulled a face. 'Is it nearly 2pm yet?'

'Morning, George,' Jenna smiled. 'Let's get you ready for breakfast.'

The eyes that stared up at Jenna were blank. He had lucid moments on rare occasions, but now wasn't one of them. The wizened old man was apparently a shadow of his former self, according to his family. The girls removed his soiled incontinence pad and cleaned him up, taking care to retain his dignity. He may not understand what was happening at that moment, but it would probably have been his worst nightmare when he was well. They chatted to him throughout the process

49

of getting him dressed and shaved, before hoisting him up and then lowering him into a wheelchair.

Jenna thought for the millionth time how unfair life could be. This man had been a scientist, working all his adult life to find cures for diseases. Now reduced to being looked after like a baby, it was an existence, not a life. Maybe it was a blessing he wasn't aware. At least she would never have to endure the torture of seeing her parents ending up like that. Jenna wasn't sure what was worse: having your life snatched away suddenly, with no time to prepare and say or do the things you wanted, or linger for months or even years. Both scenarios were equally difficult for loved ones to witness and live through.

'Do you want a lift home?' said Kristen, as they walked down the drive. 'It's been a long morning.'

'No, thanks, I need the fresh air. I'll see you tomorrow.'

'See ya.' Kristen waved over her shoulder. 'And talk to that fella of yours. Tell him you're not ready to get married. That's what I had to do. The trouble was that I left it until we'd been married five years before I got round to having the conversation.'

Jenna's jaw dropped. She hadn't known that. Had Ellie's husband had doubts before the wedding too? She sprinted to the car park to catch up with Kristen, but she'd already gone.

Towelling herself dry after her shower, Jenna paused to look in the mirror. It wasn't something she did often. Her eyes were hollow and her cheekbones were sharp enough to cut paper. Through the maze of abrasions she studied her once well-proportioned body. It was in complete contrast to her face. Although not fat as such, certain areas were storing too much of it for her slender frame. Her stomach was rounded and protruding and her thighs looked chunky. The breasts once in proportion now looked too small. The comfort food which she lived on had clearly done her no favours.

She padded through to the bedroom and ran a brush through her hair. Surprised to see it was halfway down her back she switched on the hairdryer. Once dried, the waves framed her face, softening it. The auburn and copper shades looked as if they'd been the result of a hard-working hairdresser, but in reality she couldn't remember the last time anyone had cut it and she'd never needed to have it dyed. Her crowning glory was still that, but the split ends needed sorting. She had twenty months to transform herself into a beautiful bride. Well, pretty at least. And if she broke off the engagement she'd be a stunning spinster instead. Either way, it was time to at least attempt to feel slightly better about herself. Maybe the first place to start would be to let her skin heal then treat it with respect, in place of anger and guilt. She could only try.

Jenna pulled a soft pale blue jumper over her head. The colour complemented her brown eyes and the colour of her hair. Pale denim jeans completed the outfit although she had to breathe in to get the zip to meet.

'Can I join you?' said Alesha. 'I need to talk to you.'

'If you must.' Jenna sprinted downstairs and into the kitchen to make a cup of tea.

'Well, tell me I can properly.' Alesha giggled. 'Then I'll know you mean it.'

'Alesha…come here.' Jenna sighed. Silence followed. She glanced around the room as if someone may be watching, even though Ellie was out. She self-consciously placed her arms behind her back and kicked out her legs, bending her knees back and forth. With as much grace as a child learning to play football, Michael Flatley had nothing to worry about. Dancing had always come naturally to her, but the Irish Jig had her legs tied in knots as if a seizure was imminent. Alesha, obviously worried this was a distinct possibility, materialised swiftly, and clapped.

'At least you tried.' She smiled.

'Hmm, thanks.'

'But it was crap. Anyway, Jenna, have you thought about what I said? Ben moving in?'

'Yes, I've thought how crazy it sounds, and the answer's no. I don't know how you could consider it possible anyway.'

'You know the fifth anniversary's coming up, right?'

Jenna glared. 'How could I forget?'

'Yes, sorry. But I need to get Ben out of his parents' place before then. I'm worried he's going to end up a gonner, like me.' Alesha took Jenna by the shoulders. 'They're too scared to confront him and he's likely to get himself into a lot of trouble once the date approaches. He always does but it's getting worse not better.'

'What can I do? Look, I wish I could help but I can't.'

'You can! He's been wanting to move out but never does much about it. You must go to him and offer him a room here.'

'Go to him?'

'Yes! I'll tell you where and when. Please?' Alesha wrung her hands together. 'We've got less than three weeks.'

'I wouldn't know who he was.' Jenna shook her head. 'Knowing me I'd ask the wrong man if they wanted to move in.'

Alesha giggled. 'No, you wouldn't. You will know who he is, you'll recognise him.'

'What? You're nuts!'

'Trust me.' Alesha closed her eyes and tilted back her head. 'I'll come with you. I'll tell you what to say.'

'But how am I supposed to know he's looking for somewhere?' said Jenna.

'It's easy. You act as if you know him. He'll believe you because he often drinks too much and can't remember where he's been or what he's said. And,' Alesha paused, 'he'll recognise you too.'

Jenna decided to ignore that comment. Why was she insisting they'd recognise each other? But that was the least of her problems. For now.

'If I agree to it, I'll be making it clear that it's only short-term until he finds somewhere else.' Jenna rolled her eyes when Alesha hugged her, but she hugged her back, caught unawares by the intense sadness she felt for this ghost girl and her drunken self-destructive ex. 'But there is a condition: I'm going to tell Ellie what the situation is. And you are going to apologise for upsetting her!' They exchanged grins.

'If that's what it takes I'll do it.' Alesha sniggered. 'But you should be thanking me for telling her to get a job.'

Can't you scare her into it like a normal ghost?

'Yeah, you're right.' She nodded. 'Don't suppose you know anything about writing books, do you?'

A sudden insistent rapping on the door made both girls jump.

'JENNAAA.'

'Oh, Christ, it's Mona.' Jenna slumped against the worktop. 'What's she doing here?'

'Oh, goody, can I stay?' Alesha's eyes lit up. 'I could do with a bit of entertainment.'

'No, you can't! I'll need my wits about me and won't be able to concentrate with you here. I'll see you later.' Jenna rushed down the hallway to open the door before it gave way.

'I'm coming, Mona, hang on.'

Mona had a foot in the doorway before Jenna had fully opened it. She barged past Jenna and headed for the sitting room.

'I tried to call you but your phone was switched off.' Mona took off her coat and handed it to Jenna. 'Is that tea I smell, dear?'

'I'll make some, sit down and make yourself comfy.' Before she'd finished speaking she saw that Mona had already done just that. 'I won't be long.'

As Jenna boiled the kettle, she prayed Mona wasn't planning to produce another mile-long wedding list. With a sigh she poured boiling water over the tea bags and carried the mugs into the other room. Noticing the slight curl of Mona's lip she knew instantly mugs were not her cup of tea. Literally.

'Sorry, I don't seem to own any cups and saucers.' Jenna smiled brightly. 'So, what do I owe this, erm, pleasure?'

Mona patted the sofa next to her. 'Sit down, dear. You remember I said I had a surprise for you?'

Jenna nodded. 'Yes, I remember.'

'Well, you won't have to worry about a lack of cups and saucers for much longer.'

I wasn't!

'Err, okay, why's that then?'

Mona's eyes suddenly looked wild. Almost demonic. Jenna sensed this surprise may turn out to be worse than she'd originally thought.

'The furniture needs replacing in here. A nice bit of chintz.'

'I —'

'And the décor leaves a lot to be desired, don't you think? A few ornaments wouldn't go amiss either.' Mona's gaze took in every inch of the room. 'I have boxes of figurines in the attic, waiting for a good home. I ran out of space to put them.'

Ah, so that was it. Mona intended passing on half the contents of her house to make Jake feel more at home when he moved in. Yes, she could think of better surprises, but it wasn't a disaster. They'd just have to leave a box handy and unpack Mona's trinkets when she was due to visit.

'Mona, it's lovely of you to want to give us things for the house,' said Jenna. 'But there's no need. You keep them.'

Mona's eyes glinted. 'Oh, but I will be keeping them, in effect.' She clapped her hands together. 'You see, I've decided to sell my place and when you're married I'll help you financially with this house. I've got a bit put by too.'

Jenna scratched her head. 'You can't sell up. Where will you live?'

'Here, of course!' Mona laughed. 'It makes sense. When you and Jake return from honeymoon I'll have moved in. Just think, Jenna, I'll be here when you both get home from work. I'll still be able to cook Jakey's favourite meals and I'll teach you how to cook too.'

Jenna blinked in an attempt to stop the room from spinning. It felt the same as when she'd had one too many glasses of Elderflower wine. But without the pleasant lead-up. Sweat gathered on the back of her neck.

'Jakey will be thrilled. I thought about keeping it a secret from him until…Jenna, are you alright? You look pale.'

'I don't feel well,' Jenna croaked. 'I need to lie down. It's probably a bug.'

Mona stood, clearly annoyed by the inconvenient timing of the bug. 'I'll be in touch shortly to go over the plans.' Mona placed her bag over the crook of her arm. 'We've so much to discuss, dear. It's all so exciting. I hope you're feeling better soon.'

Jenna's legs shook as she saw Mona to the door. Now she really did feel ill. And the recovery wasn't likely to be anytime soon. She opened the door to let Mona out.

'Just imagine, dear, when Jakey has to work late, I'll be here to keep you company. We'll have so much fun.'

Jenna managed a nod and slammed the door, sinking to the floor. Fun? Yeah, right. She was likely to have more fun jumping out of a plane at 30,000 feet knowing the parachute was dodgy. And even if she was hurtling towards a ten foot spike beneath her, it would still be less painful than living with Mona. Surely?

Climbing unsteadily to her feet, she began doing the Jig. And managed to hum an Irish tune, between calling as loudly as she could: 'Alesha! ALESHA! Get here now! It's an emergency.'

Alesha appeared wide-eyed in front of her. 'I'd ask if you were okay. But I can see that you're not. You look like an elephant trying to ballet dance. On a tightrope. Not that you look like an elephant, but you get my drift. What's happened, Jenna?'

'Oh, maybe I exaggerated. No emergency...I think I'm having a nervous breakdown, that's all.'

Chapter Six

'It can't be that bad.' Alesha grimaced. 'What's happened?'

'Mona wants to move in.' Jenna moaned. 'Where can I find Ben, Alesha? The sooner I get him to move in the better. In fact, do you know anyone else who might want to stay? The more the merrier.'

'Come again?'

'I need to fill every nook and cranny with people, so there's no Mona-size space left.'

'Ah, right. Good plan.'

'It's the only one I can think of. There's no other way out.'

Alesha nodded. 'Yeah, I can see that. After all, your only other option is way too complicated and far-fetched.'

'What's that?'

Alesha rolled her eyes. 'Call off the wedding, you idiot!'

'I'm going to. You were right; it's not going to work between me and Jake.'

'Really?' Alesha grinned. 'You're doing the right thing.'

'I know, but it won't be easy telling Jake. I'm dreading it.'

'Get it over with as soon as possible. But back to Ben. We need to work out a strategy.'

'I'm regretting this already,' said Jenna. 'But I'll give it a go. I could do with the rent money.'

'He's got a good job in advertising, he'll be happy to pay his fair share.'

'What's he like? Apart from drinking too much, I mean.'

'He's not an alcoholic. He does binge drink to blot stuff out though.'

'Tell me about him, Alesha. I'll need to have something other than that to go on.'

'He's lovely. He'd do anything for anybody but says what he thinks,' said Alesha. 'But it's better to be honest, isn't it?'

Sorry, Jake, I can't marry you because I think married life with you will be boring. And I'd rather live in a tent in sub-zero temperatures than live with your mum. No, being economical with the truth works for me!

'Erm…Maybe not always, Alesha. There are times in life when it's better to be economical with the truth.'

Alesha shrugged. 'Anyway, you need to judge for yourself. He's going to be at Mango Cocktail Bar tonight. Do you know it?'

'I know where it is but I've never been. Cocktail bar? From what you've told me I wouldn't have thought that was his kind of place.'

'There's more to it than cocktail menus.' Alesha laughed. 'It's huge, with different seating areas and a dance floor. The big screen TV is popular with the men, for watching sport.'

'Well I'm not going in alone,' said Jenna. 'I'll have to tell Ellie then she can come with me.'

'No, not yet.' Alesha shook her head. 'There can't be any distractions; you need to talk to Ben on your own. If he decides to take the room you can tell her then.'

Jenna opened her mouth to protest but Alesha held up a hand to stop her. 'It'll be fine. I'll talk you through it when we arrive.'

Jenna's shoulders slumped. What was she getting herself into here? It was beyond crazy. Just a few days ago her life had been normal. Dire, but normal. Now she was engaged and about to break it off, conversing with a dead girl and contemplating the ghost's ex-boyfriend move into her home. Maybe she'd feel better once she'd had chance to speak to Jake. It was hard to concentrate on anything much until then. She had to admit though, that a weight had been lifted by making the decision to call off the wedding.

'Okay. What time do I need to go?'

'Around 7pm. I'll be outside Mango's when you arrive.'

'See you later then. I'm going to see if I can get hold of Jake now. The sooner I get this out of the way, the better.'

As Jenna approached the entrance to Mango's, her heart sank. Could she really go through with this? Still, in less than an hour it would be over. Unable to get hold of Jake, she'd left a voicemail asking him to go to the house after work. He wasn't likely to get there before nine, so there was plenty of time.

Suddenly Alesha appeared. Dressed in white jeans and a black vest top, she looked more stunning than ever. Jenna glanced down at her skinny black jeans, boots and green top. At home her appearance had been acceptable, but now a wave of self-doubt washed over her.

'You look fab, Jenna,' said Alesha. 'Honestly.'

'Well, look at you! Drop dead gorgeous.' As soon as the words left Jenna's mouth she realised what she'd said. 'Oh, Alesha, I'm so sorry.'

Alesha laughed. 'Literally, hey?'

None of the living girls inside the building could possibly match up to her. It was such a shame she'd be invisible. What a waste.

'It's nice for me to dress up for a change.' Alesha tossed back her mane of curls. 'Even if nobody else can see me.'

'Well, from someone who *can* see you, you're stunning.'

'Thanks. It only takes a second for me to get ready now.' Alesha giggled. 'I just imagine how I want to look and that's it...not as much fun though.'

Jenna had a sudden vision of a room strewn with clothes and makeup. Half empty bottles and glasses littered the room. She heard the incessant chatter and laughter of a group of girls with nothing to worry about, other than whether to wear their hair up or down.

She swallowed down the lump in her throat and turned to Alesha. 'Let's get this over with before I change my mind. I'm going to look such a saddo going in on my own.'

'No, you're not. Nobody will take much notice. Get your phone.'

Jenna held out her palms and shrugged. 'Why?'

'Pretend you're talking to someone. Me. That way you'll have something to focus on when you go in.'

Taking the phone out of her pocket she held it to her ear and took a deep breath.

'Let's go. I need a drink.'

The place was vast. Divided up into sections, she understood why it was popular. Whatever mood you were in, there was a space to suit it. One half of the room was filled with the usual pub tables and chairs. Soggy beer mats and sticky beer and wine spills were evident. The other half of the room was furnished with low squishy sofas and coffee tables not unlike the one at home. Couples, clearly oblivious to everything and everyone around them sat limbs entwined. There was also a couple of sofas taken up by different groups of friends, huddled close to be heard above the music.

A small flight of stairs led to another floor. Even from that distance she saw the huge screen playing music videos and guessed it also showed sport, when there were any games worth watching. It seemed a lifetime ago since she'd sat in front of a similar screen. Excitement built as they'd watched the World Cup, the room filled with hopeful tension. She sighed and edged through the throng of people, towards the bar, her phone still clamped to one ear she fumbled for the money with her free hand, and ordered a small beer.

Alesha was right: nobody paid any attention, other than to dodge aside to let her back through the crowd. She headed for a space in the corner of the room, behind the sofas.

'Okay, then, is he here?' She said into her phone, throwing a glance at Alesha who was stood beside her.

'Yes, he's here.' She paused as if lost in thought. 'Over there. Greet him as if you know him and remind him where from. Say it was at Luciana's a couple of weeks ago.'

Alesha inclined her head towards a group of people on the sofas. Four scantily clad girls leaned forward, giggling at a man perched on a sofa arm.

Jenna inched closer. His Jet black hair was short and spiked back on top but reached the nape of his neck at the back. It brought to mind the Jet stone which was carved into jewellery, famous in the seaside town of Whitby, not far from York.

Ben wore pale denim jeans, which she couldn't help noticing were tight-fitting. The fizzy bubbles of her lager went up her nose and she coughed and spluttered. All five pairs of eyes at the table turned in her direction and looked her up and down. Ben paused, his pint glass halfway to his mouth. He did look vaguely familiar but she didn't have a clue where from. Almond-shaped brown eyes studied her, as if they could see what she was thinking. He had a strong jaw-line but it was the cleft in his chin that had Jenna momentarily transfixed. Blimey, it was almost deep enough to hold the contents of her glass.

Oh, shit! Here goes!

'Ben! Hi!' She arranged her mouth into what she hoped resembled a bright smile. 'How's it going?'

His brow furrowed. 'Err, hi. Look I'm sorry, but I can't quite place you. Where do I know you from?'

'Don't you remember? We met at Luciana's a couple of weeks ago.'

Ben nodded slowly, then clicked his fingers. 'That's it! I recognised you, but couldn't think where from.'

Jenna was confused. Was he pretending to recognise her? She was sure she'd seen him before too. Alesha winked and smiled in encouragement. Why had she been so adamant that they would seem familiar to each other?

Jenna nudged her, waiting for further instructions.

'Ask if you can speak in private,' said Alesha. 'Ask if he's still looking for somewhere to live.'

'Can I have a word?' Beads of sweat gathered on her brow. The four girls weren't even attempting to conceal their curiosity. 'In private?'

'Sure.' Ben picked up his drink and beckoned her to follow him to an empty table. 'I'm really sorry, but I can't remember your name.'

'It's Jenna.' Her heart thudded against her chest. 'I was wondering whether you're still looking for somewhere else to live. I have a spare room I'm going to rent out if you're interested?'

'Christ, I can't remember telling you that.' He stared at her blankly. 'But yeah, I'm interested. I'm too old to be shacked up with the parents, you know?'

Jenna nodded. 'It's spacious and not too far from town. You're welcome to have a look.'

'I'll take it!' He grinned and downed the rest of his drink. 'Let's have another drink to celebrate.'

'Erm —'

'Hey, it's okay. You've gotta get back to whoever you came with, right?'

She's right beside you, Ben. The love of your life!

'Well…the friend I was supposed to be meeting couldn't make it,' Jenna lied. 'I have time for a quick drink, but I can't stay long.'

'Same again?' Ben stood up to go to the bar. 'I won't be long.'

Alesha sat in the chair opposite Jenna. 'What do you think?'

That the cleft in his chin could double up as a mobile wine glass. That looking into his eyes are like drowning in pools of melted

63

chocolate…and that his jeans are like the wrapper of a giant — Oh, for God's sake, Jenna, what are you thinking? No…don't answer that!

She lifted her gaze slowly, hardly daring to look Alesha in the eye. But Alesha's eyes shone back at her. She clasped her hands together. 'Well?'

'He seems erm, nice,' Jenna answered. 'It must be so hard for you to be so close to him, yet so far away. Why couldn't you just communicate directly with him?'

Alesha turned towards the bar, clearly searching for Ben. 'I've tried.' She sighed. 'But there's no getting through to him. Sometimes I think he's going to acknowledge my presence, but not for long. It's too powerful for me to fight.'

'What is?'

'His resistance. It's as if by letting me in, he'll have to face me leaving again. He'd rather blot it all out, except that doesn't really work. He doesn't believe in the afterlife either. He probably thinks he's going crazy when he senses me around. Just like you did.'

Ben placed the drinks on the table and sat down between Jenna and Alesha. 'So, when can I move in, then?'

'You need to see the house first,' said Jenna. 'You might not like it.' She tried to ignore Alesha's glare.

'Okay, cool! Give me the address, I'll put it in my phone along with your number.'

Jenna toyed with a beer mat while he took the details. Something told her that she may live to regret this. That 'something' confirmed her fears a minute later.

'Any chance I can pop round after work tomorrow? About six-ish?' He looked up from his phone.

'That's fine. My friend, Ellie lives there too at the moment. It'll give you chance to meet each other.'

'Great.' Ben nodded. 'I'll wait until it's all confirmed before I tell Sabrina. Not that she'll be moving in with me, don't worry.'

'Sabrina?'

'A girl I'm seeing.'

Jenna's blood wasn't so much boiling, it was ready to explode. Why the hell hadn't Alesha told her he had a girlfriend? Was this just part of a ploy to split them up? She was jealous and likely to be using Jenna, somehow. What else hadn't she mentioned?

She needed to get out. After having it out with Alesha she'd make up an excuse to Ben, tomorrow. This was a complication too far and she had no intention of getting involved any further.

'I've got to go now.' She stood. 'Thanks for the drink and I'll erm see you tomorrow.'

'You will! See you then…and it's good to meet you…again.' He grinned. 'I'm sorry I can't remember the first time, J!'

J?

'Yeah, erm, bye then.' Jenna scuttled to the entrance and took large gulps of air. Her fists were curled into tight balls as she rounded on Alesha.

'How dare you? Why didn't you tell me about Sabrina? I thought he was heartbroken over you!'

'He is, Jenna. There's been a few women on the scene over the last couple of years though. None of them last more than a week or two. Until now.'

'Sabrina?'

'Yes. I'm worried because she's bad for him. And no, before you say it, I'm not jealous.'

'Hmm, anyway, what's the panic? You've just said they never last more than a fortnight.'

'This one's different.'

'Oh, how long's he been seeing her?'

'A month.'

A month? Wow! I understand your distress. Not.

'Oh, come on, Alesha. This is ridiculous. If you're not jealous then what is it?'

Alesha held on to Jenna's arm. 'He has bouts of drinking and womanising. But he never lets anyone get too close. They mean nothing to him. Sabrina is worming her way in though and she's trouble. He works with her. She's out for herself, that one. I don't trust her, she's up to something.'

'Like what?'

'I don't know. Yet. I'm sorry for not telling you, but I wanted you to meet him first.' Alesha gave a sad smile. 'I do want her away from him, but it's not out of jealousy. When you die those emotions cease to exist.'

Jenna's forehead creased. She couldn't get her head round that, but who was she to argue?

Alesha continued 'All I want is for Ben to be happy. That's all. I need to know he's going to follow the right path, and to stop hurting himself further. I genuinely believe Sabrina is out to destroy him and he certainly doesn't need help from anyone else on that score. You can help him, Jenna. Please?'

Jenna winced as Alesha's grip on her arm tightened. It was surprisingly strong. Her resolve of ten minutes ago diminished the second she looked into Alesha's eyes. A mixture of desperation and hope stared back at her. She'd see it through, but state it was short term. The only option was to take a day at a time. Just as she'd been doing for almost five years. But her priority now was to get home and talk to Jake.

'Okay, here's the deal: I've said he can move in. Other than that I don't know what else you expect of me.' She took large strides, eager to get home. 'I can't tell him what to do. I don't even know him.'

'I know, but you'll soon get to know what makes him tick. All I know is that him being where he is won't help him. Let's just play it by ear.'

'Well I'm not having this woman making herself at home.' Jenna shuddered. 'I'm finding the idea of sharing the house with not just one lodger, but two, really difficult as it is.'

'I do understand, Jenna. Really I do.' Alesha stopped her in her tracks. 'All I ask is that you give it a go, for me. I'm begging you. If, after a month you've had enough, at least we'll both be able to say you tried.'

'Yeah, whatever.' Jenna waved her away with a grin. 'Leave me in peace now, will you? I need to concentrate on what I'm going to say to Jake.'

'Good luck! He'll be alright once he gets over the shock.' Alesha's eyes glinted. 'There must be hundreds of women out there who'll be happy to step into Mona's bad-ass shoes — colour-coordinating his freshly laundered shirts and entertaining his work colleagues with delicious cordon-bleu meals.'

The nearest Jenna could see herself getting to colour-coordinating shirts would be by putting them all in the washing machine with something red. She knew from experience they'd come out identical in colour. As far as the cooking went, it would be more likely cordon bleurrghh.

She was doing the right thing by ending it, not just for herself, but for him too. If they did stay together she'd end up letting him down. There was more than enough guilt to cope with, without adding to it.

'I know he'll be okay, Alesha, but I still dread telling him.' Jenna's stomach lurched. 'See you tomorrow, no doubt.'

67

Alesha waved and disappeared from sight, much to Jenna's relief. It hadn't been one of her best days and it was unfortunately about to get worse. She hoped Jake wouldn't be long. Now that she'd made up her mind, she didn't want it hanging over her any longer than necessary.

She took off her coat and checked to see if Jake had left a message. He hadn't, but he was bound to arrive shortly.

'Hi, Jen, been anywhere nice?' Ellie poked her head round the door of the sitting room. 'Do you want a cup of tea?'

'Oh, I've just been catching up with an old friend,' Jenna mumbled. 'I could do with something a bit stronger than tea to be honest. I'm about to break up with Jake.'

'What? No way!' Ellie's mouth gaped. 'How come?'

'I've realised it would be a mistake,' said Jenna. 'I'll fill you in later. Would you mind making yourself scarce for a bit? He'll be here soon and I need to talk to him in private.'

'Yeah, course.' Ellie nodded. 'I'll go upstairs out of the way. When I hear the door slam behind him I'll come back down and pour you a large glass of wine.'

Jenna curled up on the sofa, but a minute later was pacing the floor. Where was he? Although the air was chilly, sweat gathered on her forehead and top lip. If there was one thing she hated it was confrontation and bad feeling. She could only pray that Jake would understand and there would be no animosity. Once he'd finished having a heart attack, obviously.

Her phone started vibrating on the table, hopping around like a frog on speed. As she lurched for it, it fell through her clammy fingers onto the floor. Jake's name flashed up at her, spinning left to right manically. She picked it up and jabbed the screen to answer.

Keep calm, Jenna. He's probably just running late. He'll be here soon and by the time you go to bed the deed will be done. Over.

'Jake, where are you? Will you be long?'

'I'm at the hospital. Can you come? Mum's in a bad way. She's had a heart attack.'

Chapter Seven

The cold plastic casing of the phone dug into her hand. Despite this her grip tightened. There must be some mistake. A heart attack? Mona had seemed fine earlier. Dragon-like as usual.

'Oh my God, Jake! Where are you now?' Jenna gasped.

'At the hospital.' Jake's voice quivered. 'Can you come?'

'I'm on my way.' Jenna hung up and shrugged back into her coat. With shaking hands she dialled the number of a local taxi. It wasn't something she would spend money on as a rule but this was urgent. After swiftly explaining to a shocked Ellie where she was going, the taxi pulled up outside.

Jenna had been without a car for over a year now. The last one she'd had couldn't seem to complete any journey without breaking down. It had become clear that without exception it was quicker to walk.

Ten minutes later the driver pulled up outside the A&E department. Jenna thrust the money at him with a garbled thank you and sprinted to the entrance. After almost falling through it, she saw a reception desk in front of her.

'Can you tell me where Mona Mansfield is, please?' Jenna gripped the edge of the desk. 'She's had a heart attack.'

The receptionist tapped away at her computer and pointed to a set of swing doors. 'Through there. At the end of the corridor turn right.' She smiled.

Jenna's heart raced as she followed the instructions. Turned right she collided with Jake who was obviously waiting for her.

'How's your mum?' Jenna took deep breaths. 'What happened?'

'They're busy doing tests.' Jake slumped against the wall. 'Thank God I was there when it happened. The ambulance was there in no time and I came in it with her.'

'She was fine earlier.' Jenna's forehead creased. 'I don't get it.'

'I went home to grab a change of clothes before coming to you,' Jake explained. 'Everything seemed normal. Although Mum was rambling on about needing figurines out of the attic. She was packing cups and saucers into a box when I got there. Then she keeled over. It all happened so fast.'

Jenna was horrified that Mona had been sorting things for the house. She must've got overexcited and it had been too much. The guilt was overwhelming. Jake mercifully cut into her thoughts.

'Let's see if we can go in.' He led her through another short corridor and into a room. They made their way over to the bed where a small figure lay, surrounded by machines and monitors. The stench of disinfectant made Jenna's stomach turn.

She peered down onto the bed. Surely that couldn't be Mona? It was impossible to comprehend that the strong and formidable lady of a few hours ago had been replaced with this frail old person. Hot tears burnt her eyes as they met Jake's over the bed. He too appeared to have diminished in size. The stocky confident solicitor now looked like a frightened little boy. She moved around the bed to hug him. He clung to her so tightly that she couldn't move an inch. For a brief nanosecond the feeling of imprisonment was comparable in her mind of being married to him. Giving her head an impatient shake to dispel this thought, she pulled backwards to escape his vice-like hold.

'She doesn't look like Mum anymore,' he whispered into Jenna's hair. 'I don't know what I'd do without her...or without you.'

Jenna hesitated. 'I'm sure she'll pull through. She's in good hands. And you won't have to find out what you'd do without me because I'm going nowhere.'

Be careful what you're saying. There'll be no going back.

She continued, 'It's me and you together. A team. Now, I'm going to get my future husband a strong coffee, right?'

Jake nodded and gave her a weak smile. He bent and picked up his mum's hand, cradling it gently in his own. 'Thanks, Jenna. We're lucky to have you, aren't we, Mum?'

Jenna was sure Mona's lips moved slightly.

Busying herself with the coffee machine, she refused to dwell on the implications of the last hour. Whatever happened, they'd get through it. As husband and wife. They'd be okay, she'd make sure of it. And if Mona made a full recovery, which hopefully she would do, they'd have to discuss living arrangements for her properly. One thing was for sure: Jenna wasn't about to abandon them. Her new family. She picked up the coffee cups and her fallen spirits with a new-found determination. Paying no attention to Alesha's insistent voice calling her, she pulled back her shoulders and went to them.

Unlocking the door two hours later, Jenna turned to Jake. 'Go and put your feet up, I'll bring you a drink.'

Jake shook his head. 'If you don't mind I'll go up to bed. I don't know if I'll sleep, but I'm exhausted.'

'I'll come with you,' said Jenna. 'I'm just going to see if Ellie's still awake.'

She tapped lightly on Ellie's door. 'You awake, Ellie?'

'Yeah, come in. How's Mona?'

'It's a case of wait and see,' said Jenna. 'They said the next forty-eight hours is crucial.'

'I know Mona's not our favourite person, but I wouldn't wish that on her. Or Jake.' Ellie yawned. 'I guess your bombshell about the wedding will have to wait a bit?'

'Shh!' Jenna hissed. 'I'll talk to you about that tomorrow.'

Ellie's eyes narrowed. 'You can't marry him cos you feel sorry for him. But obviously now isn't the right time.'

Jenna's gaze dropped to the floor. 'Hmm, well, I'm not calling it off. It was wedding jitters, that's all. Anyway, there's something else I need to tell you. A bloke called Ben's coming to —'

'Jenna?' Jake called from the bedroom.

Jenna sighed. 'I'll explain tomorrow, I need to see if Jake's okay. Night, Els.'

'Night, Jen. If there's anything I can do let me know.'

Jenna nodded and blew Ellie a kiss from the doorway. 'I will.'

The next morning Jenna poured coffee with one hand and rubbed her eyes with the other. Both she and Jake had spent the night tossing and turning. She turned as he came into the kitchen.

'Are you hungry?' She put a steaming cup of coffee in front of him.

'No, thanks.' He shook his head. 'I'll drink this then pop into the office for a bit.'

'You're working?' Jenna said, surprised. 'I thought you'd be going straight to the hospital.'

'I've just rang to see how Mum is,' said Jake. 'There's not much change but they say that's not necessarily a bad thing. Anyway, I'm not going to be at work long. I'm hoping to pass some of my workload onto a colleague.'

'Okay,' said Jenna. 'I'm at work all day, today. I'll see you at the hospital this evening.'

Ellie raised her eyebrows as she walked into the room. 'All day? I thought you were —'

'They changed my shift, remember?' Jenna threw Ellie a warning glance.

'Oh, yeah.' Ellie nodded. 'Sorry to hear about your mum, Jake.'

Jake stood up to leave. 'Thanks. I'll let you know if I hear anything, Jenna. See you tonight.'

Once the door closed behind him, Ellie rounded on Jenna. 'You're not working all day, are you?'

'No, I'm not working at all because you're going to call them and say I'm ill.'

'But why? You never throw a sickie.'

'Just do it, Els. I'm going for a shower and then I need to talk to you.'

Jenna hated letting the staff down but she just couldn't face work today. She couldn't remember her last good night's sleep. Also, her head felt as if someone was banging a hammer inside her brain. But, much as she'd love to crawl back into bed, she had to tell Ellie about Ben and Alesha. Maybe by getting it out in the open, some sense could be made of it all. And maybe it would distract Ellie from persistent ramblings about Feng Shui. Although she refrained from moving more furniture, she still wandered around the house muttering about energy flows.

'Let me get this straight.' Ellie held her head in her hands. 'You're telling me a ghost wants her boyfriend to move in here?'

'Yes! It still kind of seems unreal, even though I've met him.'

'But why you? I believe in ghosts and stuff!' Ellie pouted. 'Why didn't she come to me?'

'Well, you have met her, I believe.' Jenna grinned. 'You said she was rude.'

'*Her?*' Ellie tutted.

'She said I'm at the centre of it all, whatever that means. If Ben moves here I can try and make him see sense and it will help me financially.'

'Did she say anything else? Is that it?'

'Oh, she talks nonsense about my destiny.' Jenna shrugged. 'And says Jake's wrong for me and that I need to quit blaming myself. Blah, blah blah.'

'Well…she's right there.' Ellie stood and glanced around the room. 'Where is she, then? Look, I'm not calling you a liar, but I need you to prove it.'

'Alesha!' Jenna began. 'Alesha, come here!'

During the silence that followed, a look of concern spread across Ellie's face. 'Jen, you haven't been yourself since…the accident. I think —'

'ALESHA!' Jenna began doing the jig. Her face flamed at the incredulous expression on Ellie's face.

'Now I know you've lost it!' Ellie snorted. 'What the hell are you doi—' She backed against a chair and fell onto it as Alesha materialised in the centre of the room.

'Hi,' said Alesha to Jenna, before turning to Ellie. 'Got a job yet?'

Ellie's mouth opened and promptly closed again. Pressing her back into the chair her knuckles turned white as they gripped the arms of the chair. 'Err…'

'You'll have your new lodger soon, Jenna. At least *he'll* pay you for being here.' Alesha winked. 'I can't wait for him to get moved in. We're going to have so much fun!'

'Are we?' Jenna shrugged at Ellie. 'How do you work that out, then?'

'Ohh, you'll see.' Alesha danced around the room, the hem of her white lace dress swirling around her calves.

'Aren't you going to give his room a clean before he arrives to see it? I'd do it myself but it's a bit difficult, given that I'm dead.'

'It is clean!' Jenna put her hands on her hips. 'Don't start telling me what to do or not do, in my own house.'

'Okay, chill!' Alesha grinned.

'I'll check it over to make sure, if you like, Jen?' said Ellie.

'Good idea.' Alesha shooed her away. 'Make yourself useful.'

'Hang on, you cheeky cow,' Ellie spluttered. 'Who do you think you are?'

Jenna held up her hands. 'Stop it, you two! I need you to be friends if this is going to work.'

'Hey, I'm not here to cause trouble,' said Alesha. 'Well, not much.'

'Is it nice in heaven?' said Ellie. 'I've often wondered whether heaven and hell really exist.'

'I've been in hell since I died.' Alesha's eyes clouded over. 'I know there's something better waiting for me, but I can't get there until I sort out loose ends here.'

'Ohh,' Ellie whispered. 'But it's not like, flaming fires and demons though?'

'No, sorry to disappoint you,' said Alesha. 'And before you ask, heaven is beautiful. I want to get there permanently now, so I hope you're going to help put my mind at rest so that I can move on.'

The girls nodded in unison.

'It's going to be cool having you around.' Ellie tentatively touched Alesha's arm. 'Isn't it, Jenna?'

Jenna hesitated before answering. 'Yeah, I'm slowly getting used to it.' She nodded. 'But I've got a lot on with Jake and his mum just now, so I'm going to be busy with them.'

'Hmm, I heard about Mona,' said Alesha. 'Well, all you can do is be there for him until she recovers. I guess you can't do much else right now.'

Jenna opened her mouth to say that she was going through with the wedding, but thought better of it when she saw the look that passed between the other two. They could think what they liked. Her mind was made up and that was it.

'I don't want Jake knowing I haven't gone to work,' said Jenna. 'I needed to get my head together, you know? I probably won't be any worse off financially because they'll take less tax off me. I do feel guilty though.'

'Life's too short to worry about some things,' said Alesha. 'If I'd have known what was going to happen to me I'd have taken more time off. All that bloody time I wasted being at work.'

'What did you do?' Ellie asked.

'I worked in an office. Can you believe it?' Alesha grimaced. 'I wish I'd done something exciting with my life.'

'Like what?' Jenna knew where Alesha was coming from. Her life had turned out to be the complete opposite of what she'd dreamed of doing.

'I dunno, but probably something abroad,' said Alesha. 'Maybe working at a beach bar, somewhere hot. The views from the window would've been palm trees and white sand, not a back alley filled with wheelie bins.'

'But then you might not have met Ben,' said Jenna.

'Um, no, I guess not.' Alesha fiddled with the hem on her dress.

Her face gave nothing away, but it wasn't the response Jenna had been expecting.

'Hmm, sun, sand and palm trees sound good.' Ellie sighed. 'Maybe that's what I should do, look for a job abroad.'

'Do it while you have chance.' Alesha nodded. 'What about you, Jenna? Your original career choice wasn't changing incontinence pads, was it?'

That sounded suspiciously like a statement not a question. But she can't know, can she? Of course she can, Jenna...she's got superpowers...or something.

'No, it wasn't,' said Ellie before Jenna had time to think up a suitable response. 'She was going to be a s—'

'Ellie!' Jenna's fists curled. 'I don't want to talk about it, okay?'

'Okay.' Ellie shrugged. 'But you're wasting your life. I wish you could see that. It's not what your parents would want.'

'Well let's ask the expert, shall we?' Jenna spun round to face Alesha. 'Come on, if they were able to speak about my life they'd come to me, wouldn't they?'

'Jenna,' Alesha began. 'They do. How many times have you felt as if something was brushing against your cheek? You put it down to an itch or the wind. What about the times you think you hear their voices? You put that down to wishful thinking or the sound of the rain playing tricks.'

'Don't be ridiculous.'

'It's not ridiculous, it's true.' Alesha took Jenna's hand. 'But you won't listen to what they're saying.'

'Stop it! Stop it!' Jenna covered her ears. 'They've gone. They've left me.' Hot tears slid down her face as she curled up into a ball on the sofa.

'They haven't.' Alesha sat next to her. 'But they're in the same situation as me, Jenna. They can't move on until you face facts: the accident was just that. It wasn't your fault. And also, they want you to live your dream otherwise their death really would be in vain.'

'Well w-why are y-you t-telling me this, why not them?'

'I've told you, you won't listen to them. And.' Alesha paused. 'It had to be me who came into your life this way. I've tried to tell you, but you won't listen to me either. Between us, we can help everyone to move on and be happy.'

'How? Apart from Ben moving in, I mean,' said Ellie. 'What does Jenna have to do?'

'Listen to her heart, not head,' said Alesha. 'Imagine a path she could follow, given the chance. Where would the exciting journey begin? What would she encounter along the way? And what would the final destination be?'

'Erm, right.' Ellie glanced at Jenna, brow furrowed.

'Each time she goes to wander from that path, she must stop in her tracks before getting back on it.' Alesha continued. 'Even though there will be thorny parts to get through and danger along the way.'

'Well, you're not exactly selling it to me.' Jenna snivelled. 'The path I'm on at the moment may be dull, but it's familiar. Safe. And I know where it will lead.'

'Exactly!' Alesha nodded. 'You'd have run in the opposite direction from your path a few years ago.'

'She's right, Jen.' Ellie strode across the room and wrapped her arms around Jenna. 'It's not too late to follow your dream.'

Jenna took a crumpled tissue from the sleeve of her jumper. 'What you two seem to forget is that I've already taken a wrong turning from my path. I wouldn't have invited a complete stranger to move into my house otherwise, would I?'

Something told Jenna that she'd wandered too far and that she may never find her way back.

I hope this bloody path I've stumbled upon leads me to Destination Alcohol!

Chapter Eight

When the chiming of the clock announced it was six o'clock, the three girls looked towards the door. Jenna half hoped Ben wouldn't show up. But the other half wanted the extra money that his rent would bring. Getting her finances in some kind of order wouldn't be easy until Jake moved in. At least this way some of the burden would be lifted.

Five minutes later, the doorbell caused them all to jump out of their seats, high enough to almost hit the ceiling. Luckily they missed, as it was already threatening to give way.

'You put the kettle on, Ellie, while I let him in.' Jenna made her way nervously to the door, accompanied by Alesha.

Jenna took a deep breath and opened the door. 'Hi, Ben. Come in.' She stood aside to let him through. As he squeezed past her in the narrow hallway, the scent of citrus filled the air. It was a subtle but manly smell. 'First door on the right.'

Following him into the sitting room, Jenna took in the tight ripped jeans, which revealed strong, dark-haired thighs. 'Ellie's gone to put the kettle on.' She gulped.

Ben turned and handed over a bag. 'I think this calls for something stronger.' He grinned. 'Get some glasses, J.'

Jenna peered inside and took out the bottle of fizz. 'Okay.' She was relieved to put some distance between herself and Ben. Being in such close proximity to him made her feel uncomfortable, but she was unsure why.

'Forget the coffee.' Jenna entered the kitchen. 'We need glasses instead, Ellie.'

Ellie raised her eyebrows. 'Cool! Come on, I can't wait to meet him.'

They stood still and watched for a moment before walking into the room. Ben was wandering round, picking up photo frames for closer inspection. Alesha was glued to his side. Jenna fought the urge to yell at him to leave the photos alone. Not least because he didn't put them down straight. Jenna was obsessive about things being symmetrical. The sight of her precious things being out of place made her heart race. She reached for the light switch and tapped it four times, until her breathing returned to normal.

'Here're the glasses.' She put them down on the coffee table. 'This is my friend, Ellie, and Ellie, this is Ben.'

'Good to meet you, Ellie.' Ben held out his hand.

'You too.' Ellie grinned and pointed to the bottle. 'Get that open, then. If I do it I'll likely take someone's eye out.'

As Ben turned to pick up the bottle, Ellie fanned her face with her hand. 'He's hot,' she mouthed, and grinned.

Jenna's eyes met Alesha's. Would this reaction alienate Alesha even more towards Ellie than she'd been previously? Her heart sank. Just when she'd thought they were going to get along. Taken aback, Jenna saw that Alesha appeared more happy and glowing than usual. Jenna took the glass from Ben's outstretched hand. She nearly dropped it when Alesha nodded at Ellie, and said, 'I know!'

Although Alesha had been insistent that jealousy didn't exist when you were dead, Jenna hadn't really believed her. Why didn't it? Happiness obviously did, judging by Alesha's expression now.

'It's a nice place you have here,' said Ben. 'I love these old period buildings.'

Jenna nodded. 'Yeah, me too. It needs loads doing to it, that's the problem. Just when one thing gets fixed, another two problems arise.'

'Maybe so, but better that than one of those new builds. They're just glorified boxes.'

'That might be how you'll describe the room.' Jenna laughed. 'I'll show you, see what you think.'

Ben put down his glass and followed Jenna upstairs.

'That's the bathroom.' She opened the door so he could look inside.

'It's big.' He peered round the door. 'Nice.'

Does he have a secret fetish for peeling plaster and paint?

'That's Ellie's room.' She indicated a door on the left of the passage. 'And, erm, that's my room.' Pointing to the door next to Ellie's she felt her face flush.

For goodness' sake get a grip! You're showing a potential lodger the layout of the house, that's all!

'This is the spare room.' She flung open the door at the end of the passage. 'Don't feel obliged to take it if it's not what you want.'

Ben stood in the doorway and nodded. 'I like it.' He opened the fitted wardrobe, seeming to approve of the amount of storage space inside. Next, he went to the window and peered out at the street. As far as streets went, Jenna thought, it wasn't particularly outstanding but neither was it run-down. All the gardens were well-tended. Well, apart from hers. She really should get it tidied up. It was a wonder the neighbours hadn't complained that she lowered the tone of the area. But, she suspected it had a plus side for them. The overgrown lawn and weeds high enough to rival Jack's beanstalk, meant that if they wanted to get rid of unwanted items they could throw them over Jenna's fence. Safe in the knowledge that they would remain undiscovered for the foreseeable future.

With a start, Jenna realised Ben was bouncing up and down on the end of the double bed. Why hadn't she replaced it with a single one? That way he'd be less likely to bring half the female population of York here for nocturnal activities. She'd have to have a word with him on that score. It would have to wait though, because the roof of her mouth was suddenly dry. It was doubtful any noise to come out of her mouth at this point, would even vaguely resemble a recognisable word.

'It's comfy.' Ben patted the space next to him. For a split second, Jenna thought he was inviting her onto the bed. Was her possible new lodger a psycho sex-pest? And of course he knew her bedroom was next door. What had she done? He hadn't even been here twenty minutes and already he was — oh, just testing the mattress to determine whether it would give him a good night's sleep.

'Erm, so what do you think?' The sooner he answered this question, the sooner he'd be gone. For now, anyway.

'When can I move in?' He grinned. 'How much is the rent?'

Five minutes later, they joined the others downstairs. Jenna was more than happy with the amount they'd agreed on. Now the unpaid bills could be settled and maybe some of the more pressing jobs would be affordable.

'So, are you our new bottle-opener and resident eye-candy, then?' Ellie raised her eyebrows as they walked back into the room. Jenna wondered briefly what Ellie and Alesha had been discussing so intently. One thing was for sure: Alesha really wasn't bothered by Ellie's remarks about Ben. In fact, she'd go as far as to say that all of a sudden they seemed to be the best of friends.

'I'm happy to be your bottle-opener.' Ben grinned. 'As for being your resident eye-candy, well, if you insist.' He winked first at Ellie and then more lingering on Jenna. 'Although, to be honest, I think I've got the best deal as far as that goes, ladies.'

Jenna swallowed hard. Both Ellie and Alesha were giggling in Ben's direction. Wasn't Alesha even a *little* put out by her ex's obvious flirting? Had Jenna not known anything about Ben, the word 'womaniser' would've sprung to mind. The person she'd described didn't match the one in front of Jenna, now.

'Right, then.' Jenna rummaged through a drawer. 'Here's your key, Ben. You can move in whenever you like. Oh, and by the way, keep your door locked or Ellie'll be on the prowl.'

'Will she?' he raised his eyebrows at Ellie. 'That's interesting.'

'What you on about, Jenna?' Ellie snapped.

'Your feng shui, Ellie.' She turned to Ben. 'The bed could be moved at some point. Or the wardrobe. Even you, if she decides you're facing the wrong way!'

He grinned and reached to take the key from Jenna. His hand wrapped around hers, before taking the key and sliding it into the pocket of his jeans. Jenna was amazed that he could fit anything else in there. The contents were clearly crammed in tightly as it was. She wiped a bead of sweat from her brow.

'I can borrow a mate's van at the weekend,' said Ben. 'I'll be here bright and early Saturday morning. I'll let you know what time to have the bacon on, J.'

Jenna bristled. Bacon on? Since when did a landlady become obliged to cook for their lodgers? Just as she was about to tell him this, he laughed.

'It was worth a try,' he said.

Jenna couldn't help but laugh back. 'Maybe, but it got you nowhere. See you on Saturday.'

'Yeah, see you then,' said Ellie. 'And don't bother asking me to cook you bacon. I'm vegetarian.'

'Are you?' Ben clasped a hand to his mouth. 'I was going to bring a load of pheasants and deer which I shot and killed, too. I thought you'd appreciate me filling up the freezer.'

Ellie gasped. 'No way! Jenna, get the key back off him, will you?'

'No chance.' Ben patted his pocket. 'I was joking, don't panic, El.'

Jenna wasn't quite sure what to make of him. He definitely wouldn't hold back in making himself at home, that was evident, but she couldn't deny that he made her smile. That was definitely a big plus point.

'I'll see you out.' Jenna moved towards the door. 'Sorry, but I'm in a bit of a rush. My fiancé's mother had a heart attack.'

'Oh, I'm sorry to hear that,' said Ben. 'I hope she's okay. Don't let me hold you up. I'll see myself out. Bye for now.'

'Thanks. Bye.' Jenna wondered what had made her divulge that information. Not that it was a secret, of course, but still…

'He seems lovely.' Ellie smiled. 'He's going to liven up the place.'

'You say it like it's a good thing.' Jenna rolled her eyes. 'I quite liked my house as it was: quiet and peaceful, actually.'

'Sorry, Jen. I'll be out of your hair soon, I promise.' Ellie's voice wobbled. 'Thanks for putting up with me.'

Jenna threw herself at Ellie. 'Oh, Ellie, I'm sorry. I didn't mean it, honest. I've kind of got used to you being here now. You make the best coffee in York.'

She was furious with herself. Yes, it was hard sharing space after so long on her own, but the last thing she wanted was to hurt Ellie. It wasn't her fault that Jenna found it difficult to cope with the loss of control she felt having other people in the house. And it hadn't been Ellie who'd instigated this whole lodger thing. No, that blame lay firmly with Alesha, who'd been uncharacteristically quiet. Could it have hit her, that Ben had changed from being the person she'd thought he was? If indeed he'd been that person at all. Jenna knew only too well how the mind played tricks sometimes. If Alesha preferred to think of Ben as a heartbroken wreck, then who was she to point out the flaw in this description. From what she could gather, he was the life and soul of the party, not backwards in coming forwards and a probable womaniser to boot. What he wasn't, was a man who openly mourned the love of his life. At least as far as Jenna could see, anyway.

Alesha, she realised, was staring at her. Jenna busied herself straightening the photos, but she felt Alesha watching her every move. Eventually she spoke. 'You're very anal about things being in place, aren't you?'

Jenna turned to face her. 'Why shouldn't I be? It's my home and my things.'

'Hey, I'm not saying it's wrong. I'm curious that's all.' Alesha took a step towards her and smiled. 'Thanks for doing this, Jenna. It'll all turn out well, you'll see.'

Would it? Jenna had the distinct feeling that 'well' was not the way it would be described in the not too distant future. She wished the prickle of unease lodged in her brain would dislodge itself sharpish. But it seemed like it was in no rush to vacate anytime soon.

'Are you quite sure this is the way forward? I really can't see what's to be gained from it, to be honest.'

Alesha squeezed her hand. 'Trust me, all will become clear. Remember what I said about that path though, okay?'

As Jenna left the house and turned towards the bus stop, she saw Mabel at her window. Was it only a few days since the last visit? It seemed much longer than that. So much had happened in such a short time. It would be nice to have a chat with her before going to the hospital.

Mabel beamed when Jenna walked into the room. 'Hello, dear, it's lovely to see you.'

'You too.' Jenna perched on the arm of Mabel's chair. 'How are you?'

'Oh, I'm fine, dear. But what about you? Ellie tells me you have some exciting news.'

Confused, Jenna wondered what this could be. She couldn't know about Ben moving in yet. And then she remembered. One of the most exciting times in a girl's life must surely be getting engaged. But clearly not in Jenna's case. In her defence though, Mona's heart attack was bound to have taken the shine off her ring. It was bound to be tarnished at the moment, wasn't it? She held out her hand.

'Oh, my goodness, it's beautiful. Congratulations, dear.'

'Thank you,' said Jenna. 'But Jake's mum's ill in hospital, so we've not had chance to celebrate yet.'

'That's a shame.' Mabel studied Jenna's face. 'I hope she recovers soon, then you can get on with making plans, can't you?'

'Yes,' Jenna mumbled. 'Who'd have thought it, me a wife.' She tried to ignore the feeling that she was talking about somebody else. There hadn't been time for it to sink in properly yet, that's all.

'Well, as long as you're happy. You are, aren't you?'

'Of course.' Jenna lowered her gaze. But not before seeing Mabel's brow furrow. 'We're looking at the Christmas after next though, so it's going to be a long engagement.'

'Oh? Why's that?'

Why indeed?

'No rush, especially now. We need to concentrate on getting Mona back to fighting strength first.'

Hmm, maybe I'll retract the fighting bit. And slightly less strength than before? No! That's a terrible thing to think, Jenna!

'I see.' Mabel nodded.

Jenna was sure that she did. Only too well. At least Mabel never judged her. No matter what, she seemed to love her, faults and all.

'Thanks, Mabel.'

'For what, dear?'

'Being you.'

'It's not all it's cracked up to be, believe me.'

Jenna kissed her cheek. 'Well, I love you.'

Mabel's eyes misted over. 'I love you too, dear. More than you could possibly know.'

'Look at us.' Jenna blew her nose. 'What are we like, hey?' She stood up to leave. 'I'd better get to the hospital, but I'll see you soon.'

'All right. I hope everything turns out…okay.'

'Well, I do have one less problem to worry about. We're getting a lodger so the financial strain will be lifted a bit.'

'Really? Who is she?'

'It's a he.' Jenna felt her face flame. 'Erm, a friend of a friend.'

'What does your young man think about that?' asked Mabel. 'Ah, I can see from your face you haven't told him yet, have you, dear?'

'Erm, no. I've not had chance.' Jenna hadn't even considered what Jake would make of it. But surely he'd understand how much she needed the extra money, wouldn't he? 'Anyway, if I run I'll catch the bus, Mabel. Take care.'

As Jenna went through the ward door, it was as if she was entering a parallel life. Everything seemed mixed up. It was almost impossible to remember who she should say what to.

If she'd thought life complicated before, well, that was nothing compared to now.

Jake looked up and left his mum's bedside to greet her. 'Hi, I didn't expect to see you yet. I thought you'd be still at work.'

Damn! She hadn't considered the timing. That's where lying got you. Into telling more lies to cover up for the first.

'I, erm, left early. It was hard to concentrate when I needed to be here, with you.'

Thank God Alesha said hell doesn't exist. My place would definitely be booked.

'Thanks, Jenna. That means a lot.' Jake took her arm. 'Mum's awake and she's been asking for you.'

90

'That's great! Have the doctors said anything?'

'The signs are good. They're hopeful with plenty of rest she'll make a full recovery.'

Jenna walked up to the bed. The improvement from yesterday was huge, but the colour of Mona's skin made her look more ghost-like than Alesha.

'Hello, Mona. That was quite a scare you gave us.' Jenna smiled. 'You'll soon be back to normal though, from what I've been told.'

I wonder if a heart attack can cause amnesia? Maybe she'll have forgotten about moving in.

'The figurines,' Mona whispered. 'I'll find them soon.'

Maybe not, then.

'What's all this talk about figurines, Mum?' asked Jake. He shrugged at Jenna.

'Now's not the time to be worrying about figurines,' said Jenna. 'They're going nowhere. Relax.'

Literally nowhere.

'I'll pick up some brochures for you, Mum. You can have a look through some and tell us about the best wedding packages.'

Don't I have a say in this?

Mona's face instantly brightened. 'I've made a list of all the manor houses in the area.'

Obviously not.

'I've got a list of caterers too. But we're not using the ones from your grandparents' party!' Mona's eyelids drooped. 'They'd never manage a banquet for a hundred guests.'

I wonder if they can manage ninety-nine? I'm not sure they'd notice if I gave it a miss.

'You need to get some rest now.' Jake bent to kiss Mona's cheek. 'We'll see you tomorrow, Mum.'

Jenna hesitated before bending to do the same. It was the first time she'd kissed Mona. It felt a bit strange. Jenna felt a stab of guilt for wishing Mabel was Jake's mum. Logic told her that although not impossible, Mabel was probably too old. But she was more family to Jenna than Mona could ever be.

You're vile, Jenna. Absolutely vile.

Jake opened the car door for Jenna. As she stepped inside, it occurred to her that he was one of life's true gentlemen. They were few and far between, yet her husband-to-be belonged to this rare breed. How lucky was she? Therefore, it seemed more than slightly wrong to be thinking about a man who was as far removed from being a gentleman as you could get. But there was no denying the intrigue that surrounded Ben.

Jenna was concerned about something he'd left her with. But she could hardly thank him for it. It wasn't a gift. Not unless a sudden unfamiliar ache in her lower stomach could be classed as such. If so, she wanted to exchange it for something more suitable. Or, even better, ask for a refund…

Chapter Nine

Jenna inhaled the freshly brewed coffee. For some reason she found the smell relaxing. Not that she was uptight. Much. A loud noise outside startled her. Either the owner of a set of bongo drums had taken up residence, or a car stereo was playing reggae music at top volume. A quick glance out of the window confirmed the latter.

When Ben stepped from the car he spotted Jenna and waved, then took a case from the boot. It didn't look as if it would hold much. Maybe the plan was to do more than one trip. She opened the front door and watched as he carefully slung a guitar case over his shoulder.

'Morning, J.' He walked up the path. 'Bacon on yet?'

Jenna grinned. 'No, you'll have to make do with coffee. Do you play the guitar?' She realised how dumb that sounded. Of course he did. Why else would he carry it around? It was too big to be some kind of fashion accessory. Men could be strange creatures, but not enough to haul a musical instrument everywhere they went, like a handbag.

'Yeah, I try,' said Ben.

'Cool! Come in and get sorted. How many more trips do you need to do? I thought you were borrowing a van.'

'Nah, not necessary. I've got everything I need right here.'

'Okay.' Jenna led him into the hallway. 'Take your stuff upstairs and I'll make you a drink.'

'Yes, ma'am.' Ben saluted her and stood to attention. 'Are you always this bossy? Hope so, I like it.' He winked.

Jenna felt her face flush and rushed to the kitchen, wishing Ellie was back from her Saturday morning trip to the supermarket. She blinked in surprise as Alesha appeared suddenly.

'Sorry I didn't wait for the signal.' She panted. 'I had to be here when Ben arrived though.'

'It's okay,' said Jenna. 'I'll let you off, this once.'

'Anyway, I'm bored with seeing you tie yourself in knots attempting to do the jig.'

Jenna pulled a face. 'Good.'

Ben sauntered into the kitchen. It struck Jenna as sad that he wasn't aware of the fact that he'd just brushed past Alesha. She wiped the corner of her eye and handed him a steaming mug.

'You okay, J?' He touched her arm.

'I'm fine.' The simple words belied the truth of what Jenna really thought and felt. This situation was surreal. If only it was possible to rewind a few days. Then all there would be to think about was what she and Ellie could have for dinner that evening.

'Hi, Ben, hi Al — erm, I'll just put the shopping away,' said Ellie from the doorway, grimacing at her near blunder.

Thank God Alesha's name hadn't been said in full. As luck would have it, Ben hadn't noticed. Jenna shuddered at the thought.

'Hi, El.' He smiled. 'I'm going to get the three of us a takeaway this evening. To celebrate me moving in.'

'Great,' said Ellie. 'Indian, Chinese or Italian?'

'What's your favourite, ladies?'

'What's yours?' asked Jenna.

'You pick.'

'Oh, for goodness' sake.' Alesha sighed. 'Make a decision. I'm glad I don't have to worry about stuff like that anymore. For the record Ben prefers Chinese. Especially crispy duck.'

'What about Chinese?' said Jenna. 'I love crispy duck.'

Ben did a double take. 'Really? Me too!'

'Erm, and me,' said Ellie. 'Obviously not the duck though. Just the erm…crispy.'

'That's settled then. Crispy it is.' Ben clinked mugs with Jenna and Ellie. 'How's your future mother-in-law, J?'

Oh. My. God! I haven't told Jake about Ben moving in. Shit, shit, shit!

Over the past couple of days Jenna had been so busy with work and visiting Mona, that telling Jake had slipped her mind. Almost. She *had* planned to tell him after Ben had seen the room, but hadn't found the right time. He'd been so worried about his mum and keeping on top of his workload that the moment had passed. She had to tell him before he turned up to find Ben here, with no warning. Although he knew Jenna's financial situation, she sensed he wouldn't be happy. But at the end of the day he could've moved in himself, had he not been so reluctant to leave the comforts of home. And Mona pandering to him as if he were a child. He'd probably be ecstatic at the idea of his mum living with them after the wedding. That way he'd have the best of both worlds.

No matter what, Jenna, you should've told him before now. Stop making excuses and deal with it!

'J?'

'Oh, erm, she's on the mend. Actually, I need to give Jake a call to see if there's any more news.' Jenna darted upstairs with her phone. 'Jake?' She wasn't sure whether to be relieved or not when he answered. 'Where are you? Can we talk?'

'I'm on my way to the hospital and then I'm nipping to the office to pick up some files. Is something wrong?'

'Yes! No! Look, I'll meet you at the hospital and then you can drop me off back here on your way to the office, okay?'

'Right, see you soon,' said Jake. 'Do you fancy a takeaway tonight? Maybe a Chinese?'

'Yummy,' muttered Jenna. 'A Chinese.'

Nice one, Jenna. Hope you're hungry!

'So, when Ellie asked if her friend could stay for a while I couldn't say no.' Jenna lied. 'And the rent money he's going to pay will help a lot.'

'He?' Jake's jaw tightened. 'How many more waifs and strays are you planning on giving out keys to?'

'Only Ben, that's all.'

'I can't believe you didn't think to discuss this with me first,' said Jake. 'I'm not happy about it. Tell him no.'

Jenna's gaze dropped to the floor. 'Erm…I can't, because he's erm—'

'What?'

'Moved in already. This morning.'

'Get in,' Jake hissed.

Before Jenna had time to fasten her seatbelt, Jake accelerated swiftly. She gripped the seat with white knuckles. He didn't look at her or speak until they pulled up outside the house.

'See you later.' Jenna opened the car door. Jake didn't answer. No sooner had she stepped from the car, he pulled away with a screech.

She stood on the pavement, watching him disappear from sight. In all the time they'd been together, he'd never had a reason to be angry with her. Until now.

Suddenly, the last place Jenna wanted to be was at home, with her two lodgers. She needed some space and time on her own, so decided to walk into town via the river.

Although the air was chilly, the boats that cruised along the water were surprisingly full. The passengers looked happy and carefree. But were they really? It was easy to paint on a smile for the benefit of others. Even when you were dying inside.

The town centre was always busy on a Saturday, which was why Jenna tended to avoid it as a rule. She dodged a group of youngsters, who were jostling with each other amid much laughter. Couples strolled hand in hand, clearly happy just to be together, and then there were people like her. Wandering aimlessly, not quite sure where they wanted to be.

A wedding dress shop caught her eye. Maybe now was a good time to take a look.

At least it'll get me back in Jake's good books if I show some enthusiasm for the wedding. But I should want to look for my own pleasure...shouldn't I?

Stepping inside, she immediately felt awkward. An immaculately dressed member of staff pounced straight away.

'Can I help you?' She smiled. 'Are you looking for A-line, princess, sheath, mermaid or ballerina?'

97

What? Can't she speak English? That's all foreign to me.

'Erm, I'm not sure.' The sea of white froth around her was overwhelming. 'Maybe I can just take a look?'

'Of course.' The girl nodded. 'Let me know if you want to try anything on.'

Jenna ran a hand over the rails. It was a wonder they didn't give way under the weight of some of the dresses. How on earth were you supposed to move in them, never mind actually walk? In Jenna's mind they were horrific. Far too much bling for her liking. The only thing she was sure of was that the right dress wouldn't be too fussy. And then she saw it. The ivory taffeta was understated, yet at the same time perfect. It was strapless, with just the right amount of beading detail to prevent it from being plain. It swung out around the hips and tiny buttons ran down the full length at the back. If she was going to wear a wedding dress at all, this would be the one. But a wave of panic hit her like a thunderbolt and she sprinted to the exit, taking in deep gulps of air once outside.

What was wrong? The dress looked completely right on the hanger, but the idea of actually putting it on was abhorrent. Trying and failing to picture wearing it in front of Jake and a roomful of guests, she legged it up the road, until the shop was no longer in view. She tapped the wall four times. That didn't calm her, so had to tap it four more times.

Although Jenna was no expert, at a guess this behaviour wasn't typical of a normal bride-to-be. Shouldn't she be turning this way and that, admiring her reflection in the mirror? And then be reluctant to take the dress off? Bridezilla she clearly wasn't. Well, if dress shopping was out today, she'd try something else instead. Like sitting in that coffee shop and watching the world go by for a while.

The aroma of the coffee relaxed her a little. Sinking back into the squishy chair, Alesha sprung to mind. Jenna half expected her to appear, and had to admit it would be nice if she did. But it was obvious where she was: at home, with Ben. And Ellie.

Part of her wanted to run and run. But as much as the thought of getting away was appealing, where would she go? The only family left was Uncle Mick. The last she'd heard from him was a postcard from Nepal a couple of months ago. The travelling bug had hit him in his early twenties and he was thirty-four no█ ████ █████ed having him around on a regular basis. █ █████se he was the only link to her father, but bec█ ███s good fun and also made her feel safe. Like an older bro████r.

People had worried that Jenna would become isolated if she continued to live in the house. But it was everything to her. The trouble was, it felt as though she was losing control of it. First Ellie, then Alesha and now Ben. Of *course* Jake would be upset by two others living there. Choking back a giggle, Jenna wondered what he'd say if he knew about Alesha. He couldn't have a go at Jenna for giving out a third key though! But it was more than possible that he'd take exception to Alesha appearing when she pleased…especially given that she'd conquered walking through walls. Almost. Luckily ghosts didn't seem to bruise.

The first thing to greet Jenna when entering the house was a sweet vanilla scent. Following it, she wandered into the sitting room, halting in surprise at the scene in front of her. Lit candles were scattered around and the table was nicely set with three place settings. Both Ellie and Ben looked up from folding napkins.

'Hi, J.' Ben grinned. 'Hope you don't mind us digging this stuff out from the depths of your kitchen cupboards.'

'No, it's fine.' Jenna wasn't entirely sure that was true, but was more concerned by the fire risk the candles were posing. Lovely as they were, they made her panic. 'Erm, are the candles safe?'

"Course they are,' said ⬛⬛⬛⬛⬛⬛⬛⬛ to make sure they're in the right holders, tha⬛

'I just wanted to say a pr⬛⬛⬛⬛⬛⬛⬛⬛ making me welcome into your home.' Ben lig⬛⬛⬛⬛⬛⬛⬛⬛er arm. It felt like an electric shock running thro⬛⬛⬛⬛⬛⬛⬛

Hmm, God knows what he cla⬛⬛⬛⬛unwelcome. I haven't exactly rolled out the red carpet.

Jenna wondered where Alesha could be. Looking from Ellie to Ben, her heart sank. Had they been getting too close for Alesha's comfort? Vowing to keep an eye on the situation, there was nothing else she could say or do right now. More than anything, she wanted Ellie to be happy. But hopefully that wouldn't entail starting something with Ben. That would confuse matters far too much. The feeling of protectiveness towards Alesha was strong, despite not knowing her for long. Jenna refused to acknowledge the other emotion rising to the surface. What was it about him that had Jenna so on edge? And made her feel so geeky and tongue-tied when they were together? Was Alesha wondering the same thing?

Relief swept over her when Alesha materialised literally out of nowhere, in the corner of the room. Beckoning to Jenna, she moved towards the doorway. 'Come here.'

'I'm going for a bath,' said Jenna. 'I won't be long.'

'Take as long as you need,' said Ben. 'I'll order the food when you come back down.'

Locking the bathroom door she turned to Alesha. 'Are you okay? Is it odd seeing Ben here?'

'No, but I got bored, so left them to it.'

'Bored?'

'Yeah. I have no interest in folding napkins. That was the last thing I expected Ben to be doing. They've spent ages trying to make the room look nice for you.'

'Right.' Jenna wasn't sure what else to say. Guilt rose inside her. Ellie was the best friend she could've wished for, and Ben hadn't come knocking on her door, begging to be let in. It wasn't their fault that Jenna felt the way she did.

'Jake's not happy about Ben being here.'

'I'm sorry about that. I honestly didn't want to cause trouble between the two of you.'

Jenna raised her eyebrows. 'Really?'

'Really! I just wanted you to split up, that's all.' She grinned.

'Your wish might be granted. He's not spoken to me since this morning, even though I've left loads of messages.'

'Don't chase after him. If he wants to sulk, let him.'

'It's my fault. I could've handled it better.' Jenna turned on the taps. 'I have no idea if he's going to show up here later, or not.'

'I'm amazed Ben's staying in on a Saturday night.' Alesha clearly wanted to change the subject to one she found more interesting. 'You're honoured.'

'If you say so. Can you leave me to have a bath now? Go downstairs and make sure the house isn't in danger of being burnt down by any of those candles.'

Jenna threw on jeans and T-shirt then went down to join the others.

'Just in time. Did you smell the wine?' Ben handed her a drink. 'To my new housemates.' He raised his glass.

After deciding which food was to be delivered, Jenna flopped into the one armchair. Ellie sat on the sofa. Been sauntered to Jenna's chair and perched on the arm. She edged away slightly. Why wasn't he on the sofa with Ellie? Alesha appeared and sat there, eyes gleaming.

'Have you had a nice afternoon, Jen?' said Ellie.

'I went into town and braved a wedding dress shop. It was cringey.'

'Why? Didn't you see anything you liked?'

'Most were shocking. Both in price and appearance. There was one that was quite nice, I suppose.'

'Did you try it on?'

'No.' She hesitated. 'I tried to imagine myself wearing it in front of Jake.'

'And?'

'I couldn't.'

'Oh. Right.' Ellie gave Jenna a hard look. 'Is Jake coming round? Should we have ordered food for him?'

'Christ, sorry, J!' Ben reached for his phone. 'I can add some more to the order.'

'It's okay.' Jenna shook her head. 'I somehow don't think he'll show up.'

'What's wrong?' Ellie's forehead creased. 'You haven't been arguing, have you?'

'Not exactly.' Jenna paused. 'But, look, he's not too keen on the idea of you moving in, Ben. It's nothing personal, obviously. I sprang it on him this morning. I'm sure it'll be fine once he has time to get used to the idea.'

'Hey, I don't want to cause problems.' Ben put his glass on the coffee table. 'Just say the word if you want me to leave.'

'You've only just got here,' said Ellie. 'He's being selfish, Jenna. He should be glad you're going to have extra money coming in…and another pair of eyes to make sure you're okay.'

I think it's the extra pair of eyes on me that's the problem. Especially as they're male. But he has nothing to worry about on that score. As if! Maybe he'll accept it better once he knows Ben is seeing this Sabrina, whoever she is. Call me pessimistic, but I don't see how mentioning his ex, a ghost, also being on the scene, will allay his doubts somehow. Just a hunch…

'He's stressed at the moment, that's all.' Jenna shrugged. 'Jake's not a mean person. You know that, Ellie.'

'No, he's not,' Ellie agreed. 'Anyway, what's the story with you, Ben? Tell us all the gory details.'

As soon as the words left her mouth, Jenna could see that Ellie was mortified. They both looked at Alesha, who snorted with laughter.

'Nothing much to tell.' Ben topped up their glasses and took a big swig of wine.

'Tell us about your girlfriend,' said Jenna. They had to act as if they knew nothing much about him. 'Sabrina, did you say her name was?'

Alesha stiffened and pulled a face.

'I wouldn't call her my girlfriend, as such. Just the lucky lady I've been seeing for a few weeks.'

On the surface his words sounded arrogant, but he didn't fool Jenna. For the first time, she saw his vulnerable side. Maybe after losing Alesha the thought of getting close to someone was too much.

'There's a difference?' asked Ellie.

'Well, I'm not planning on living with her, or anything. I've been there and…'

'And what?' said Jenna, though she knew the answer.

'It didn't work out.' Ben's whole demeanour changed. His eyes clouded over. He reached for the bottle and filled his glass, lost in a world of his own.

Alesha wrapped her arms around him. Although he gave no indication that he'd felt anything, he did snap out of his mood and attempted to grin at the girls. 'Hope the food arrives soon, I'm starving.'

Jenna exchanged glances with Ellie and Alesha. They appeared as bothered as she was, by the sudden change in him. The mood needed to be lifted, and quickly.

'I'm looking forward to hearing you play the guitar,' said Jenna brightly.

'Okay, later.' Ben nodded. 'Here's the food arriving. I'll get it.'

He placed the array of containers on the table. As they sat down Jenna realised how hungry she was. They chatted about safe topics such as TV and music, which was one of Jenna's favourite subjects. Alesha appeared content to listen to the flow of conversation, but on more than one occasion Jenna felt her eyes boring into her. What was she thinking? At least she was smiling though, and for now that was the important thing.

Jenna found herself enjoying the evening, in a way that was unfamiliar to her. She couldn't remember the last time she'd felt so relaxed…and, for a short time at least, happy.

The sound of the door closing and footsteps in the hallway startled them. They looked at each other, as Jake called out to Jenna.

'Hope you're hungry, Jen. I've got us a Chine—' He stood in the doorway, stock still. The only movement from him was the pulse clearly visible in his neck.

'Jake! Come and sit down.' Jenna pulled out a chair. 'We were going to order you some food, but I hadn't heard anything...' Her voice trailed off.

Ben stood up and walked round the table. 'Jake, I'm Ben, it's nice to meet you.' He held out his hand.

Jake nodded briefly, but ignored the outstretched hand. He banged the bag containing the food onto the table. 'Here, you may as well have it, I've lost my appetite.'

'Jake, please, come and —'

'I've got work to do. I'll see you...soon.' He headed for the door. Jenna followed, placing her hand on his arm. 'Don't go.'

Jake shook off her hand. 'You're busy. I wanted a nice quiet night, with my fiancée. But that's going to be impossible here now, isn't it?' He opened the front door.

'I can always come round to yours more,' said Jenna. 'It's only temporary, Jake.'

'This is the house we're going to be living in when we're married, and we should be planning things here, together,' he said, over his shoulder.

'We'll work it out. In the meantime, there's tons of food. Come and have some?'

The door banged closed behind him.

I think that's a no! Sadly, I'm going to need more than king prawns to make everything right.

Chapter Ten

Jenna held onto Ellie at one side, while Ben got the other. It was one step forward and two back, as they attempted to get her upstairs without anyone getting injured.

Poor Ellie had knocked back the wine too quickly. Jenna couldn't remember the last time she'd seen her this drunk. It was understandable. Although she'd been estranged from her husband a few months, her future was still uncertain.

Jenna got Ellie settled into bed. She kissed her cheek and tiptoed to the door. She was startled to find Ben hovering on the landing. 'Is she okay?'

'She will be. I'm going to turn everything off downstairs, unless you're going back down?'

'No, go ahead.' Ben smiled. 'To be honest, I've probably had a few too many myself. I think having to help El has sobered me up.'

'Sleep well, and thanks for the takeaway.'

'No worries. I'm just sorry I've caused problems with Jake.'

Jenna moved to the top of the stairs. 'It'll be fine. One way or another. Goodnight.'

In one stride, Ben had her enveloped in his arms. 'Night, J, and thank you.'

She made her way downstairs slowly, gripping the bannister for support. Her legs felt like jelly. She wasn't sure if it was because of the wine, or the effect of Ben being in such close proximity. It must be the wine. Nothing else made sense.

'Oh, hi.' She jumped as Alesha appeared. 'You startled me.'

Jenna sank onto the sofa and Alesha sat next to her.

'Have you had a good time? Apart from Jake, I mean.'

'Yeah.' Jenna nodded. 'It was fun. I think it did Ellie good to let her hair down. I've not been much fun for her.'

'I'm talking about you, not Ellie.'

Jenna got the distinct impression that Alesha was testing her. The problem with passing this test was that she didn't know the question, so how could she give the right answer?

'Well…it was nice to get to know Ben a little. That's what you want, isn't it?'

'Yes. What do you think of him, so far?'

'Good sense of humour. Nice, I guess.'

Alesha linked arms with Jenna. 'Good looking too?'

'I can see why you think so, yes.'

Alesha sighed. 'Just admit it, you're attracted to him.'

Jenna gasped. 'I'm so not! I'm just trying to make an effort, that's all. As you badgered me into doing, if you remember?'

Oh, shit! What's she picked up on? I'm really not attracted to him, am I? I am? No. I'm. Not!

'Hey, it's fine to be honest, Jenna. I'd be happy if you said yes.'

'Why?'

'Just because.' Alesha nudged Jenna's side. 'He's hot and you know it!'

'I admit it's easy to see why you were attracted to him. But *I'm* not. I've got enough on my plate with the guy I'm supposed to be marrying.'

'Never mind Jake, for now. Ben sleeps in the nude, you know.'

Jenna disentangled herself from Alesha's grip, and turned to face her. 'Alesha! I don't need to know that, thanks very much. I'm not sure where this is leading, but I'd rather you kept information like that to yourself.'

'Easy!' Alesha winked. 'Anyone would think what I said got to you.'

'Don't be ridiculous! There's nothing between me and Ben, nor is there likely to be. End of.'

Alesha smiled. 'We'll see.' With that she faded from sight.

Upon waking Jenna checked her phone to see if Jake had left a message. He hadn't. She'd go to the hospital to see Mona, and hopefully catch him there. The longer the situation was left, the worse it would be. A tiny voice in the back of her head told her to leave it, and break off the engagement once and for all. But she didn't want to listen. As soon as the air was cleared with Jake, life would get back to some kind of normality. Apart from the minor detail of the resident ghost — and her oddly disturbing ex-boyfriend, who was now Jenna's lodger, of course.

Christ, I thought life was difficult before. Bring back blissful ignorance. Okay, maybe not blissful. I'd settle for the ignorance.

Jenna arrived at the hospital to find Jake sitting with Mona. He gave her a tight smile.

'Hello. I didn't expect you today.'

His face gave nothing away. Was he pleased to see her?

'How you feeling, Mona? You look better.' Jenna lightly touched her hand.

'I'm going home tomorrow.' Mona's beady eyes bored into first Jenna, then Jake. 'So we can get on with planning the wedding.'

Had she picked up on the tense atmosphere between them?

'Erm, okay. Good.' Jenna nodded. 'That's great news isn't it, Jake?'

'Yes.' His tone was clipped. 'The wedding can't come soon enough for me.'

Jenna was surprised by his words. She'd half expected him to be calling it off. Part of her had wanted him to, she realised with a sinking heart.

'What's the colour scheme?' asked Mona. 'I think red as it's going to be a Christmas wedding. Mind you, I can't see why you need to wait that long.'

'Neither do I, as it happens,' said Jake. 'I think we should bring the date forward.'

'Excellent!' Mona clapped. 'As soon as I get home I'll start getting things booked and ordered.'

'Hang on.' Jenna clenched her fists by her sides. 'Strange as it may sound, I do have a say in this. I'll speak to you about it later, Jake.'

Mona tutted and shook her head and Jake nodded curtly.

'Maybe we should go and discuss it now?' Jenna continued in a low voice. The yelling would have to wait until they were alone.

'I'll pick you up in the morning, Mum.' Jake kissed her cheek.

'Bye, Mona. See you soon.' Right at that moment, Jenna couldn't think of anything worse.

They walked down the corridor in silence. It was only once they were in the car that Jake spoke.

'We'll go to Mum's house where we can talk without an audience.' He started the engine. 'Okay?'

When they arrived at the house, Jake went to make a pot of tea. Jenna stared at a thick file on the table. It was neatly labelled 'Wedding File.' With shaking fingers she opened it and gasped. Mona had written 'For Jenna to try on,' next to the monstrosity of a dress she'd shown her. Next was a list of possible manor houses for the reception, but it was what was on the next page that bothered Jenna the most. Under the heading 'Guest List' was around 150 names. She didn't recognise the vast majority. At the bottom read 'Jenna's friend, Ellie.' Was that it? Couldn't Mona even remember to add Uncle Mick?

A tear ran down her cheek and splashed onto the page. She'd gradually lost contact with all her friends. They'd tried to understand what she was going through. But unless you'd been through it yourself it was hard. Jenna could see that. The truth was that she'd resented them for still having their lives and their families intact.

Jenna had had to grow up quickly and could no longer identify with the carefree partying lifestyle. It had taken a long time, but eventually a semblance of normal life had resumed. But it was as far removed from her previous life as it was possible to get. The new one consisted of fretting about bills and home improvements, and doing a job she now hated.

'Are you alright, Jenna?' Jake strode up and placed an arm around her shoulder.

His face softened as she looked up at him. 'I'm not being mean, Jake, but look at this.' Jenna thrust the file in front of his face. 'Your mum's taking over the wedding. I don't want a big fancy do. It's about us. Or should be.'

Jake sighed. 'I know what you're saying, but can't you just humour her? Let her have a say?'

'A say, yes. But I'm not having her making all the decisions as if it's her own wedding.'

'Okay, I'll have a word. But I want to bring the date forward. Waiting so long is ridiculous.'

'Forward to when?'

'Next spring. It's still a year away. I'm not trying to rush things.'

'Right. I'll go with that.'

'Brilliant! We need to choose a date and get things booked. And give Ellie and Ben a deadline for finding somewhere else to live.'

Jenna's brow furrowed. 'I know you aren't happy about them being there, especially Ben. But his rent money will really help. Surely you can see that. And there's no way I'd throw Ellie out. She's my best friend. They don't need to leave yet. You were so rude, last night.'

'Yes, sorry. I'll apologise. I don't mean they have to leave next week, or even next month. But you do need to give them warning that they have to start looking for alternative accommodation. Once they're gone, I'll decorate the house. Get it looking nice,' he cajoled. 'With plenty of time to spare before the wedding.'

'Okay, okay. But I can't think about speaking to them, or planning the wedding until after the date has passed. It's coming up soon.'

'What date?' Jake grinned. 'Have I forgotten something?'

Only the five year anniversary of the worst day of my life, that's all...

Chapter Eleven

'This is Sabrina,' said Ben. 'And this is Jenna and Ellie.' He pointed at the girls in turn.

'Hiya.' Sabrina stepped into the room behind Ben. 'I've just had my nails done, d'ya like em?' She held out her hands, displaying talons long enough to make a tiger envious. The vivid red made Jenna blink.

Alesha appeared, and grimaced. Jenna and Ellie both coughed at the same time, to choke back a giggle.

'Nice to meet you, Sabrina.' Jenna smiled. 'Would you like a drink?'

'D'ya have any Lambrini? Or cider?' Sabrina popped her chewing gum.

'Nooo…I don't think we do, do we, Ellie?' Jenna hardly dared meet Ellie's eyes.

'No. We have beer for Ben…or ordinary wine.'

'I'll have a beer. I can only drink good wine. No offence.'

'None taken.' Jenna glanced at Ellie and Alesha, then wished she hadn't. Both were grinning like Cheshire cats. 'Sit down, Sabrina.'

Jenna took in Sabrina's hard features. She thought of a child boring into a piece of paper with a crayon. They tended to go over the same part constantly. This was what the blusher on Sabrina's face reminded her of. Her eyes were outlined in thick kohl, but they looked piggy, rather than bigger. Her lip outline had been done with a pencil far too dark for the pale pink lipstick, and the line had been placed way wider than her actual lips. Her face was framed by long blonde hair, which had been clipped in, in a rush. The clips weren't all fastened, and the candy-floss textured mane hung like a curtain that had come off the track on one side.

It was a shame. Jenna thought she was probably pretty, underneath all the falseness and garish colour. But certainly not a patch on the gorgeous Alesha. Ben obviously didn't have a type. They couldn't be more different.

Sabrina stood and wandered round the room, looking at photos. As she bent to look at them, her pink velour tracksuit bottoms rode down to reveal a matching thong. Alesha twanged it. Hard. Sabrina stood straight and put her hand to her bum. She glanced round, but there was nobody near her. Or so she thought. But she sat back down in a hurry.

Jenna wiped her eyes and saw Ellie do the same. Alesha suddenly appeared in different clothing. The outfit matched Sabrina's. She strutted about, popping gum and holding out red painted nails.

By now, Jenna and Ellie were holding their sides. Sabrina seemed oblivious, but Ben clearly wasn't.

'You two okay?' he asked. 'What's so funny?'

'Oh, just something we saw earlier,' said Ellie. 'You wouldn't be interested.'

114

'So, Sabrina, you work with Ben, right?' asked Jenna. 'What is it you do?'

'We work for an advertising company, creating slogans and branding for products.' Sabrina inspected her nails.

It was the last thing Jenna would've put Sabrina down as doing. But it seemed looks were misleading in her case.

'Sounds interesting.' Ellie leaned forward in her chair. 'Tell us what you're working on.'

'We can't! It's confidential.' Sabrina's eyes blazed. 'Can we, Ben?'

He looked taken aback by her outburst, but gave a brief nod. 'Okay, calm down, Sabrina.'

She sank back into her chair and gave a tight-lipped smile. 'Erm, yeah, sorry.'

Jenna wondered why she'd got so defensive. But maybe there was more to Sabrina than met the eye. Judging by the look on Alesha's face, Jenna wasn't the only one to think so.

Alesha poked Sabrina's shoulder and smirked when Sabrina rubbed it, with a frown.

'Ben, I'm meeting my friends, remember?' She glanced at her watch. 'Can you drop me off?'

A please wouldn't go amiss!

'Yeah.' Ben stood up. 'See you in a bit, girls.'

'She's a bitch!' Alesha spat. 'And an ugly cow! She's up to something too.'

'You don't like her then?' Ellie grinned. 'I must admit, she's not what I expected.'

'What did you expect?' asked Alesha.

'Well…someone more like you I suppose.' Ellie shrugged.

'Maybe the person who Ben's meant to be with is nothing like me.' Alesha turned to look at Jenna. 'And I think Ben knows it's not Sabrina. It's just a matter of time before he realises who she really is. And vice versa.'

Jenna shifted in her seat. Why was Alesha looking at her like that?

'Don't you mind the idea of Ben being with someone else?' said Ellie. 'It can't be easy.'

'I don't mind. Why would I? We weren't meant to be. I'll always care about him though, and want him to be with the right person.'

'What about you, Ellie?' said Jenna. 'How would you feel if you knew that so-called husband of yours was seeing someone else?'

Ellie sighed. 'He might be for all I know. Maybe that's why he's been calling me, to tell me. But I'm not ready to speak to him. I hope he is, in a way.'

'What? Why?'

'Because it'll help me move on. As far as I'm concerned, we're not married anymore. I mean in my head, not officially. It's weird how you can be so close to someone for so long, and then overnight it changes and you become strangers.'

'Yes, it is weird.' Alesha nodded. 'But you'll meet someone else, Ellie. When the time's right.'

'I know,' said Ellie simply.

'What family did you have?' Jenna asked Alesha. 'Any brothers or sisters?'

Alesha shook her head. 'No, I was an only child, like you.'

'What about your parents? Were they both still alive when…you know?'

'Yes. They took it hard, of course. But they're okay. Religion's helped them. Their faith has seen them through. I think what also makes it easier is knowing they'll see me again one day.'

116

'Will they? Really?' Jenna rubbed her temple.

Alesha nodded. 'Yes, and you'll see your parents one day too. Remember what I said about time not being the same after death? Well, live life to the full, the way they want you to. They'll be waiting for you, but not for a long time yet. To you, at least.'

Jenna considered her words. 'I *am* living the way they'd want me to. I'm keeping the house, aren't I?'

'Do you really think that's what they want? Above you living your dream? The worst thing you could do, in their eyes, is to waste your life. Bricks and mortar mean nothing to them. Why the obsession with keeping the house?'

'They loved it, and sacrificed so much for me…I need to feel as though I'm repaying them, in the only way I know how.'

'Has it never crossed your mind that you're doing the exact opposite to repaying them, by giving up on all your hopes and dreams? Think about it, Jenna. By living this way, surely you're throwing everything back in their faces? It was not, I repeat, was not, your fault…so don't let them have died in vain.'

Jenna clasped her hands to her ears. Alesha didn't know what she was talking about.

'Shut up! Shut up!' Jenna moaned.

'Is everything okay?' Ben stood in the doorway. He hesitated before entering the room.

'Erm, yes.' Jenna attempted a smile. 'So…Sabrina's out with her friends? She seems…nice.'

Ben laughed. 'She is, once you get to know her.'

Alesha narrowed her eyes. 'She's a manipulative, scheming little witch.'

'I'm sure she's not.' Ellie shook her head.

'What? You don't think so?' Ben turned to Ellie. 'You've only met her once.'

117

Jenna knew only too well how difficult it was, to enter into any conversation with Alesha when others were around. It was easy to answer her without thinking, and she saw that poor Ellie was struggling. 'Ellie didn't mean it, she has a strange sense of humour sometimes.' Jenna laughed. 'Don't you, Ellie?'

'I guess so.' Ellie glowered. 'Who wants a drink? Sorry we haven't any *proper* wine.'

'How much can you tell us about your job, Ben? I mean, I get it's confidential, but it sounds interesting,' said Jenna.

'Oh, Sabrina exaggerated, take no notice.' Ben opened the can of beer Ellie held out to him. 'We create advertising slogans for companies to use on TV, billboards and stuff. What she meant by the confidential aspect is when we're working on something new. Obviously we can't risk any rivals pinching our ideas, so we have to keep new campaigns hush-hush, until it's all signed, sealed and delivered.'

'Cool! It sounds exciting.' Ellie's eyes gleamed. 'Show us something you've done.'

'Okay. I'll just get my laptop.'

He found the page he was looking for and they peered over his shoulder at the screen.

'These are the most recent,' said Ben. 'This one here was for a pen company.'

Inkflow Pens
'We're always write'

'And this one is the new energy bar, you know? Four inch?'

The 4 inch Energy Bar
'Have 4 inches and go for miles'

'They're good.' Ellie laughed. 'We should have a go, Jen.'

'Yeah, right,' said Jenna. 'Oh, okay then. Why not?'

Ben tore two pieces of paper from a pad on the table. 'Here you are then, go for it.'

Jenna chewed the top of the pen. It was hard, thinking under pressure. But, she thought, if Sabrina can do it, then so can I. 'Okay, I've got one. What about you, Ellie?'

'Yeah, you first.'

Jenna held out her piece of paper.

Happy Chappy Toilet Tissue
'Crack' a smile!

'Very good!' Ben grinned. 'What you got, El?'

Serious Support Sports Bra
'Because titting about isn't part of the game!'

'That's hilarious!' Jenna giggled. 'You've got competition, Ben.'

He nodded. 'Yeah, I have! Got any more, El?'

She scribbled on the paper. 'What about this?'

South West Trains
No squeeze, just ease!

Ben nodded his approval. 'I love the drawing to go with it! You're good!'

'Yes, you are,' said Jenna. 'You were always good at drawing. How's the book coming on, by the way?'

'Well,' Ellie sighed. 'I'm debating whether to change the name of the main character. Maybe to something a bit more modern.'

'Oh. Did you work out that first paragraph you were struggling with?'

'No. But you can't rush these things.'

Nobody could accuse you of rushing, Ellie.

'You're writing a book?' Ben raised his eyebrows. 'I can't wait to read it.'

Let's hope your eyesight remains intact by the time you reach pension age, then!

'Well, keep going.' Jenna smiled.

'Write about a clown called Sabrina.' Alesha piped up. 'She looks like one!'

Jenna and Ellie grinned.

'What's so amusing?' asked Ben.

'Oh, nothing,' chorused Jenna and Ellie.

'A private joke,' added Ellie.

'Whatever!' He shrugged. 'I'm going upstairs to listen to some music. I'll probably be asleep soon, I'm knackered.'

'Okay.' The girls nodded. 'Night.'

'Let's go up to your room, Jenna,' said Alesha. 'I want to see all your makeup and stuff.'

'I don't use it that much nowadays,' said Jenna. 'But we can, if you like.'

'What about I give you a makeover?' said Ellie. 'You need to start practising with different looks for the wedding.'

'Yes!' Alesha's eyes shone. 'Come on, I'll tell you what colours are best, Ellie.'

Alesha gave Ellie a running commentary on what products to use. Just as Jenna thought they'd finished, they started on her hair.

'Ow!' Jenna rubbed her head. 'Don't let them send you for an interview at a hairdresser's, Ellie.'

'Oh, I forgot to tell you about the latest interview.'

'Where was it?' Jenna crossed her fingers. 'Did it go well?'

'Define well.' Ellie shrugged.

'Do you think you'll get the job?'

'I already know I haven't.'

'How?'

'Because I told them not to offer it to me.'

'What? Why?'

'It was in a restaurant,' said Ellie. 'I asked if I would have to serve meat. They said yes. I explained I was vegetarian, and asked if I could just serve non-meat dishes. When they said no, I asked if they'd fire me if I refused.'

'What did they say to that?'

'I'd be fired on the spot. So I suggested we avoided all the unpleasantness, and to pretend the interview never happened.'

'But won't you be penalised by the jobcentre?'

'No! The restaurant owner will be careful what he says.'

'How can you be so sure?'

'Because I mentioned what a big rat they had, in the kitchen.'

'Urghh, really?'

'No. Not really. But he wasn't taking the risk of me talking, so he said not to worry about the jobcentre.'

'Nice one!' Alesha snorted.

An hour later Ellie led Jenna to the mirror. 'Open your eyes.'

Jenna stared, open-mouthed. She hardly recognised the person looking back at her. 'Blimey, is that really me?'

The smoky eyes staring through the mirror looked twice the size, and her cheekbones were accentuated with highlighter.

Her lips were painted matte red. The thick mane of hair was big and bouncy.

'Stunning!' Alesha gasped.

'You look beautiful!' Ellie grinned. 'What do you think?'

'It doesn't look like me...but I like it.' Jenna peered closer into the mirror. A sudden memory caught her unawares. She was applying lipstick with the aid of a small compact mirror. There was a group of girls joking that Jenna probably even slept with lipstick on. She was never seen without it. Her eyes began to sting.

Alesha cut into her thoughts. 'Ben's just gone into the bathroom. Let's show him your new look, Jenna.'

'No!' Jenna shook her head. But before she had time to stop her, Ellie flung open the bedroom door. Just at that moment Ben came out of the bathroom.

'Ben,' Ellie called. 'Come and see the new Jenna.'

'Wow!' Ben gaped from the doorway. 'I mean, seriously, wow!'

Jenna felt her face flame. She hoped the layers of makeup disguised it.

'She looks fab, doesn't she?' said Ellie.

'Yep.' He whistled. 'She does.'

Jenna felt uncomfortable with so many eyes on her. 'Right, erm, I think I'll get ready for bed now.'

'You look like you already are.' Ben grinned. 'Night, J. Night, El.'

Once he was out of earshot Jenna turned to Ellie. 'That was mega-embarrassing. I felt a right idiot.'

'Did you see his face?' Alesha giggled.

'I know!' said Ellie. 'Bet he fancies you now, Jenna.'

'No.' Alesha shook her head. 'You got the *now* bit wrong.'

'What do you mean?' Ellie's forehead creased.

'I mean he always did.'

'I don't know what you're talking about, Alesha. He's just been friendly since he moved in, that's all.' Jenna sighed.

'Oh, it was long before he moved in,' said Alesha. 'You see, Jenna, it was you he was meant to be with all along, not me. Obviously you don't remember, and I don't think he does either, yet. I intervened, and blocked your true destiny. Part of the reason I'm here is to put that right.' She picked up a pot of face cream from the dressing table. 'Hey, I've thought of a slogan, especially for Sabrina: Witchety Face Cream

'It will help...but once haggard always haggard!'

Jenna and Ellie stared open-mouthed as Alesha waved and disappeared from sight.

Chapter Twelve

Jenna pulled the duvet over her head. 'L-leave m-me alone, Ellie, please.' She sobbed.

'I've brought you a cup of tea,' Ellie whispered. 'I'll leave you alone if you want, or we can talk? It's up to you, Jen.'

'Ohh, Ellie, I can't bear it! What am I going to do? Are things ever going to get better? I hate this date!'

Ellie gently removed the duvet from Jenna's face. 'I know how hard it is for you, darling. But you've got the wedding to think about now.'

'You're not helping.'

'Your parents would hate seeing you like this, you know.'

Alesha appeared at the foot of the bed. 'They *do* see you like this. *And* they hate it!'

'Well, let me see them then. They can tell me!' Jenna howled.

'I can't.' Alesha shook her head. 'But please believe me when I say they *are* with you at times like this, when you're reaching out to them.'

'I think you're making things worse, Alesha,' said Ellie. 'If you can't bring them to her, you should quit talking about it.'

Alesha glared at Ellie. 'What do you want to say to them, Jenna?'

'Why did you leave me? I'll never let the house go. I'm so sorry for what happened. Oh, and I'm sorry for knocking a hole in the wall when I tried to put a picture up.'

The room was silent for a minute, before Alesha replied. 'They had to go, but they haven't left you, not really. The house isn't important, and what happened had nothing to do with you. Stop blaming yourself, once and for all. As for the wall...you always were a clumsy cat.'

Jenna froze. Clumsy cat? How could Alesha possibly know that's what her mum called her? 'Alesha.' She gulped. 'How did you know that? Was it a guess?'

'No! It's hardly a generic phrase.' Alesha took her hand. 'They love you and want you to be happy.'

'Yeah.' Jenna wasn't sure what to think.

'Don't slouch when you could dance, and don't mutter when you could sing.'

'MUM? DAD? Where are you?' Jenna shot up in bed. She put a hand to her mouth. 'My dad used to say that. I thought it was strange, but now I understand it. They really do want me to be happy, don't they?'

Alesha nodded. 'How could you doubt that?'

'I didn't really. But I've forgotten how to be.' Tears streamed down her face. Ellie handed her a tissue. 'Five years ago today, my world was torn apart. It felt as if my heart had been ripped out. Then mangled up and trod on, and put back in all wrong. Nothing could ever be the same again after that.'

'No, it couldn't.' Alesha agreed. 'But life could still be good. Excellent in fact, if you let it.'

Jenna's mind was spinning with countless thoughts. She turned to Alesha.

'Oh, God, Alesha! I'm so sorry! Today's hardly a walk in the park for you, is it? Has Ben gone to work?'

Alesha nodded. 'Hope he's okay. I can't believe I've been dead five years.' Her eyes misted. 'I wish I could come back to life for even just a day.' She giggled. 'Then we could go shopping, go out for lunch, do each other's hair and make-up and drink wine.'

'And you could spend time with Ben properly,' said Jenna.

Alesha gave a brief nod, but said nothing.

Jenna blew her nose. 'Look, we can catch up later, the three of us? But if you don't mind, I could do with a bit of time on my own. You know?'

The others nodded.

'I'm going to pick up some stuff from the house if you don't need me, Jenna,' said Ellie. 'Adam will be at work so I'll let myself in and get what I need. I've been putting it off.'

'Do you want me to go with you?' Jenna didn't want to let her go on her own. 'For moral support?'

Ellie shook her head. 'No, I need to do this on my own. Just as you need to get through today in your own way. Don't worry, I'll be fine.'

'I'll come with you, just in case you need someone to talk to,' said Alesha. 'Come on. We'll see you later, Jenna.'

Jenna huddled back under the covers. She opened her eyes with a start, on hearing footsteps thundering up the stairs. Her heart raced, until Ben's bedroom door slammed. He must've left work early.

She rubbed her eyes and slid into a dressing gown. Caffeine was what was called for.

As she poured coffee into a mug, Ben walked into the kitchen. Without a word, he slumped over the worktop.

'You look like I feel,' Jenna murmured. 'Hard day?'

Ben winced as the hot liquid hit the back of his throat. 'Yep, you could say that.'

He raked his hand through already dishevelled hair. Banging down the mug, he began pacing up and down the length of the room. His eyes wandered to the calendar hanging on the wall.

'Fuck that!' He snatched a pen from the worktop. 'Fucking seventh of May! I wish it could be eradicated! Wiped out!' He swiped the box on the calendar with the pen. 'Fuck you!'

He threw the pen against the wall. Jenna flinched. 'Tell me about it, Ben. I'm not too fond of this date myself.'

'Why's that? Let me see…you don't like your shifts at work? You have nothing to wear? You've ran out of chocolate?' He crumpled onto a chair. 'Sorry, J, but you don't understand.'

'Well, tell me. And no, none of the things you mentioned are the reason. I don't like the date because five years ago today, I lost my parents in an accident.'

Ben turned to face her. 'Christ! You're kidding? No, course you're not! Fuck!'

Jenna clasped his hand. 'I can't get it out of my mind. People tell me to move on, but I can't!'

He opened the fridge and took out a can of beer and a bottle of wine. 'Here.' He poured a glass and placed it in front of her.

'No! I've got coffee, tempting as it is.'

'Fuck the coffee!' He opened the can. 'Well, I'm having one.'

127

Jenna toyed with the stem of the glass. 'Do you want to talk?'

'I want to listen. Tell me what happened, J.'

She took a long slug. 'I was at uni in Birmingham, doing a degree in music. I was in my last year and due to graduate in the November. A few months before the accident, some friends and I formed a band. I was the lead singer —'

'No way! Really?' Ben leaned forward. 'Sorry, carry on.'

'The first week of May we practised round the clock, hardly sleeping. On the seventh we were performing our first gig. I begged my parents to go.' Jenna took a deep breath. 'They said they wouldn't miss it for the world. They set off early that morning and arrived at lunchtime. We spent a lovely couple of hours together, then I went to set up with the band.'

'Where was the gig held?'

'The student union. Anyway, it went really well. I remember being so nervous I thought I was going to throw up. But when I started singing, my parents looked so proud. We got a standing ovation, Ben! It was cool. The feeling was incredible, and what made it better, was knowing my mum and dad were beside themselves. The amount of photos Dad took. Honestly, they were both in their element.'

'Proud of their little girl, hey?' Ben smiled.

'Yeah. They told everybody who would listen that I was their daughter.' Tears streamed down her cheeks, falling with a plop onto the table. 'They left around ten that evening. I had a couple of drinks with the band. We were buzzing. When I got back to the shared house I was living in, the police were there. They took me into a room on my own.' She sobbed. Ben handed her a tissue. 'I can't recall their exact words. I think I've erased them from my memory. But one minute I was delirious with happiness and the next it was snatched away.' She tore at the tissue, watching the shredded bits scatter in front of her.

128

'What happened, J?' He passed another tissue to her.

'There was a tyre blowout on the car. It careered into the central reservation on the motorway, and came to a stop sideways in the fast lane.'

'Jesus,' Ben muttered.

'That didn't kill them. They'd have been okay, but the car behind them T-boned their car. Apparently they wouldn't have felt a thing.' Jenna cradled her head in her hands. 'It was all my fault! If I hadn't asked them to travel that day, they'd be here now.' She reached blindly for her glass, knocking it over in the process. Ben filled it and put it in her hand.

'You can't blame yourself, J. It would've happened next time they got in the car.'

'Yes, but they wouldn't have been on the motorway, would they?' She dug a nail into her palm. 'They'd have survived.'

'You don't know that! Life can be cruel. Who knows why innocent people are taken from us?' His eyes misted. He wiped them with an impatient swipe of his hand. 'Did you go back to uni?'

Jenna shook her head. 'I couldn't face it. All the whispers and sympathy.' She shuddered. 'Anyway, I was in no fit state. For weeks, it took me all my time to get out of bed, never mind concentrate on a degree.'

'So what did you do?'

'Eventually I got a job in care. Keeping the house became the most important thing. My parents had re-mortgaged it, to fund my degree. They could've moved, bought something smaller, but they loved this house. And I felt bad they'd struggled financially so that I could do what I wanted.'

'You were their only child and it sounds as if they were happy, if you were.'

'I know. When I told them I wanted to be a singer, and maybe work in production too, they accepted it. Not once did they try to change my mind.'

'Well, from what you've said about that night, they were proud of what you'd achieved. What I don't understand is why you can't see beyond keeping hold of the house. Surely, what they'd want more than anything is for you to live your dream.'

'That's what everyone says.' Jenna sighed. 'But I don't even know if it is my dream anymore.'

'Right. So, working in a job you don't particularly like, worrying about bills and house repairs is, then?'

'No! 'Course it's not. But what else can I do?'

'You could go back to uni, or at least do something you're interested in. I'm sure your parents would want that. There's nothing stopping you from selling up, buying a smaller property, and doing something worthwhile with your life. We know only too well how short life can be. Start living again, J.'

'When Jake and I get married, we'll be able to keep the house. It'll be easier then.'

'Oh, yeah, the wedding.' Ben filled her glass. 'You excited? Not only will you be caring for people at work, but you'll be coming home to run around after a husband. And, by what I've heard from Ellie, his mother too.'

'How does Ellie know Mona is planning on living with us?'

As if I couldn't guess. Alesha.

'Dunno.' He shrugged. 'But it sounds like a recipe for disaster to me. Still, if that's what you want…'

Jenna hesitated. 'Right at this moment, I haven't a clue what I want, Ben. Everything seems to have happened so fast and I'm getting carried along with it all. I don't feel in control of my life anymore. I haven't for five years, but it's getting out of hand lately.'

Not least because of Alesha crashing into my life. And you too…

Jenna continued. 'It's your turn now. Tell me why *you* hate this date so much.'

She felt uncomfortable at the thought of hearing what Ben had to say about Alesha dying. But it had to be done.

'I lost someone close to me. That was an accident too. She was knocked over.' Ben closed his eyes. 'All the witnesses say that the driver had no time to stop — that Alesha stepped out right into the path of the car.'

'That's awful!' Jenna whispered. 'Was she your girlfriend?'

This feels so awkward. When he says yes, I'll have to pretend to be shocked.

'No.' Ben shook his head. 'Not at the time of the accident.'

No? Did he just say no? Why's he lying?

'No? Who was she, then?'

'Well, she *had* been my girlfriend. We'd been living together, but we split up a few weeks before it happened.'

'You can't have!' Jenna's eyes widened.

'Pardon?'

'I mean, erm, so you weren't living together anymore? How sad.'

'The morning it happened, she came round to the flat we'd been renting, to pick up some stuff. I was still living there.' He leaned back in his chair and put his arms behind his head. 'We had a stupid argument about who owned some CD's. She stormed out. Less than half an hour later she was dead.' His voice broke. 'I've blamed myself. Why didn't I just let her take the CD's?'

I don't believe I'm hearing this. One of them is lying…and I suspect it's Alesha!

'How's it your fault, Ben?'

'She was obviously in a bad mood. Not concentrating on the road. It *is* my fault!'

Jenna was confused. Why hadn't Alesha told her they'd split up? It didn't make sense. How was she supposed to convince Ben he wasn't to blame? Alesha said she'd seen somebody on the other side of the road, and wanted to catch up with him. But she could hardly tell Ben that.

'You don't know why she stepped in front of the car, Ben.'

'It's obvious.'

'No, it's not! You can't feel guilty because you'd had an argument. People argue all the time. It's life.'

'That's why we split up. We'd started arguing and worried that in the future resentment would build up, and that we'd end up hating each other. Neither of us wanted that. The pact we made was, despite no longer being a couple nobody would ever stop us being close. Any new partners were going to have to deal with it. And accept our brother/sister relationship.'

'But surely there was still attraction between you?'

Ben shook his head. 'No, not by then. But she *was* stunning.' He smiled.

She still is, Ben. She makes me look like a heifer!

He continued. 'We understood each other, and wanted to remain a big part of each other's lives. We *did* love each other and it was hard to let go of the relationship. But we knew it was the right thing to do. I've never got over her though, to be honest.'

'Do you think you'd have ever got back together?'

'No, but I do believe we'd have stuck to our guns and continued to be close.'

Jenna jumped, hearing Alesha's voice from the hallway. 'Jenna, guess what I found at Ellie's house?' She entered the room and looked from Jenna to Ben. 'Oh, I can see you're busy. Is he okay?'

Jenna wished she could answer…and ask why she'd omitted to mention she and Ben splitting up. But she couldn't, so just shrugged discreetly.

Ellie appeared in the doorway. 'Hi. Erm, are you guys okay?'

'We're just having a chat. We're talking about what happened — you know?'

Jenna threw Ellie and Alesha a hard look and raised her eyebrows. The girls clearly realised what they'd been discussing.

'I'll leave you to it. I've got stuff to do, but call if you need me.' Ellie headed for the hallway. Alesha followed her.

'Where were we?' said Jenna. 'Oh, yeah, you and Alesha remaining close.'

'Hmm.' Ben seemed distracted. 'You know, I think I'll head upstairs for a while, too, J. If that's alright with you?'

She nodded. 'I'm here if you want to talk.'

'Ditto!' He took a handful of beers from the fridge and went upstairs.

Jenna cupped her chin in her hands. How had everything become so complicated? And how could a ghost be a very real part of her life? The most frightening part was that it seemed normal somehow. What did seem unreal was the prospect of marrying Jake.

Thoughts jumbled up in her head. It was as though some magnet drew her to the light switch. Her fingers tapped it over and over again. She couldn't stop, but counted each one. It had to be an even number. Alesha's voice startled her. Tapping once more so as to not end on an odd number, Jenna turned to her.

'What's up, Alesha?'

'Quick! Come upstairs!'

Jenna followed her to the staircase and by the time she reached the bottom, Alesha was already at the top.

'Hurry up!'

Alesha led Jenna along the landing to Ben's bedroom door which was slightly ajar.

'What you doing?' Ellie came out of her room.

'Shhh,' hissed Alesha. 'Listen.'

Ben sat on the edge of the bed, guitar in hand. His gaze was on it, as he strummed gently. In a deep husky voice, he sang the words of a song he'd clearly written. Jenna stood transfixed, and her breath caught in her throat.

Hey girl, why did you leave me? Why did you have to go?
I'm left with just my memories
And how I miss you so.
I bet you're still angelic, and still lovely,
I wonder what you're seeing -
And what you think of me.

My life has been so empty, since you left my side,
I'm man enough to admit that -
So many tears I've cried.
Oh, how I'd give my everything, to see you once again,
And hear you say you love me -
And take away this pain.

Alesha, oh, my darling, what am I to do?
My heart's in tiny pieces -
I'm so sorry I failed you.
How I hope you're listening, to what I have to say,
I wish I could turn the clock back –
Five years - to the Seventh of May.

No harsh words would leave my lips, believe me I have tried –
To imagine keeping you –
That day, safe, right by my side.
I hope you know my love for you, is never going to end,
My beautiful Alesha-
I'm sad I lost - my best friend.

A low sob escaped from Ellie, who stood behind Jenna. Tears streamed down Jenna's face as she looked from Alesha to Ben. Alesha too was crying silent tears. She wrapped her arms around Jenna and Ellie. The three of them clung together before Alesha whispered in Jenna's ear.

'I can't believe my lack of concentration for a second could cause so much pain. I mean, in myself I'd be okay. But seeing the grief I've caused others breaks my heart. Go in to him, Jenna. He needs you.'

'I can't.' Jenna wasn't sure how to deal with his grief. She couldn't deal with her own.

Ben looked up and saw Jenna through the gap in the door. His jaw clenched. 'What you doing there, J?'

'Erm, I came to see if you're okay. Can I come in, Ben?'

He nodded. 'How long have you been standing there?'

She couldn't lie. 'Long enough. That song was beautiful.' She closed the door behind her.

He took the guitar off his shoulder and placed it in the corner of the room, before sitting back down on the bed. 'Don't just stand there. You'd better sit down if you're staying.'

Jenna sat primly on the bed, as far from Ben as possible, arms hanging by her sides.

'Don't look so nervous. I won't bite.' He smiled. 'Unless you ask me to.'

'Maybe I should —'

'Relax! Bet you're glad this day's nearly over? I know I am.'

'Yeah. It's tough.'

Ben lay sideways on the bed, propping himself up on one elbow. 'People try to understand, but they can't. Not really. Especially after all this time. If I had a pound for every time I've heard, *you need to move on with your life, Ben*, I'd be rich. I don't really mention it now. And anyway, I know life goes on, it has to. I'm working, I see my mates, go out. So what do they mean, move on?'

Jenna considered his words. 'I suppose they mean find someone new. Be happy.' She shrugged. 'But you have, haven't you? With Sabrina? It doesn't mean you'll forget Alesha, obviously.'

Ben picked at a loose thread on the duvet. 'It's not serious between us. Sabrina asked me to go for a drink with her, and it's carried on from there. Nothing heavy.'

'You'll meet the right person, one day.' She grinned. 'Christ, how old do I sound?'

'Ancient.' He laughed. 'How come you haven't seen Jake today? I thought he'd be here to support you.'

'He would've been, but I told him I wanted to be alone.' She stared at the floor. 'To tell you the truth, he finds it a bit difficult. Knowing what to say.'

'Sometimes it's enough to just have someone there, even without words.'

'That's where Ellie's fantastic. She knows when to talk, and when to just listen. She was there for me and that's never changed.'

'That's what friends do. You're there for her now, when she needs you.'

'Yeah, but I get a bit impatient sometimes, like, when she leaves things switched on, and moves stuff around in the house. But then I feel guilty.'

'You feel guilty about everything. I wish you didn't.'

'That's a bit rich, coming from you.'

'Let's do a deal: after today, we both make a determined effort to change our attitudes towards what happened.' He reached for her hand. 'A new start. We'll help each other.'

'But I can't forget, Ben. And I can't imagine not feeling sad.'

'That's not what I'm saying. I'm talking about the guilt. It's helped me to talk to you today. I've said more to you than I've ever said to anybody else, because you understand. And, you know what? I feel so much better for it.'

Jenna had to admit she did, too. She'd opened up to Ben in a way that should feel strange. They hadn't known each other long, but they both understood what the other was going through. Guilt and blame were not easy to talk about, unless it was to somebody who felt the same.

Jenna wondered briefly what Alesha had meant about Jenna and Ben being destined to be together. But it wasn't worth thinking about, she'd been talking rubbish. Yet it had been an odd thing to say.

'So do I.' She nodded. 'Thanks for helping me get through today.'

'Likewise.'

She began to hum the song he'd been singing. He froze for a second and then picked up the guitar and strummed gently. Jenna sang a few of the words. He watched for a few seconds and then joined in. Their combined voices sounded amazing.

'Maybe we should form a band. A duo,' said Ben. 'Your voice is incredible.'

'So's yours. What would we call ourselves?' She laughed.

'Hmm, what about Attitude? That seems fitting.'

'We can't do it. Not really.'

'Why not? It's just for fun.'

'Okay, partner.' She gave a thumbs-up. 'It'll be a bit more interesting than just singing in the bath.'

He put the guitar down by the side of the bed and leaned across to give her a hug. They both lost their balance and fell backwards, arms wrapped around each other. There was a moment of awkward tension before they each shifted slightly.

As they glanced at each other, Jenna's heart thudded. Their noses were almost touching. Her hand moved up towards the cleft in his chin. The urge to run her finger over it was strong. But she snatched it back quickly. Did she need some kind of substitute light switch, or something? The emotions of the day were to blame. She bent her head so that they were no longer facing each other. They lay still, not saying a word, and not moving. Content to be together, yet apart, with their own private thoughts.

Hmm, lying on Ben's bed with him may be for innocent enough reasons, Jenna…but try explaining that to Jake…and why you're on intimate terms with Ben's armpit.

Chapter Thirteen

'Where the hell have you been, Alesha? Why the disappearing act for a week?' Jenna's nostrils flared. 'I suppose you wanted to avoid any awkward questions.'

'Hi, Jenna,' said Alesha. 'What's up? I can't be here all the time. There's other places I need to be too.'

'Oh, yeah? Like where?'

Alesha shrugged. 'Here and there. But never mind that. How's it going with Ben?'

'Funny you should ask. Why didn't you tell me about the two of you splitting up?'

'I didn't actually *say* we were together as a couple at the time of the accident, did I?'

'Yes! You said —'

'I said Ben was my *ex*-boyfriend.'

'But, that's because you died.'

'It's not. I didn't lie, Jenna. Anyway, that bears no relevance to why I'm here. I said I was worried about Ben. And I am.'

Jenna put her hands on her hips. 'You should've told me. I thought he was distraught about losing his girlfriend, not ex.'

'Does it make so much difference?' said Alesha. 'It's still me we're talking about, whatever our relationship at the time. Do you think Ben is any less upset because we were in the process of breaking up?'

Jenna exhaled and sat on a chair. 'No. I can't imagine him being any more devastated than he was last week. But you know he's blaming himself. We both know he wasn't to blame, but short of telling him you're here, how am I meant to get that through to him?'

'You can't tell him!' Alesha shook her head wildly. 'He won't believe you and will probably leave. He'll get angry and take it out on you.'

Jenna knew this was probably true. He was hardly likely to say: 'Ohh, that's nice.'

It had been hard enough for Jenna to accept she was seeing a ghost, and she hadn't been a non-believer as such. He'd be bound to take it badly, especially if he didn't believe in the afterlife. Alesha was right, they had to find another way to take away his blame and guilt.

Since the date a week ago, Jenna and Ben had found time most days to have a chat. They hadn't spoken any more about the accidents, but talked about work, music and life in general, it was clear they'd formed a bond. Their mutual understanding and opening up to one another the way they had, made it seem as though they'd been friends for some time. Although, in reality, a month ago they hadn't even met. Jenna remembered what Alesha had said about interfering in their destiny.

140

'Alesha,' she said, 'what did you mean last week, about destiny? One of the reasons you're here — to put things right?'

'You were in the same bar as Ben one evening. The attraction was clear, turning round to glance at each other constantly, while talking to friends.'

'I don't recall that,' said Jenna. 'Yet he did seem vaguely familiar when I met him.'

Alesha nodded. 'I was standing close enough to hear what he was saying. He told his friend that he thought you were gorgeous. Sex on legs.'

'He didn't!' Jenna's face felt hot enough to fry eggs on. She took Alesha's comments with a big dose of salt. It was hard to know what to believe, from Alesha, who clearly had her own agenda.

'He did. Just as he was plucking up courage to approach you, I stepped in to talk to him. I'd fancied him for weeks and had to make my move there and then.' Alesha covered her face with both palms. 'As we chatted, you looked over and saw me with Ben. Shortly afterwards you left.'

'So? Just because Ben and I looked at each other, doesn't mean we were destined to be together.' Jenna laughed. 'What's the big deal?'

'He was distracted. Looking for you. Once he realised you'd gone, he bought me a drink and that was it. We continued to see each other and fell in love quite quickly.'

'Nice to know he forgot me so fast.' Jenna giggled.

'But maybe he didn't,' said Alesha. 'It didn't work out for us. I should've let him go to you that night.'

'That's crazy!'

'I may have agreed,' said Alesha. 'At one time. But now I know for sure that I interfered in your destiny. If you'd have got with Ben, it would've lasted. You'd still be together now.'

'Alesha,' said Jenna, 'you've really grown on me, much as I hate to say it. But, I have to say you're more loopy than I am.' She grinned. 'And that's saying something.'

'Think what you like,' said Alesha. 'But I know the truth.'

'Well, thanks to you, it's too late for me and Ben.' She rolled her eyes. 'I'm marrying Jake in eleven months. We've set the date for the twenty-third of April.'

'The time will soon go.' Ellie walked into the room. 'What's all this about you and Ben?'

'I was meant to be with Ben. It was my destiny.' Jenna clutched her chest in mock despair and sank to her knees. She swallowed back a giggle. 'And now I have to see him everyday knowing he'll never be mine.' She held her head in her hands, pretending to weep. As she took her hands away from her face, a pair of trainers came into view. Her gaze lifted to a pair of jean-clad legs. A rip in one leg revealed dark hair covering the thigh. Unless Ellie had developed a problem with testosterone, it was a man. She prayed it *was* Ellie. Doctors could do wonders nowadays. And at least she could cover her legs. They'd be able to halt it before it spread to her face.

But it became apparent that she couldn't reach God by speed dial. He hadn't answered her prayer. The cough was definitely male.

Jenna's heart plummeted to the floor with enough impact to almost cause it to give way. If only. Never had she wanted the ground to open and swallow her up more than now.

She forced her head up to be greeted by Ben staring down. His eyes resembled not so much saucers, but dinner plates. His mouth was open wide enough to accommodate her not so tiny frame. And Jenna longed to climb into it, never to be seen again.

The silence was loud enough to deafen the whole street. Until Ellie giggled. Alesha joined in and they clung together, tears pouring down their cheeks.

'J?' Ben whispered. 'Are you okay?'

Rising clumsily to her feet, Jenna nodded manically. 'Yes! Yes! I'm fine! Erm, it was a joke. About someone else called Ben. Not you. Obviously.'

'R-ight.' He looked from Jenna to Ellie. 'Well...I'll be off, then. I'm erm, going to work.' He made a hasty retreat and was out of the door in five seconds flat.

'That was hilarious!' Ellie wiped her eyes.

'I've never laughed so much since I died,' said Alesha.

'Oh, good! I'm glad to have cheered you up.' Jenna scowled. 'I bet he didn't believe me when I said it was a different Ben.'

'No.' Alesha agreed. 'But there's no point dwelling on it. Are you at work today?'

Jenna shook her head. 'No. I've nothing planned until Jake leaves work. Then I'm going round to Mona's to discuss wedding plans.'

Ellie and Alesha exchanged looks. Jenna pursed her lips. 'If that's okay with you two?' She wasn't sure why she got so defensive when it came to Jake and the wedding. And the last thing she wanted to do was interrogate herself on it.

'Look, why don't we all go into town and spend the day on "mission wedding?"' Ellie put an arm around Jenna's shoulder. 'It might seem like ages away, Jenna, but it'll fly by. There's a lot to organise.'

Jenna thought of Mona's list. Was there really that much to it? It seemed as if exchanging rings was the easy part. When did weddings become so much more than that? Although the idea of a huge fuss brought her out in a cold sweat, she appreciated Ellie's offer of help. It meant a lot, given Ellie's own marital situation. And she knew Ellie didn't really agree with her and Jake marrying.

'Okay. I guess I have to start sometime.'

'I still say Jake isn't the one for you, but a day out will be nice.' Alesha grinned. 'I never got to wear a wedding dress. I'm going to try some on.'

'Hey, I didn't get chance to tell you what I found at Ellie's house,' said Alesha, as they strolled into town. 'There was a stack of drawings. They're brilliant. Ellie should be an artist. Loads were of you when you were a teenager.'

'Really? I remember you getting me to sit for ages at a time, Ellie. You were really good.'

Ellie blushed. 'Thanks. I'd forgotten about them to be honest.'

'The best one was of you singing.' Alesha laughed. 'You had a hairbrush instead of a microphone.'

'Oh, I remember it.' Jenna grinned. 'I was going to be a pop star, wasn't I, Ellie?'

Ellie nodded. 'Maybe you still could be. It's not too late.'

Jenna chose not to answer that remark. 'Did you bring the pictures back with you? I'd love to see them.'

'Yeah, I'll show you. Now, Let's look at that dress you liked, Jenna,' said Ellie. 'Which shop was it in?'

'Up here.' Jenna led them towards the cobbled street and pointed.

'Wow!' Alesha's eyes gleamed as she examined dress after dress. 'There's hundreds.'

'I know.' Jenna hovered near *the* dress. After hesitating for a moment, she pulled it from the rail gently. It was gorgeous.

'Is that it?' Ellie stroked the material. 'You have to try it on, it's perfect.'

'I'm not sure, maybe —'

'Try it!' said Alesha. 'I can't wait to see it on.'

Jenna placed the dress over her arm and slouched head down, to the changing rooms.

'Do you need any help?' The same shop assistant appeared with a smile.

'No, but thanks.' Jenna edged into the changing room with Ellie and Alesha. 'How do I get into this thing?'

They finally got the dress on Jenna. Ellie buttoned up the back. They all gazed into the mirror.

'Jenna, you look absolutely beautiful.' Ellie breathed. 'You could try on a hundred, but not one would look better than this.'

'She's right.' Alesha nodded. 'I almost want you to get married after all, so everyone can see you in it.'

Jenna ran her hands over the tiny beads and twisted to see the back. Was it really her? The dress hugged her body in a way that gave the illusion of a perfect hourglass shape. She adored it. So, why couldn't she get it off quick enough?

'Can you undo the buttons, Ellie?'

'Are you going to buy it?'

'I don't know. I'll think about it.' She stepped from the dress. 'It's a big decision. Let's go. We can come back later.'

'Hang on.' Alesha pouted. 'I want to try some dresses on.'

Before their eyes, she appeared in quick succession, wearing a different style dress each time.

'Which one's best?'

145

'Alesha, you'd look good in a bin liner.' Ellie laughed. 'Wouldn't she, Jen?'

Jenna nodded. 'Definitely.'

With that, Alesha appeared swathed in black shiny plastic. She posed and sashayed around the changing room. They were right: she looked as stunning as ever.

The walls suddenly felt as though they were closing in on Jenna. She had to get out.

'What's wrong?' Ellie caught her up as she made a beeline for the exit. 'You look pale.'

Jenna's whole body was trembling. Something about that shop that made her feel ill. But what? The dress was stunning, so what was the problem?

'I feel a bit dizzy.' She leaned against the wall. The temptation was too much. Ellie pulled Jenna's hand away once she'd tapped the wall nineteen times. Within a second, Jenna tapped it once more. Ideally she'd have started counting again, from one, but had to content herself with at least ending on an even number. 'I need to sit down.'

Ellie took her arm. 'Come on, let's go for a coffee.'

Jenna wiped the froth from her top lip. Her breathing had returned to normal. What must the other girls think of her?

Alesha had followed them into the café without a word. Jenna met her gaze and lowered it quickly. It was as if Alesha wanted to say something, but thought better of it. Jenna could guess what it was: if the wedding was such a good idea, then why wasn't she boring everybody with constant wedding talk, and maxing out her credit card with wedding 'essential' purchases? Like any normal bride to be. Jenna wondered for what seemed like the millionth time the same thing. But something dawned on her. It would explain her lack of enthusiasm. It was obvious what was wrong.

'The reason I'm not getting into wedding obsession mode is because my mum and dad won't be there.' Jenna sighed. 'How can I be happy about it without them?'

'Oh, Jen.' Ellie rubbed her back. 'It must be hard. Maybe a small wedding will be easier to cope with.'

'It's Mona who wants the big do,' said Jenna. 'And I don't seem to have much say.'

'That's ridiculous.' Alesha's eyes narrowed. 'If you're so against it, then tell her and Jake in no uncertain terms. You're complaining to us, but not being assertive enough with them. Are you sure it's not because you want to blank it out? As if it's not happening?'

'Alesha!' Ellie gasped. 'That's a bit harsh.'

Alesha shrugged. 'Is it?'

Jenna turned to Ellie. 'What do you think? You've known me for years and were with me when I met Jake. I know you have reservations about us, but tell me what's going through your mind.'

Ellie hesitated. 'Well…it's not that I don't like him. I've no reason not to. But…'

'What?'

'It was one thing you seeing each other. I'm not convinced you should be marrying him though. He's erm…'

'Carry on.'

'He's too staid for you. I think you accepted his proposal for practical reasons.'

Jenna pushed back her chair and stood. Her hands gripped the edge of the table.

'There may be some truth in what you say about the practical bit,' said Jenna. 'I don't hide the fact that I want to keep the house and Jake will help me do that. But, he's not too staid. I want reliable and responsible, not excitement and adventure. I want stability.'

'You sure that's enough?' Ellie reached for Jenna's hand and squeezed it. 'Honestly?'

Jenna nodded. 'I'm sure. We love each other.' She held up her hand when Alesha opened her mouth to speak. 'It may not be heartstoppingly full on passion kind of love, but it's still real.'

'Okay.' Ellie nodded. 'Why don't you go back for the dress then? You're going to blow Jake's mind when he sees you in it.'

The only part of Jake I can see blowing is his top when he finds out I haven't given Ellie and Ben their marching orders yet. But there's plenty of time before they need to leave the house.

'I *will*!' She picked up her bag. 'I'm going for it now. Before somebody beats me to it.'

And while Mona's safely out of the way. I don't want her showing me anymore horrific creations. I'm having this one and that's final. Whether she approves or not. Which of course she won't.

Ellie helped Jenna through the hallway with the neatly wrapped dress. They climbed the stairs slowly, arms aching from the weight of the box.

'What you got there?' Ben watched from his bedroom doorway.

148

I feel so embarrassed about this morning. Crawling around on the floor like a complete plonker.

'It's Jenna's wedding dress,' said Ellie. 'We're going to lay the box on top of her wardrobe.'

'Let me help.' He took the box into his arms and edged sideways into Jenna's room. As he reached up with the box, his T-shirt rode up to reveal a tight tanned torso. Jenna gulped and averted her eyes.

'So, the dress.' He pulled his top down and smiled. 'Wedding plans in full swing then? Exciting, hey?'

No.

'Yes.' She fished the ringing phone out of her bag. It was Jake.

'Hi, I've just got back from town. I've got my wedding dress.' She watched Ben leave the room, closely followed by Ellie. 'Are you picking me up to go to your mum's?'

'You've got it? Well, that's fabulous!' Jake gushed. 'I'll pick you up shortly, and you can tell me all about it.'

'Jake…can you come in for five minutes? It's just that you haven't apologised to the others yet, for being rude.'

Jenna screwed up her face, anticipating Jake's inevitable change of mood. She was surprised to find that didn't happen.

'Okay, for five minutes. I guess I can put up with them for a little while longer. They'll be gone before we know it, won't they?'

Probably not, Jake, because I haven't asked them to leave yet.

'Hmm. See you shortly.'

Jenna, Ellie and Ben were in the sitting room twenty minutes later, when Jake arrived.

'Hi,' he called from the hallway.

Jenna rushed to greet him. 'Hi. The others are in here,' she whispered. 'Please be nice, Jake.'

He nodded and made way for her to go in first.

'Hi, Ellie, erm, hi, Ben.' He stood arms stiffly by his side. 'Look, sorry about last week. I was stressed about Mum. But I was rude, and there's no excuse.'

Ben stepped forward. 'No problem, mate.' He held out his hand to Jake for the second time. Jake looked at it as if it was a rifle pointing at him, but after a brief hesitation he took it.

'Do you want a drink, Jake?' Ellie asked.

He shook his head. 'No thanks, we need to go. Mum's waiting to see Jenna. I've told her you've bought a dress, Jenna. Are you taking it to show her?'

'It's on the top of the wardrobe,' said Jenna. 'I'll show her another time.'

I don't want her to see it. She'll only make negative comments.

'I'll get it back down for you, if you like, J?' Ben raised his eyebrows. 'It's easy for me to reach.'

Jake's eyes glinted. 'No need. If Jenna wants it, *I'll* get it for her.'

Jenna's heart sank. Trust Ben to say that. He was only trying to help, but he'd made things worse. She could almost reach out and touch the tension in the room.

'Come on, let's go.' She tugged Jake's jacket sleeve. 'You can't go anywhere near the dress, Jake. It's bad luck.'

'Okay.' He nodded and walked towards the door. He turned to Ellie and Ben as if he'd just thought of something. 'Oh, before I forget, I've seen a new property rentals place. It's just opened in town. Maybe they'll have some decent properties in there. You need to find somewhere sooner rather than later, as Jenna's probably mentioned.' He gave a backwards wave and went out to the car. Jenna threw an apologetic look over her shoulder and followed him out.

'Hello, dear.' Mona moved some piles of papers so Jenna could sit down. She'd recovered well, but still appeared frail. But it was bound to take some time before she got her strength fully back. There was nothing wrong with her tongue though. It was sharp as ever.

'Jake tells me you've bought your dress.' She glanced around the room. 'Haven't you brought it? I must say, I'm disappointed you didn't want my opinion first.'

'It was the only one in my size, so I had to get it.' Jenna forced a smile. 'How are y —'

'I still think red for the colour scheme.' Mona cut in. 'And that country house hotel just out of town. Here.' She thrust a brochure at Jenna. 'You can have the full wedding package there. I'm rather upset you've put your foot down to church though.' She sniffed.

Jenna never went to church so she wasn't going to be a hypocrite. She was less convinced than ever that God existed. If so, how could He take lives away, in cruel circumstances? Especially when so many died young.

'No church.' Jenna handed the brochure back to Mona. 'But that looks fine. You can book it, if you want.'

Jake beamed. 'I'll put the kettle on and leave you two to your planning.'

'So I said, no. They needed to be a deeper red. The flowers need to be *exactly* the right shade. As for the table decorations, I thought a rose-based centrepiece. The favours can go in little organza bags in the same colour. I'll get some chocolate hearts with red foil. Jake needs a cravat. In red of course. And a grey suit. I've seen a picture of a delightful cake on the interweb. I'll give them a ring. It states a hundred portions but I'll ask whether they can do a bigger one. Just to be

151

safe. I thought a Rolls Royce for the car. Those limousines are so common now, don't you think? I mean, how many pink ones do you see driving around? Ten a penny on a Saturday night. But Bentleys are classy, aren't they? Jenna? JENNA?'

'Oh, erm, sorry.' She rubbed her eyes. 'Yes.'

She wasn't sure what she was saying yes to, but it was always a safe word to use when talking to Mona.

'So, I can go ahead and book what I feel is required?' Mona sounded surprised.

Jake walked into the room carrying a tray. The tray shook in his hands.

Jenna nodded. 'Yes, you can, Mona.'

The cups clattered in the saucers as Jake set down the tray. His eyes met hers. She could see he was as surprised as Mona by her words. They weren't the only ones. She'd made such a fuss about her right to decide what went on at her own wedding. But when it came to it, she wasn't remotely interested in table decorations, cakes or favours. Whatever they were. She was more than happy to let Mona arrange those kinds of details.

'Just tell me where and when to turn up and I'll be there.' She picked up her cup. 'But please try to remember to ask me who I want to invite.'

Mona was leafing through the wedding file, muttering to herself. All of a sudden she looked ten years younger. Jenna smiled. It suited her to indulge Mona's longing to take over. And it was nice to know she'd made Mona happy. At last.

Jake mouthed the words 'Thank you.' He smiled in a way she hadn't seen for some time. In that moment she understood his frustration in them not having the chance to be alone much. Her heart melted at the look he gave her. She couldn't stay here overnight. Mona was old-fashioned that way. But Jake could go back to the house with her. Okay, they'd have to be quiet, but that would make it more fun. When was the last time they'd actually had sex? Either it was so long ago she couldn't remember, or, it was easily forgotten. Jenna decided not to delve too deep for the answer. But right now she did want to be alone with him.

'So, once you've tidied up outside, Jakey, the house can go on the market.' Mona waved a pen in the air. 'And then we can move my belongings bit by bit into our new home.'

Jenna glanced at Mona's face, then Jake's. He swallowed. She turned back to Mona.

'Your new home?'

'Your house! We were arranging it, remember?' She gave Jenna an indulgent took. 'Jake thinks the back bedroom will be the best one for me. Don't you, Jakey?'

Ohh, how nice of you, Jakey...but nice as you may be, I think I'm going to have to kill you.

Chapter Fourteen

'These drawings are really good, Ellie.' Ben leafed through the stack of papers in obvious admiration. 'I love this one.' He held up the picture of Jenna singing into a hairbrush.

She was instantly transported back to the age of around fifteen or sixteen. Singing was the single most important thing to her then. Happiness radiated from her face on the page.

She smiled for the first time since returning from her encounter with Mona and Jake. It seemed as though they had it all figured out. He'd tried to play it down, of course. They could perhaps convert a bedroom into a lounge for Mona, so they'd all have their own space. But Jenna knew this was unlikely to happen. He'd be quite content to have the two women in his life vying for his attention, and making sure his life ran as smoothly as possible.

'Have you heard Jenna sing, Ben?' said Ellie.

'Yes.' He winked at Jenna. 'She could go far, with the right '*Attitude*.''

Alesha appeared and sat next to Jenna. 'I've heard Ben and Ellie talking. They don't know whether you want them to move out now, or not,' she whispered.

'Take no notice of what Jake said the other night. You're both welcome to stay. Until the wedding, obviously.' She smiled at Ben and Ellie.

'You sure?' Ellie asked.

'Yes.' Jenna nodded. 'I'm a bit stressed to be honest. Jake is all for Mona living with us. And now her house is about to go on the market. I hope it takes ages to sell. But, even if it doesn't, I'm not throwing you both out to suit them. They seem to have it figured, between them, but it's my house.'

'You need to be there, if anyone wants to view the house,' said Ellie. 'Then you can put them off buying it.'

'Why didn't I think of that? Ellie, you're a star!'

'She is.' Ben turned to Ellie. 'How do you feel about a job where I work? You'd have to have an interview, but I could put in a good word. We need someone on the branding team, and you'd be perfect.'

'I would?'

'Yes. We need someone who can draw, but you're good with the slogans too. I honestly think you'd be great, El.'

'It sounds fab.' Her eyes shone. 'I'd love that!'

Jenna hadn't seen Ellie so enthusiastic about getting a job since she'd moved in. It wasn't that she was lazy, but didn't want to settle for doing something she'd hate. Unlike Jenna. But then she had no choice.

'I'll speak to my boss tomorrow. I have a good feeling about this, El.'

155

Two days later Ellie jumped up and down in front of Jenna. She'd been dreading Ellie arriving home. But it seemed the interview had gone perfectly and they'd offered her the job there and then.

'That's fantastic news!' Jenna hugged her. 'When do you start?'

'Tomorrow,' said Ellie. 'They showed me around. I saw Sabrina. She didn't seem too chuffed about me working there.'

'Don't let her worry you, just get on with what you need to do.'

They both clammed up about Sabrina when Ben walked in.

'Congratulations, team mate.' He caught Ellie in a bear hug. 'Let's have a drink to celebrate. I'll show you what we're working on at the moment, so you'll have a heads up before getting there.'

Hello? I'm here, too! I feel as invisible as Alesha. And that's cool. I'm so happy for Ellie.

'Right.' Ben opened his laptop. 'We have a commission from a building firm. They need a slogan and brand image. But, here's the best bit. There's a competition set by our company to come up with the winning package. Whoever designs the winner will be almost certain to get a promotion. It'll mean more pay and a team under us. Three teams of two will be working on it. You'll be working with me, El.'

'Okay.'

Ben continued, 'Obviously you won't be getting promoted if we win.' He laughed. 'But you'd still be working with me. Do you think you can put up with me at work and at home?'

'Oh, it'll be hard, but I'll try.' She giggled. 'But why aren't you working with Sabrina?'

156

Ben grimaced. 'Don't you start. I've already had an earful from her about it. It's not my call. But to be honest, I think I'm going to stand a better chance working alongside you. She's not been working there long and I have to say I'm wondering how she got the job. Rumours are rife that she's related to one of the other bosses, though she denies it.'

'I don't trust Sabrina, the not-so-teenage witch,' Alesha muttered.

The glow radiating from Ellie's face was bright enough to light up the whole of York.

'What's the building firm called?' Ellie sat next to Ben so that she could see the screen on his laptop. 'Is there a deadline?'

'Here's the builders' website.' He pointed to the screen. 'The deadline is two weeks from now.'

'Is that all?'

'Yeah, the pressure's on,' said Ben. 'But we can do it.'

'MP Builders.' Ellie read from the screen. 'Hmm, interesting.'

'Yes, and what do MP's do?' Ben grinned.

'Talk a load of bollocks?' Jenna handed Ben a beer and Ellie a glass of wine. 'Get loads of freebies?'

'Yes.' Ben nodded. 'But what else?'

'Tell lies.' Ellie grinned. 'I can see where you're going with this, Ben.'

'Good girl.' He put down the beer unopened. 'What're your thoughts? I have an idea.'

Ellie closed her eyes and tossed her head back. 'I know!'

'Write it down and I'll tell you what I've got.' He handed her some paper and a pen.

'Okay.' She held out the paper. Ben took it from her without looking.

'Here's what I'm thinking, El:

'MP Builders
No lies, we *do* build houses.'

'That's nearly what I wrote.' Ellie poked at the piece of paper. 'Look!'

Ben read:

'MP Builders
Trust MP Builders…we really *do* build houses.'

'That's amazing,' said Jenna. 'And Ellie's bound to come up with a great logo. I'm excited for you both.'

'I'm gonna sound a bit soppy here.' Ben smiled. 'But I'm feeling quite optimistic about life all of a sudden. Since I met you two. I'm enjoying being here.'

Jenna felt better too. Hours spent with Ben, Ellie, and Alesha were what kept her going, just lately. More and more, she looked forward to their evenings together. The thought entered her head that neither Jake nor Mona entered into thoughts of enjoyable moments, but she banished that train of thought from her head. For now it was best to concentrate on anything that made her feel good. And at the moment, it was simply relaxing at home with her friends. As far away from wedding talk as possible.

For the first time in years, she saw that life could still be fun. Although the intense sadness still existed, so too did laughter and joy. It was impossible for any human being to live permanently in one frame of mind. Emotions fluctuated depending what was happening at the time. But the over-riding emotion for Jenna had been despair. Happiness, however, was beginning to take over. During the times she was in the house with the others, at least. The rest, she'd deal with soon. For now, she wanted to savour the unfamiliar feeling of actually wanting to get out of bed each morning. Because everything was going to turn out right, she was certain. She and Ben seemed to have turned a corner, albeit a tiny one. It was a step forward, and more than she could've dared hope for. She turned to Alesha and smiled.

'You seem happier.' Alesha put her head on Jenna's shoulder. 'I'm glad.'

'So does Ben,' Jenna muttered. 'And he's cut down on the alcohol.'

'Just remember, the path may be rocky at times,' Alesha whispered in Jenna's ear. 'But you'll get there.'

I hope I'll enjoy 'there' when I arrive.

A few days later, Ellie arrived home from work subdued. Jenna hoped she wasn't tiring of the job already. It had been going so well by all accounts. Alesha followed her in.

'What's wrong, Ellie?'

Ellie slumped on the sofa with a sigh. 'I'm not sure.' She shrugged. 'But Alesha showed up at work with us today, and we both feel Sabrina has something to hide.'

'How do you mean?'

'I saw her looking shifty at her desk,' said Alesha. 'She made sure nobody was watching before opening her computer screen.'

'And?'

'She'd logged into Ben's account,' Alesha spat. 'And I had a feeling he hadn't given her permission.Why would he?'

'Is that it?'

'No,' said Ellie. 'It's not. Alesha came and told me she was worried. I asked her to keep a check on her movements for the rest of the day.'

'Ohh, you mean she sneaked off for a break when she wasn't supposed to,' said Jenna. 'Or, she was hiding out in the toilets, or —'

'Or, she was stealing Ben's work.' Alesha's eyes flashed.

'That's a big accusation to make.' Jenna paced the room. 'Do you have proof?'

'Kind of,' said Ellie. 'Alesha saw our work on Sabrina's page. She's stolen it, we think. Passing it off as her own. Ben and I had finished it too. It was brilliant. We were just about to email it to the boss.'

'So why didn't you?'

'We'd got as far as telling the boss it was ready,' said Ellie. 'But then Ben was called away.'

'Who by?'

'Sabrina. She told him someone from another department was looking for him. So off he went.'

'Then what?'

'He was gone ages. When he got back, he said it was a wild goose chase. Sabrina was smirking in the direction of the boss's office.'

'You think she's sent your work to him, as her own?'

'Yes.' Ellie was shaking. 'I told Ben I had an errand to run, and drove back here. I needed your advice, Jenna. What shall I do?'

'I take it you went to work in separate cars this morning?' said Jenna. 'He'll be back soon though. Christ, I hope you're both wrong.'

Jenna's heart raced as they heard Ben in the hallway. 'Ellie?' He halted in the doorway as he took in her tear-stained face and trembling body. 'What the hell's happened? You left work suddenly.'

'You'd better tell him what you suspect,' said Jenna. 'Sit down, Ben.'

As Ellie relayed her suspicions, Jenna realised how flimsy it all sounded, without adding Alesha into the picture. His expression changed from confusion, to disbelief and then anger. Unfortunately the anger was directed at Ellie.

'I can't believe you're saying this, El. Why? Okay, *someone* saw Sabrina bring my account up onto her computer. I don't know how or why, but she wouldn't try to steal our work. That's crazy.' His eyes blazed. 'And then try to pass it off to the boss as —' The blood drained from his face. He slumped onto a chair. 'Oh, shit!'

'What?' Jenna placed a hand on his shoulder.

'Just before I left, the boss said something to Sabrina.' He gave a weary sigh. 'He said: 'You're doing well, Sabrina. *No lies…*''

'It could be coincidence.' Jenna shrugged. 'But it sounds as if you need to prepare yourself, Ben.'

'And then the boss winked and nudged her. We need to be there early in the morning, El. Before she gets there. We'll go and see him.'

'But what if it *is* true?' said Ellie. 'How do we prove what she's done?'

'Good question.' Ben rubbed his temples. 'She wouldn't do that to me…would she?'

'Yes!' Alesha put a comforting arm around Ben. But of course he wasn't aware of it. She kissed his cheek and turned to Jenna and Ellie. 'I want to throttle that little bitch! Obviously I can't, I'm dead. So you'll have to do it for me!'

Okay. If I get my hands round her scrawny little neck, I'll…wind up in jail.

'Jenna, give him a hug. For me. He needs it,' said Alesha.

She moved towards Ben slowly, and hesitated before wrapping her arms around him.

Who am I doing this for, again? Oh, yeah, Alesha.

'Ben.' She lifted his chin so that he was looking at her. 'We'll sort it, don't worry. We've got your back, haven't we, Ellie? We're here for you.'

Ellie nodded. 'You know, it seems like we've been friends for ages. It's strange, isn't it?'

'No, it's not strange.' Alesha shook her head. 'Destiny may seem strange, but it's not really.'

'Yes, it is strange,' said Ben. 'Thanks, girls.'

'I thought today was going too well.' Jenna sighed. 'But let's look on the bright side. It may look bad now, but things can only get better. It can't get any worse, can it?'

Alesha gripped Jenna's arm. 'I'm afraid it can, Jenna. I'm sorry. But there's something I haven't told you.' She attempted a smile. 'Now's a good a time as any. When you're on a downer anyway. Look on the bright side…I could've told you when you were in a good mood and totally spoilt your day…'

Chapter Fifteen

Jenna's heart sank quicker than the Titanic. She mounted the stairs in trepidation. Whatever Alesha was about to tell her, she didn't want to hear it. But there was no option.

She curled up on the bed, head in hands. Feeling the mattress shift under her, Jenna faced Alesha, who was propped up next to her on the bed.

'I don't like this,' said Jenna. 'Not one bit.'

'What?'

'I dunno, but whatever it is, I don't like it.'

'Think the worst, and then it won't seem so bad.'

'My arse is bigger than Kim Kardashian's?'

'Umm, it's worse than that.'

'Simon Cowell is about to judge my singing skills?'

'Worse.'

'Craig Revel Horwood is about to judge my Irish jig?'

'Well, there's not much in it, but it's still slightly worse.'

'Now I know how bad it is!'

Alesha took a deep breath. 'Keep calm, Jenna. I know it's going to come as a shock, but —'

'Oh, for God's sake, spit it out.' Jenna wrapped the duvet around her. 'I don't think you can shock me anymore, anyway.'

'Mabel was driving the car that killed me.'

Okay, maybe you can!

The charms on Jenna's bracelet clattered together. The noise clanked inside her brain like a drill going off. On and on, relentlessly. It was alright. Just a bad dream, that's all. It would be over soon. If she could only ride it out a few more minutes, everything would be back to normal. That thought didn't exactly put her mind at ease, yet anything would be better than the words swimming around in her mind now.

'I don't believe you!' She laughed. 'It's some sick joke.' The laugh sounded hollow to her own ears. 'You're just attention seeking, Alesha! As soon as the attention goes off you, you come out with this rubbish. Well, I for one don't buy it.' She held her knees tightly to stop them knocking together.

Alesha reached out and held her hand. 'It's true. I know I should've told you before, but there's been so much for you to take in already. I've been waiting for the right time. Then I figured there never would be one.'

'But…'

'It wasn't her fault. As I said, the driver had no time to react.'

'I thought she seemed so sad because of her husband.' Jenna gripped Alesha's hand. 'But it's more than that, isn't it? She's blaming herself too. Just like Ben.'

Alesha nodded. 'Yes, she is. It's another reason why I said you were at the centre of it all, Jenna. You have to help her.'

Jenna snatched her hand from Alesha's. Placing both arms under the duvet, she scratched her left forearm. Back and forth until she felt the warm liquid oozing down her arm. The burning sensation calmed her. Slightly.

'Of all the places for her to live, she moves next door to me,' said Jenna. 'I mean, I'm glad, because I genuinely love her. But now I know, it puts me in a difficult situation. Again.'

'She was drawn to this area, Jenna. To you. Although she didn't realise that. But you can help her.'

'I think you've got me mixed up with someone.'

'Who?'

'Mother Teresa.'

'There's no mix-up.'

'But I can't be responsible for how other people think and feel. Not Ben and not Mabel.'

'Ben already feels better, thanks to you. Don't you want to make Mabel feel better?'

Jenna sighed. 'Of course I do. But how can I? As far as she's aware I know nothing. And how do you suggest I tell her about you?'

'You'll think of something. I know it's not easy, but I hate the thought of her blaming herself.'

'So do I. I'll go to see her tomorrow. But I've no idea what I'm going to say.'

Ellie tapped on the door. 'Can I come in, Jenna?'

'Yeah, come and join the party.'

Jenna moved so that she could sit down on the bed.

'You two look like I feel. I hope we're wrong about Sabrina.'

'Ellie,' said Jenna. 'Alesha's just dropped a bombshell. Wait until you hear this.'

'Oh. My. God.' Ellie's eyes widened. 'I can't take it in.'

'You and me both,' said Jenna. 'Poor Mabel.'

'Are you going to tell her you know?'

'I'm not sure. I'll have to play it by ear.'

'Do you want me to come with you to see her?'

Jenna shook her head. 'No. I think it'll be easier for her if there's just me.'

'And me,' said Alesha. 'I need to be there. Not that she'll see me, but still.'

'You're right,' said Jenna. 'I'm at work in the morning, so we'll go tomorrow afternoon. Get it over with. I'm dreading it.'

'Jenna! Sit down, dear. I've just made a pot of tea.' Mabel beamed. 'It's lovely to see you.'

'How you doing?'

'Oh, you know. A few aches and pains, but that's to be expected at my age. How are you, dear?'

Terrible! What the hell am I going to say?

'Erm, fine, thanks.' Jenna ran her hands round the rim of her cup. 'I'm glad to have got the date over with, for another year. It's hard every day, but that just brings it all back.'

Mabel nodded. Her eyes began to water. 'Yes,' she said, simply. Alesha went to sit on the arm of her chair. Jenna wished Mabel could see her, or at least feel her presence.

'Jenna.' Mabel put down her cup. 'There's something I need to say. You may not like it.'

Ditto!

'What is it, Mabel?'

'Look at your arms. They've been bleeding.'

'Oh, it's nothi —'

'You've done it to yourself, deliberately. Haven't you?'

Jenna opened her mouth to deny it, then closed it again. What was the point of lying? Mabel knew.

She nodded and looked at the floor. 'Yes. It happens without me really thinking about it. Usually when I'm stressed or unhappy.'

'Which is a good deal of the time, isn't it?'

'Yes. I bet you think I'm a freak, Mabel. *I* think I am.'

'Don't be silly, dear.' Mabel smiled. 'You've told me that you blame yourself for what happened to your parents. That's ridiculous, of course, but logic can go out of the window in that kind of situation. I understand.'

I know you do, but I wish you'd tell me.

'Do you? How?'

'I've heard people saying the same thing, over and over again. I used to be a counsellor, years ago.'

'Did you? So, even though you can be told a million times something wasn't your fault, blaming yourself is a normal reaction, then?'

Mabel nodded. 'Yes. And when somebody dies, in any situation, there's often a friend or relative wishing they'd done more. Said something, not said something, or given more of their time.'

'I guess so, but what's all of that got to do with my arms?'

'Self-harming is more common than you think,' said Mabel. 'Of course there are different levels of severity. It's always without exception because that person is deeply unhappy. Maybe something happened in the past that they couldn't control, or they blame themselves for something. Doing what you do, Jenna, is a way of gaining some control, and you think you deserve to be in pain, or unhappy. It's a step-up from your OCD, isn't it, dear?'

Jenna hesitated. She'd never stopped to consider her actions before. But what Mabel said made sense. She still felt as if she was crazy, but it was comforting to know she was far from alone.

'I drive myself mad with this OCD. I know what I'm doing, but I can't stop.'

'How bad is it?'

'You wouldn't believe what I've started doing.' Jenna didn't want to admit it out loud, but it felt good to finally open up. 'I take photos of the unplugged iron and hairdryer, on my phone. If I sense a panic attack coming on, I look at the photos.'

'I see,' said Mabel. 'And then you feel calmer?'

'Yes.' Jenna nodded. 'God knows what I'd do if there was a fire and I had to leave quickly. I go through a mental routine in my head. But the trouble is, it's getting longer by the day.'

'Why do you think that is, dear?'

'It's because I have two other people living there and I'm getting obsessed with checking their every movements. I'm terrified they'll leave things switched on that shouldn't be.'

'Did it all start after you lost your parents? I'm guessing it did.'

'Yes, I think so. I wish I could stop.'

'Will you try something for me, dear?'

'Okay. What?'

'Next time you get unwelcome thoughts and images in your mind, picture a space in front of you. They aren't allowed beyond that space. Make them stay there and put them in a box. Close the lid, and think of something else. Something that makes you happy.'

'I'll try.' Jenna wiped a bead of sweat from her forehead. 'Is this what you do, Mabel?'

The silence seemed to drag on for ages. Alesha put her palms together in prayer and closed her eyes. It was the perfect opportunity for Mabel to talk about the accident. They looked at each other and waited for Mabel to speak.

'Yes, I have to. I'm not saying it's easy.' She sighed. 'But if I didn't try I'd go mad. I understand you better than you think, Jenna.'

'In what way?'

'Oh, nothing you need to be concerned with, dear.'

If only that was true!

'Can I ask you something? Do you believe in the afterlife?'

'Yes, I do. That's what keeps me going. I know I'll see my Bert again, one day.'

'I never thought about it much, until fairly recently,' said Jenna. 'But strange things have been happening. Suffice to say, I'm a firm believer now.'

'What things?'

Jenna took a deep breath and went to sit by Mabel's feet. She reached for her hands. 'There's no easy way to say this. I know about…what happened.'

Mabel gave a low moan. 'Y-you know?'

'Yes.' Jenna stroked Mabel's hands gently. 'That wasn't your fault either, Mabel. There was nothing you could've done to prevent it.'

A silent tear fell down her cheek. 'What a waste of a life, and such a beautiful girl. I know everybody said I wasn't to blame, but I can't help thinking another, maybe younger, driver would've reacted quicker.'

Alesha shook her head wildly. 'They wouldn't have.'

'That's not true, Mabel.' Jenna passed her a tissue. 'Alesha wasn't concentrating. Nobody else was to blame.'

'You know her name? How do you know all this, Jenna?'

Jenna stalled. 'You know the lodger I was telling you about — Ben?'

Mabel nodded. 'Yes?'

169

'He was Alesha's ex-boyfriend. He blames himself, too. But I think it's slowly dawning on him that he shouldn't.'

'He's living with you?' Mabel gasped. 'But how did he know I was here? Has he seen me?'

'No,' said Jenna. 'He doesn't know. Even if he did see you, how would he know who you are?'

'He might remember me from the photo they printed at the time. Oh, they didn't have anything bad to say about me in the report.' She blew her nose. 'But it was awful, Jenna. I couldn't bear to go out and face people.' Her brow furrowed. 'But if Ben didn't tell you about me, who did? How long have you known?'

'Only since last night.' Jenna's heart raced. 'When, erm, don't panic, hear me out. When Alesha told me.'

The blood drained from Mabel's face. She shrank back into her chair. 'Wwhat?'

'I know how it sounds, Mabel. But you have to believe me. It's true!' She prayed Mabel's heart was strong enough to take the shock of her words. 'And she's here now.'

Mabel glanced around the room with wide eyes. She fiddled with her wedding ring with shaking fingers. 'You're scaring me, Jenna. She can't be here.'

'She can and she is. I know how it sounds. If I was you I wouldn't believe it either. When she first came to me a few weeks ago, I thought I was going crazy. Even more so than usual. Didn't I, Alesha?'

Mabel followed Jenna's gaze. She gulped. 'It's too far-fetched. I'm sorry, but it can't be true.'

'How else would I have known?' said Jenna. 'You must know I would never intentionally hurt you, Mabel. I want to help. We both do.'

'Well, let's say for a moment you're telling the truth. What would Alesha be saying to me?'

Jenna turned to Alesha. 'Well?'

'I saw someone I knew on the other side of the road. I stepped out to catch up with him. Because I fancied him, and we'd probably have ended up together. We'd been texting each other. I wasn't thinking — no car would've been able to stop.'

As Jenna relayed this back to Mabel, she stumbled over the words. Did Ben know about this? Judging by the look on Alesha's face the answer was no.

Alesha continued 'I can't rest until you stop blaming yourself, Mabel. Please, please don't!'

When Jenna repeated this, Mabel began to weep. 'If only I could believe it was true. But I can't.'

'I understand,' said Jenna. 'But I'll prove it to you.'

'How?' Asked Alesha and Mabel at the same time.

Jenna shrugged. 'I don't know yet. But I'll think of something.'

Mabel gave her a wobbly smile. 'I appreciate what you're trying to do. You're a good girl.'

'I will prove it, one way or another. Just you wait and see.'

'I hope you do think of a way,' said Alesha, as they left Mabel's house.

'So do I.' Jenna turned to Alesha. 'So, you really had moved on from Ben, then. Did he know about this other bloke?'

'No, and there's no need for him to know now. That'll achieve nothing. I didn't do anything wrong. I was faithful to him all the time we were together.'

'I get the feeling he wouldn't be happy to hear it. I certainly won't be telling him.'

'We'd split up and got back together a few times before the final break-up. It was hard for us both to let go, Jen. Believe what you want, but I did love Ben. Still do and always will.'

'I know.' Jenna nodded. 'I hope Mabel's okay.'

Jenna's stomach lurched as she entered the kitchen. The iron had been left on. In a blind panic she jerked the plug from the socket. She turned when a weary, dishevelled Ben walked into the room.

Call me psychic, but something tells me he's been nowhere near the iron.

Chapter Sixteen

Ellie followed Ben into the kitchen. They both slumped at the table. It looked as though their suspicions about Sabrina were confirmed. She pulled out a chair and sat opposite them.

'I take it things didn't go well at work?'

'No.' Ben strode to the fridge and took a can of beer. He held a wine bottle toward them. 'Want some?'

'Yeah, I need it.' Ellie took the bottle and reached for two glasses. 'Jenna?'

'Yeah, why not? It seems like we've all had one of those days.'

Alesha appeared and sat on the work top. 'Even I need wine and I'm teetotal nowadays.' She gave a tiny smile. 'We'll tell you how it went with Mabel later, Ellie.'

Ellie nodded briefly. 'Just when I thought I'd finally found a job I loved, it's all gone wrong. I'm a jinx.'

'What happened?' Jenna filled her glass to the brim. It sounded like she was going to need it. 'Did you send your work to the boss?'

'Yes.' Ben banged the can on the table. 'He asked to see us both in his office.'

'What did he say?' said Jenna.

'That Sabrina had already given him exactly the same work yesterday. Just as we feared.' Ellie's eyes blazed. 'The cheating, thieving little cow.'

'I can't believe she'd do such a thing,' said Ben. 'I know we weren't serious, but I thought she respected me as a person. I guess I was wrong. It looks as if she was just using me.'

'Didn't you explain to the boss?' said Jenna. 'Surely he'd believe you over her, Ben. She's only been working there five minutes, hasn't she?'

He nodded. 'Yes, but she can be very convincing. He said as he'd received it from her first, he had to accept it as hers.'

'So where does that leave the two of you?'

'Back at square one,' Ben spat. 'It's not that we can't come up with something else, we can. But that's not the point. We did a great job on it. Ellie's logo was brilliant. Why should Sabrina take all the credit?'

'Have you seen her today?'

'Yeah,' said Ellie. 'But she kept a low profile and avoided us as much as she could. We know the boss got her into the office. He obviously questioned her about it.'

'And?'

'Well, she must have brazened it out. Scheming little witch.' Ellie sighed.

Alesha climbed from the work top and went to Ben. She wrapped her arms round him.

'We have to think of something. She's not getting away with this.'

Jenna and Ellie exchanged looks. There must be something they could do. But what? Ben stood up. 'I'm going up to my room for a while, girls.'

He walked dejectedly from the room. Jenna wanted to catch him up and comfort him. But there was nothing she could say or do that would help, at the moment.

'So, what happened with Mabel?' said Ellie.

As they filled her in, Jenna worried that dragging up the whole thing would make Mabel ill. Had they made things a million times worse? Maybe so, but she vowed to find a way to get Mabel to believe that Alesha really was around.

Her mind wandered back to Ben. If he didn't come back downstairs, she'd go and check on him. What she'd give right now, to just have a normal, quiet day. Whatever that was. Those kind of days were becoming a distant memory.

A couple of hours later, Jenna knocked hesitantly on his door. He was still awake because she heard the strum of his guitar. He opened the door and stood aside to let her in. She perched on the end of the bed.

'I've just come to see if you want anything? Are you hungry?'

'No thanks. I'm still trying to get my head round what she's done.' He strummed the guitar.

'Me too. Have you written any more songs?'

'Yeah, loads. Nobody will ever hear them though.'

'I'd like to. Can I hear some now?'

Ben hesitated, then sang. His face softened and he became lost in the music. She listened and eventually joined in.

Quietly at first, but soon she forgot where she was and just sang.

Nothing else made her feel so alive…and happy. This was what she wanted to do more than anything. For the first time in years, the same feeling was back. She thought it had gone forever. But it hadn't. They played about with words and harmonies. Jenna didn't want to go back to ordinary life. The one she was in now was where she belonged. And she could see by Ben's face he felt the same. At least for now, he'd forgotten about work and Sabrina.

'Maybe we should call ourselves New Attitude.' Ben smiled. 'It's a good name for a band.'

'So we've got one then — a band?'

'Sounds like it to me. Even if nobody else hears us, we are New Attitude.'

'Cool. But there's only two of us and a guitar.'

'So what? That's all we need. You know, I've got some recording equipment at my parents' place. Nothing too fancy, but it does the job. Maybe I'll bring it.'

'Really? That'd be amazing.'

'There's a pub in town where singers and musicians can perform. It's every Thursday night. You never know, we might end up there ourselves.'

'I'm not sure about that, Ben. Maybe. We'll see.'

'JENNA? Where are you?' Jake's voice came from the landing. She froze. How the hell was she going to explain being in Ben's bedroom with the door closed?

'Shit,' she muttered. 'I'll have to jump out of the window. It's bound to be easier than facing Jake.'

'Wait there.' Ben put a finger to his lips.

'Hi, Jake.' He poked his head round the bedroom door. 'I think she went out.'

'Oh.' Jake's voice got closer. 'That's strange. I've just rang her and I heard her ringtone coming from your bedroom.'

Bugger. The phone was in her pocket, but she hadn't heard it above their singing and the guitar. Before she had time to hide, Jake pushed past Ben and strode into the room.

'Fancy seeing you here, Jenna. Something you want to tell me?' His fists curled by his sides and his eyes were like slits. But the hurt on his face was evident.

'Jake,' said Ben. 'It's not what you think. We were singing, that's all. I'm sorry for lying to you, but I didn't want you to get the wrong idea.'

'It's true, Jake.' Jenna nodded. 'We've started a band. Or should I say we're going to.'

Jake slumped against the wall. 'Why in here? In his bedroom, Jenna? How would you feel if it was the other way round?'

Jenna walked towards him on shaky legs. 'The same as you, probably.' She took his hand. 'Ben's been through a bad time too. Like me. Music makes us both feel better, but we weren't ready for an audience. I really am sorry though. From now on we practice downstairs.'

Ben nodded. 'Yeah, we will.'

Jake turned to walk out of the room. 'I trust you, Jenna. I wouldn't be marrying you otherwise. But.' He looked over his shoulder. 'I don't hold the same opinion of everybody in this house. My mum's downstairs. She wanted to see you so I thought I'd bring her out for a change of scenery. If you can tear yourself away, maybe you can go down to see her?'

Mona sat upright in a chair. She threw Jenna a chilly look. It was so icy Jenna wondered how long it would take for her to develop hyperthermia. She wore the same usual expression as her namesake, but today, The Mona Lisa seemed positively ecstatic compared to The Mona Mansfield.

'Hello, Jenna.' Mona gave a tight smile. 'Things have changed in here since my last visit.' She cast her eyes around the room. Jenna followed her gaze. Dirty cups and glasses lay on the coffee table. The crumbs on the floor would feed a flock of birds for a month, and piles of paper and pens littered the sofa.

Jenna understood Mona's distaste. She felt it too. It seemed nowadays she only had to turn her back for a second and it looked like the house from uni days. Although Jenna detested living in this chaos, a sudden nostalgia for the student life overwhelmed her. Mess hadn't entered into her way of thinking back then. It was normal. How she wished it could be so easily dismissed now. But much as she tried to banish the panic from her mind, she couldn't. While the untidiness continued, her mind would never be organised either. She took a deep breath.

'Sorry, Mona.' Jenna gathered up the dirty pots. 'I'll put the kettle on. It's been a bit hectic lately. I haven't had much time for cleaning.'

When she walked back into the room with a tray of tea and biscuits, Mona was rolling up a tape measure while Jake moved the sofa back against the wall.

'Mum wanted to check whether some items of her furniture will fit.' He straightened and took the tray from her. 'You don't mind, do you?'

'Actually, yes.' Jenna kept her voice level. 'My furniture stays put.'

'But, Jenna,' said Mona. 'Some of your furniture needs to go to the tip, dear. Mine's perfectly decent.'

Jenna blinked back the hot tears which burnt her eyes. Some of the furniture was shabby, but no way would she allow Mona to replace her parent's stuff with the chintz she favoured.

To his credit, Jake rounded on Mona. 'Mum! You can't say that! This stuff means a lot to Jenna.'

Thank you, Jake!

He continued. 'We'll buy new. Eventually. When she's ready to let go of this stuff.' He smiled at Jenna. 'Or when it falls apart. Whichever comes first.'

For nothing.

'Did you see Ellie when you got here?' Jenna could've done with her moral support. Even Alesha was nowhere to be seen.

'No,' said Jake. 'To be honest I was hoping she'd get back with her husband. That would be one problem solved. The smaller of the two, I admit.' He looked up at the ceiling, in the direction of Ben's room. 'Don't get carried away with all this singing nonsense, Jenna. It's natural you need a hobby, but maybe something a bit more practical?'

'Hobby? It's what I was, Jake. A singer. And it's still a part of me. I'd just forgotten how much until recently.'

'Singing?' Mona pursed her lips. 'I didn't know about that. Well, if it means so much to you, I'll have a word. Maybe I can get you in the church choir.'

'That's not what I had in mind, Mona. But thanks for the offer.'

Mona set down her mug. 'I could've done with seeing my bedroom. I take it I can have my own furniture in there?' She sniffed. 'But I hear your lodger's in that room. Ben, isn't it? Maybe I can just take a quick look?'

Jenna shook her head. 'No, you can't. He's paying rent, and we can't just go in there when we feel like it.'

'*You* do!' Jake muttered loud enough for her to hear.

'How long is he likely to be here?' said Mona. 'My house will be on the market before long.'

'He'll be here until I ask him to go. Likewise with Ellie.' Jenna gave Jake a hard look. 'And before you say anything, Jake, no, I haven't given them their marching orders yet. There's no need. *I'll* decide when.'

'But what if the house sells straight away?' said Mona. 'It might.'

'Yes, it might.' Jenna agreed. 'So, I suggest you think carefully about whether you really want to go ahead yet.'

Mona gasped and clasped her chest. 'But I could be homeless. We agreed.'

Jenna shook her head. 'We didn't. You informed me of your plan, after you'd arranged it together. Didn't you?'

'Jenna.' Jake wrung his hands together. 'Come on, be fair. We *have* discussed this.'

'We've also discussed your mum having separate living space. But I doubt it'll happen.' Jenna shrugged at Mona. 'Look, I'm not being unkind, Mona. But surely you can see that when Jake and I marry we need time together, alone?'

'But I'll have a TV in my room. I'll stay in there when you want me out of the way.' She made it sound as if Jenna was being unreasonable. Her lips wobbled. Jake put an arm round her shoulder. 'Jenna didn't mean it like that, Mum. She just meant *sometimes*, didn't you?'

He threw Jenna a pleading look. Against her better judgement she relented.

'Look, I'm not saying you can't live with us. But you have to respect our privacy, okay?'

Mona nodded. 'Of course I will.'

'And I say what stays and doesn't stay in the house.'

'Yes, dear.'

180

'And for now, at least, that includes my friends. Ellie *and* Ben. Right?'

Jake and Mona exchanged uncertain looks.

'If you insist.' Jake sighed. 'But I don't see why you want them here so much. You've changed.'

Jenna hesitated before answering. 'There's a few, erm, problems I need to deal with first. They both need my help with…things. Once they are sorted, I'll ask them to go. Okay? Don't worry, it'll be before the wedding.'

'What things?' Jake asked.

'I can't say, but nothing for you to worry about. I give you my word, even if things aren't solved closer to the wedding, I'll ask them to go regardless.'

'Well…' Jake faltered. 'Alright.'

'You wouldn't want to marry someone who didn't care about other people, would you?' She threw a pointed look at Mona. 'Let me do what I need to do, Jake, and then I'm all yours. Forever.' She winked. 'Deal?'

'Deal.' He grinned and ruffled her hair.

The tension uncoiled around Jenna's body. It felt as though they'd come to a new understanding. Things were going to be fine. Everything was complicated at the moment, but it wouldn't be that way for much longer, hopefully. Alesha would disappear once she was satisfied Jenna had done all she could. And then it would be easier to concentrate on the wedding, and becoming Jake's wife. As long as she and Jake were united in being assertive with Mona, that would work out fine too.

Everything's going to work out well for us all. I know it!

'Jenna,' Ellie called from the hallway. 'Where are you?'

'In here, Ellie.'

'I've been next door, with Mabel. I had to check she was okay.' Ellie appeared in the doorway, with Alesha. 'We have to find a way to convince her she wasn't to blame for the accident.

181

Poor old lady. She —' Ellie entered the room and stopped in her tracks when she saw Jake and Mona.

As Ellie moved from the doorway, Jenna stared in horror at the figure at the bottom of the stairs. Ben slumped to the floor, head in hands. Although she couldn't see his face, she heard the muffled sobs. She froze. Just as she got enough movement back in her body to go out to him, he reached for the bannister and hauled himself to his feet. She could only watch as he took a couple of steps towards her.

'Would that be the same 'poor old lady' who killed my Alesha?' His haunted look pierced through Jenna's heart.

Her mind swam with incoherent thoughts. The only thing that was clear, was that he was blocking her path to the light switch. How she needed the comforting feel of the hard plastic under her fingers.

Something tells me now's not a good time to ask him to move.

Chapter Seventeen

After Jake and Mona had made a hasty retreat, Jenna, Ben and Ellie faced each other in silence. Alesha walked up to Ben and prodded his chest. 'Don't be an idiot! It was nobody's fault, so don't transfer blame onto Mabel now.'

Jenna prayed this time Alesha would manage to get through to him. But yet again, God wasn't taking her calls. He turned on his heel and headed for the kitchen. She didn't need to be psychic to know the fridge door was about to open. The girls followed him, to find he'd taken four cans of beer and lined them up on the table. She scooped three up and put them back in the fridge.

'Hey, what you doing?' His head shot up.

'Keeping them cold for you.' Jenna sat next to him. 'Do you feel like talking?'

'Why? Got something to tell me?' His nostrils flared. 'Maybe we should have a little chat about that nice old lady next door.'

'Yes, that's exactly what Mabel is.' Jenna toyed with a tablemat. 'Isn't she, Ellie?'

Ben banged down the can. The liquid spread across the table in a sticky frothy pool. 'She's the woman who killed Alesha, isn't she?'

'If you mean was she the driver of the car, then yes.' Jenna leaned and gripped his arm. 'But she didn't kill her. Alesha in effect killed herself. You know that.'

'Have you known all along she was the driver? Did you already know about Alesha before I moved here?' His eyes narrowed. 'Tell me!'

'No, I didn't know about Mabel. I've just found out, actually.' Jenna hoped he wouldn't ask again about Alesha.

'How did you find out?' he asked.

'Erm…' Jenna glanced at Ellie and Alesha. 'Err…'

'She told us.' Ellie pulled up a chair. 'Even though she's not to blame any more than you are, Mabel's devastated. Jenna and I couldn't understand why you thought it was your fault. But now I for one can't understand why your anger is directed at Mabel.'

'Well maybe she was too old to be driving,' he hissed. 'That's why she couldn't stop in time.'

'That's not true,' said Jenna. 'And you know that, really.'

'Do I? None of us do. We weren't there.' His face twisted. 'We only know what we've heard or been told by other people. They might all be fucking lying.'

Jenna flinched and shrank back. 'I know you're angry, but I'm not having you take it out on her. It's not fair, Ben.'

'Fair? For all you know, J, the old lady may have dementia. Alzheimer's, or something.' He shrugged. 'She's probably either forgotten what really happened, or has blocked it out.'

'I can tell you for definite she's done neither,' said Ellie. 'That poor woman is tortured by it. And added to that, she has nobody. Other than me and Jenna, obviously. Do you know what she's just told me? Her husband died not long after. Mabel thinks it was the strain that killed him.'

'Christ.' Jenna gasped. 'I can't bear to think of everything she's gone through. Especially when there's no family to support her.'

'Me too,' said Alesha in a tiny voice. 'All the trouble I've caused. But right now, I want to kick Ben's sorry arse for blaming her.'

'What do you think Alesha would say if she was here now, Ben?' said Jenna. 'Think about it.'

'She'd tell me to pull myself together.' He attempted a smile. 'And she'd threaten to kick my sorry arse.'

Alesha giggled. 'He knows me well.'

Jenna grinned. 'Maybe I should kick your arse in Alesha's place.'

'Maybe you should,' he agreed. 'But before you do, can you pass me another can, please?'

Jenna handed it to him. 'When did life get so complicated?' The answer was right in front of her, of course. Wearing a bright blue dress and a mischievous smile. But the funny thing was that strange as it may sound, she'd miss Alesha. She suspected Ellie felt the same. It was a bittersweet thought that when the day came for Alesha to disappear, everything would be solved. And all of them would be at peace. One way or another. Wouldn't they?

Alesha looked agitated a couple of days later. She beckoned Jenna and Ellie to follow her upstairs away from Ben. They went to Jenna's bedroom.

'I can't believe I've been so stupid.'

'In what way? Narrow it down, it could be for so many reasons.' Jenna grinned.

'You know I said I used to work in an office?'

'Yes,' said Ellie. 'And?'

'I used to be quite good with computers. I've thought of something, although I wish it had occurred to me sooner.'

'Get on with it. What?' Jenna sighed.

'It might be a long shot, but I'd like to think Sabrina is as stupid as she looks.'

'What do you mean?' Ellie leaned forward in interest.

'The document Ben sent to the boss,' said Alesha. 'There's a way we can prove he created it, not Sabrina.'

'How?' Ellie's eyes gleamed.

'Well, it depends on how much she knows about computers. But let's hope it's very little. You can see who created the document. Write this down.'

Jenna scrabbled for a pen and paper. 'Go on.'

'On a PC, right click, go into Properties and then Details. On a Mac, go into File and then Properties.' Alesha leaned over Jenna's shoulder as she wrote. 'Here, it will say: 'Author,' and if we're lucky, it will be followed by 'Ben Williams.'

'If we're lucky?' Jenna paused, pen poised. 'What if we're not?'

'If we're not.' Alesha grimaced. 'Then Sabrina isn't so thick, after all. Because it's possible to change the name. The question is: will she know that?'

'Oh, PLEASE let her be the bimbo we know and hate.' Ellie crossed her fingers. 'We need to go tell Ben.'

'I didn't know that!' Ben beamed. 'I love you two!' Jenna felt herself flush under his gaze. She felt a fraud taking the credit for Alesha's masterstroke. But what else could she do?

'But,' Ben continued. 'We shouldn't get our hopes up. Even if Sabrina didn't know that, maybe someone else is in on it, and did know.'

'Ring your boss now,' said Jenna. 'He'll be able to check.'

'I can't. It'll have to wait until tomorrow.'

'Why? It's important. Surely he'll be willing to put your mind at rest, one way or another.'

'Do it, Ben!' Ellie urged.

'Oh, okay.' He picked up his phone. 'Here goes.'

The three girls held their breath as Ben spoke to his boss. By the time he got off the phone Jenna needed oxygen.

'He's going to call me back.' Ben pulled a face. 'Never in my life have I wanted one of my exes to be proved a complete fool. Until now.'

They all jumped ten minutes later when his phone rang.

'Paul, yes?'

The girls watched Ben's expression in nervous anticipation.

'That's great news.' Relief flooded his face. 'See you tomorrow. Yes, we'll go over *our* pitch with you then.'

'Yesss!' Ellie punched the air.

'We did it.' His smile made Jenna's heart melt faster than a chocolate fireguard. She rushed to him and went to kiss his cheek. But he turned and she ended up with her mouth against his chin. Her tongue was so close to that cleft. Her tongue moved to make its escape from her mouth, but she came to her senses just in time, pulling back from him abruptly.

Alesha gave a smug smile and looked at Ben. He in turn was watching Jenna. His expression was unreadable, but it made her uncomfortable. Not least because the only thing going

187

through her mind was exploring that cleft, and moving her lips up to meet his. Clearly she was on a level with Sabrina, in the stupidity stakes.

The following evening, they celebrated Sabrina being fired and Ben's probable promotion with a takeaway. They'd decided on Indian. The curry wasn't the only thing making Jenna hot. She wiped the sweat from her cleavage. It was a futile attempt, because with Ben's eyes watching her every movement, it made her sweat more.

She told herself it meant nothing. They were just relieved that at least one problem had been cleared up. Ben hadn't mentioned Mabel since his outburst. Jenna felt certain that he'd thought about it, and felt bad. He'd realised she lived so close, and lashed out. He wanted someone else to blame, and she'd been the obvious target.

As the drink flowed, Jenna thought about her uni friends. Were they all doing what they'd set out to do? For the first time, it crossed her mind that it would be nice to catch up with them all and find out. But would they even care about Jenna now? It had been a long time. And anyway, how would it make her feel, hearing about their lives?

Ben leaned across to wipe the stray tear from her eye. Ellie's fork halted halfway to her mouth.

'You okay, Jen?'

Jenna nodded. 'Sorry, just...'

'You don't need to explain.' Ben piled more food onto her plate. 'Just eat.'

She tried to banish the images of her previous life, but they refused to budge. The sudden impulse to go onto Facebook and see what everyone was doing, and where they were, came from nowhere. Maybe it wouldn't hurt to take a look. Soon. A sad smile spread across her face as possible status updates crossed her mind: Changed ten incontinence pads today. Went to the supermarket and it was busy. Spent three hours cleaning the house. It hardly made interesting reading. But what if people read about New Attitude? It was only a fantasy, but she'd take fantasy over reality anyday. Fantasy involved laughing and telling jokes, and singing to a captive audience. It involved getting dressed up to go out. It involved handing over a bag of dirty washing to her parents and telling them about her day. And…it involved meeting Ben in that bar years ago, without Alesha being there. If only it was possible to turn back the clock. Her parents would be alive, Alesha would be alive, Mabel wouldn't be distraught, she'd be singing…and who knew what else would be happening. But if Alesha was right, it would've involved Ben. She'd be happy. But then, she wouldn't have met Jake, would she?

'Jenna?' Ellie's brow furrowed. 'You sure you're alright?'

'Yeah.'

No! Everything's mixed up and crazy. My head feels like it's about to explode. I want my old life back. Or a new one. But not this one. Apart from that, I'm fine thanks.

Chapter Eighteen

The next couple of weeks were quiet, compared to the previous few. But something had changed. Ben was drinking again. Alesha was right. It wasn't as though he was an alcoholic but he used it to blot things out, because it was there and easy to do so.

His mood had altered since finding out Mabel was next door. Yet intuition told her there was something else bothering him. He'd got the promotion at work and the company were delighted with his and Ellie's work. But the only time he relaxed was when they sang, and he had the guitar in his hand. Jenna was the same. Music was her escape and now took over much of her thoughts and time. She wondered how much Sabrina's betrayal had affected him. He hadn't said much since she'd been fired, but it was bound to take some getting over.

She ran her hands over the recording equipment Ben had just brought in. A quiver of excitement coursed through her. It took up the whole wall under the window of the sitting room.

They'd stuck to their promise to Jake though. No more bedroom serenading.

To give Jake credit, he *had* backed off from hassling her about getting Ellie and Ben to move. When he'd witnessed Ben's obvious distress regarding Mabel, he'd simply said he was there when Jenna needed him. Since then he hadn't been back to the house much, and even on the odd occasion he did, it was only flying visits. Open displays of emotion made him uncomfortable, and he clearly worried he may be dragged into more of the same, if he hung about too long.

Jenna hopped from foot to foot impatiently while Ben set up the equipment. She wanted to test it before Ellie got home. She'd gone to see a former work colleague and probably wouldn't be late. So far, Jenna and Ben had not sung for Ellie. They'd wanted to perfect a few songs first, including some which he'd written. She never failed to be impressed by Ben's voice. Whether it was soul, blues, reggae or anything else for that matter, he was happy to tackle it. And was fantastic. He'd encouraged her to try different genres of music, and to her surprise, she discovered a country music tone to her voice, which she'd never known existed. A song Ben had written worked well, and Jenna loved it. It was modern and upbeat, not at all like the 'slit your throat' kind of dreariness she'd associated with country music before.

Just as Ben finished sorting out the wiring, Ellie arrived home. Alesha was with her. They seemed to spend a lot of time together lately which was good.

'Hi, guys.' Ellie tossed her coat onto the sofa. 'Hey, that looks cool. I can't wait to hear you both.'

'I've heard them and they're brilliant,' said Alesha.

Jenna's stomach muscles clenched. It was over five years since she'd performed in public. Even just Ellie and Alesha watching made her nervous.

191

'One, two,' she giggled into the microphone. 'You ready, Ben? Don't record anything yet though. Let's practice properly first.'

'Okay.' He nodded. 'I've got the backing tracks ready.'

As soon as the music started Jenna forgot everything, except the feel of the microphone in her hand, and the elation of doing what she'd missed so much, without even realising it.

As the song came to an end, she and Ben smiled at each other. The moment seemed to last ages.

Tears slid down Ellie's cheeks.

'Why are you crying?' Jenna's forehead creased.

'Because I never thought I'd hear you sing like that again. It's what you were meant to do.'

Jenna wasn't sure how to reply. It did feel right. But was she just attempting to cling onto something from her past? Was it one of her fantasies and nothing more? One thing was certain though: she felt happy. If that feeling hadn't been lost forever, maybe anything was possible.

'You ready to carry on?' Ben put on another track.

As she sang, Ellie and Alesha stared, enthralled. But when their faces began to morph into her parents, she stumbled over the words. As her mind wandered back to that fateful night, Jenna thought about what Mabel had said: Don't let the images get too close. Then put them in a box. So she did. And it worked.

A couple of hours later, Ben took the guitar from his shoulder to get a drink. Jenna saw Alesha's amazement when he wandered back with a glass of water and no beer in sight.

'So, you up for going to that pub I was telling you about, J?'

'What pub's that?' said Ellie.

'Where anybody can perform.' Ben nudged Jenna. 'What do you think?'

'I'm not sure. I'll think about it.'

'You should!' said Ellie. 'Is it a karaoke place?'

'No.' Ben grinned. 'It's a bit different to that. Only serious musicians go there.'

'Most karaoke singers think that's exactly what they are.' Ellie laughed. 'But this place sounds like a good place to start, Jen. Give it a go and see what happens.'

'Maybe.' She shrugged. 'I hope we haven't kept the neighbours awake with the music. Mind you, the couple next door keep me awake regularly with *their* nocturnal activities. She sounds like a tortured cat and he sounds like a howling wolf. It's like living next door to a pack of animals. I almost want to throw scraps of food over the fence.'

'I've heard them too.' Ellie giggled. 'It sounds painful.'

'Thank goodness there's a gap between here and Mabel's,' said Jenna. 'I don't think we'll have disturbed her, but I'll ask tomorrow.'

As soon as the words were out of her mouth the mood changed immediately. The charged atmosphere was strong enough to give them all severe electric shocks.

Ben banged his glass onto the table and yanked the plug for the equipment out of the socket.

At least he's learning to unplug things at night!

His eyes flashed as he strode over to Jenna. 'Can you refrain from mentioning that woman in front of me?'

He should lay off the water…it doesn't agree with him!

Anger surged through her. 'I'll mention who I want, in my own house,' she shot back.

'You're doing it to wind me up!'

'No, I'm not. Don't be ridiculous. Mabel was my friend long before you came on the scene.'

'Yes, I can see where your priorities lie.'

'If you want to put it like that, then yes. She's an old lady with nobody to look out for her. Except us.'

'I hope you're not including me in that.'

'Stop it, both of you.' Ellie held up her hands. 'Ben, quit speaking of Mabel that way. She's lovely and wouldn't hurt a fly. And you, Jenna, don't give him the chance to make such remarks.'

'Me?' Jenna rounded on Ellie. 'It's your fault! Gobbing off about her before checking who was listening.'

'Don't blame me!' Ellie glared.

'Listen at you all.' Alesha sighed. 'Like five-year-olds in a playground.'

'You can shut up, too!' Jenna hissed.

'I never said a word,' said Ben.

'Not you.'

'Who?'

'Who what?'

'Who can shut up, too?'

'ALL OF YOU! I'm sick and tired of you all.' Jenna looked at the mess surrounding her. Squatters probably lived in tidier conditions than this. Her eyes rested on the clock on the mantelpiece. It had been moved to make way for a mug, and was facing sideways. A white hot rage rose inside. Her arm swept the clock and mug. She watched them fly through the air as if in slow motion. They crashed onto the earth scattering shards of broken pieces by her feet.

Silence filled the air. Not even the ticking of the clock could be heard. When it had landed the pointers had rested at twenty to four. Like a downturned mouth. It stared up at Jenna in a sad and reproachful manner.

She blinked and looked at the three wide-eyed faces before her. All were open-mouthed. An urge to laugh bubbled up in her throat, but she choked it down.

Ben took a step forward. 'J, calm down.'

His words had the opposite effect. She wasn't done yet.

'Do not tell me to calm down.' She pointed her forefinger. 'You're all doing my head in. I can't cope with it all any longer. Now get out!'

'What?' Ellie whispered.

'You heard me. All of you get out. NOW!'

Ellie moved backwards hastily, almost falling over Ben.

'J, what's got into you? And why do you keep saying all? There's only me and El here. You're obviously not well.'

'No I'm not. I'm sick. Of the lot of you! *Three* of you, Ben. Because Alesha's here!'

Chapter Nineteen

Alesha shook her head and moaned 'no,' while Ellie rocked back and forth with her eyes tightly shut. Jenna's gaze rested on Ben, and the enormity of what she'd said washed over her with the force of a tsunami.

The only part of him moving was the pulse in his neck. Jenna focused on it, not daring to look into his face. She held her breath until she almost passed out. He slumped to the ground without making a sound. Alesha was the first to react.

'Well done, Jenna.' She clapped slowly. 'Great performance, there. Don't expect a standing ovation anytime soon though.'

'I'm so sorry.' Jenna hung her head. 'I had no right to tell you like that, Ben.'

He lifted his head. His eyes looked at her blankly. 'What do you mean? I'm wondering what possessed you to say it at all, J. I guess you wanted to punish me, I'd made you angry. But *that*? Knowing I'm still cut up about Alesha. You must hate me.'

'I don't! It's true! You had to find out sometime, I suppose. But I'm sorry for the way I told you.'

'I don't get what you're trying to say.'

'She came to me a while before I saw you in that bar, Mango's. I thought I was seeing things. But she wouldn't leave me alone.'

'You make me sound like a stalker.' Alesha huffed.

Jenna ignored her and focused on Ben. 'She wanted you to move here, Ben, and sent me to find you.'

'You've got a problem, J. See a doctor.' He got unsteadily to his feet and raked his hands through his hair. 'But please forget we had this conversation.'

She reached out and touched his arm. He hesitated before moving it away.

'She was worried about you and wanted you to stop blaming yourself,' Jenna continued. 'But she certainly doesn't want you blaming Mabel either.'

'Shut up! I'm not goi —'

'She's telling the truth,' said Ellie. 'I know that for a fact…because I see Alesha too.'

'Not you as well.' He shook his head. 'Is this some kind of sick joke?'

'No,' said Ellie. 'She's standing beside you now.'

He glanced around and sighed. 'No, she's not. Please don't do this.'

'Ben,' said Jenna. 'Think of something only she would know. Go on.'

He hesitated for a brief second. 'No.' He picked up the glass of water and studied it intently.

Alesha clicked her fingers. 'His nickname! Nobody else knew what I called him.'

'What was it?' said Jenna, to all intents and purposes talking to a bookcase.

'That won't answer you.' Ben gave a wry smile.

'Bumface.' Alesha giggled. 'He has two big dimples on his bum and I said they looked like eyes.'

I wonder if they're as deep as the one on his chin…no, do not go there, Jenna!

She winked at Alesha and turned to Ben. 'Stop talking out of your arse! But then why wouldn't you, *Bumface*?'

The glass slipped through his fingers and onto the floor. His hand didn't move. The colour drained from his face as he stumbled to the sofa.

'Erm, shit. You're freaking me out now. But it was a lucky guess.'

'It was Alesha who saved your job, not me,' said Jenna, hands on hips. 'She knew Sabrina was trouble and watched her at work. That's how Ellie found out what was going on.'

Ben turned to Ellie. 'Come on, El. This can't be true. It's madness.'

Ellie nodded. 'It sounds crazy, I get that. Still true though.'

'Tell him I was right about his mate liking that fancy dress costume a bit too much.' Alesha tugged Jenna's arm. 'I'm just amazed that he can fit a French maid's outfit under his suit.'

Jenna and Ellie gasped. 'No way!' Ellie's eyes widened.

'What now?' Ben's eyebrows lifted.

'Your mate,' said Jenna. 'The one who wore the French maid outfit? Well, he wears it for work under his suit.'

'Nooo.' Ben shook his head. 'I don't believe it. I never did, even when Alesh —'

'Even when Alesha thought otherwise?' Jenna finished for him. 'Well she says it *is* true.'

'But…' His gaze darted around the room. 'It's just another lucky guess.'

'Yeah, right.' Ellie nodded. 'Course it is. Because that's such a common occurrence.'

He opened his mouth then closed it again. They watched as he left the room, banging the door behind him.

'Do you think he believes us?' said Ellie.

'He doesn't want to.' Alesha shrugged. 'Logic tells him I'm not supposed to be here. If he admitted my existence, he'd be acknowledging life after death. He was such a firm non-believer I don't know whether he'll ever accept it. But one thing's for sure: he's furious because you've forced him to think about it.'

Jenna lowered her weary body into the bath and sank into the bubbles. The shift at work had been particularly gruelling. It was getting to the point where she wanted to walk out and never go back. She never took it out on the elderly clients though. In fact, one of the reasons the job was so depressing was because she wanted to spend more time with them individually. It was one long round of washing, dressing and feeding. They had to get round them as quickly as they could, to ensure all their needs were met as swiftly as humanly possible. Thank God she had five days off now. They all worked by a monthly rolling rota and this was her favourite week of the month. The previous week had included three double shifts and she was exhausted.

It wasn't the only reason. Her sleeping pattern was more erratic than ever. Most nights she tossed and turned, only snatching a few hours of uninterrupted sleep here and there. Consequently she was tired and grouchy throughout the day.

She knew the reason: since confronting Ben about Alesha three weeks ago, things had changed dramatically in the house. For one thing he was rarely in it. Most nights he arrived back late. Alesha was worried because he was drinking too much again. She saw it as a major step backwards, as he hadn't gone out much at all when he'd first moved in.

Jenna fervently wished she'd kept her big mouth shut. Yet on the other hand, how could she have kept quiet indefinitely? It had become harder and harder to stop herself from saying the wrong thing. Now he preferred to be out of the way. Probably nervous about what would be thrown at him next. He still laughed and joked during the times their paths crossed, but the easy going friendship and growing closeness had gone. Maybe in some ways that was a good thing. But she missed it.

She scrubbed her body with an abrasive scourer. As the deep welts appeared Jenna expected to feel better. It didn't happen.

Jake's company were in the process of locating to bigger offices, so they hadn't seen much of each other lately. He'd been working late, and more often than not, so had Jenna. She'd always spend time with both Ellie and Alesha at some point during the day though. It was strange, but a ghost had somehow become one of her best friends. It hurt Jenna more than the scourer did, to see Alesha so sad. It was likely she realised she'd picked the wrong person to help, in Jenna, who'd only succeeded in making things worse. And that was saying something.

Jenna padded downstairs in her dressing gown, to make a hot drink before bed. She popped her head round the sitting room door to see if Ellie wanted one, and was surprised to find Ben there too.

'Hi, do either of you want anything?'

'I'll have a cup of tea please, Jen,' said Ellie.

'Thanks.' Ben was engrossed in his laptop. He glanced up briefly. 'You okay, J? You look tired.'

She nodded. 'Yeah, I'm fine. I'll make the t —'. The doorbell chimed. 'Who the hell's that at this time of night?' She glanced at the clock which had mysteriously materialised on the mantelpiece in place of the broken one. Nobody normally came to visit at ten o'clock. Panic spread through her veins. Something must be wrong.

'Shall I answer it?' Ben stood.

'No, I'll get it.' She went to the door and called through it. 'Who's there?'

'It's me, open up,' said a familiar voice.

She opened the door open and squealed. 'Uncle Mick! What you doing here?' She flung herself on him, wrapping her arms around his neck. 'It's so good to see you.'

'Let me in then.' He manoeuvred himself through the narrow doorway with difficulty, as the backpack he carried was huge, and fairly wide. Jenna wondered how he managed to stay upright with that strapped to his back. He shrugged out of it and left it in the hallway before following Jenna into the room.

'Look who I've found, Ellie.' Jenna grinned and stood aside.

'Mick!' Ellie leaped from her seat. 'Oh my God, you look fantastic!'

And he did. His dark blonde hair was streaked white from the sun and he was deeply tanned.

'Ellie! You look good too! Married life must suit you.'

Ellie's smile faded. 'We're separated now. But never mind that. When did you get back?'

'The flight landed a few hours ago then I got a bus here.' He turned towards Ben.

'You must be Jake.' He offered Ben an outstretched hand. 'Good to meet you at last. I hear you're going to make an honest woman of my favourite girl, here?'

'Erm, no…I'm Ben.' He took Mick's hand. 'Nice to meet you, mate.'

'Are you going to introduce us properly?' Mick threw an arm round Jenna's shoulder.

'Ben, this is my uncle, and Mick, this is Ben, my lodger…and friend.'

'O-kayy.' Mick grinned. 'Is there a drink going spare?'

'I was just about to put the kettle on,' said Jenna. Mick pulled a face. 'I was hoping for something a bit stronger.'

'Beer?' said Ben. 'I'll join you.' The men made their way to the kitchen.

'Shall we have a glass of wine, Jen? Celebrate Mick being here?' said Ellie.

Jenna nodded. 'Yeah, come on. I'm so happy to see him.'

They gathered at the table. Alesha appeared and raised her eyebrows.

'Wow! He's hot.'

Jenna rolled her eyes. The men were talking animatedly and she was content to bask in the moment of having her one remaining relative with her. Although they emailed frequently, it wasn't the same as seeing each other in person.

'So.' Mick turned to her. 'We need to catch up, girl. What's been happening?'

Nothing much. Other than getting engaged by accident, being haunted by a ghost who I happen to be fond of, who happens to be

Ben's ex, who I'm also fond of, telling an elderly lady who knocked over the ghost about the ghost.

'Oh, nothing much. I'll erm, fill you in tomorrow. When you've had a rest.'

Mick's eyes narrowed, but he just gave a small nod.

'Where are you staying, Mick?' Ellie asked.

'I can bunk down with an old mate,' said Mick. 'But it's a bit late now. Can I borrow your sofa until tomorrow, Jen?'

'Course you can. I'll get some spare bedding.' As she was leaving the room she smiled at the enraptured faces of Alesha and Ellie. Mick had always had women throwing themselves at him, but had managed to duck any serious entanglements. He and Ben chatted as if they'd known each other forever.

Ellie tapped her on the shoulder as she was hauling bedding out of the airing cupboard.

'Ellie, you made me jump.'

'I was just thinking.'

'Careful!'

'Mick probably won't be in the country long. It's a shame for you to not spend as much time as possible together while you can.'

'I'm sure we will.'

'But it'll be easier if he stays here.'

Jenna spun round. 'It's not practical. Any more than a night on the sofa won't work, will it?'

'Nooo. But if he had a room to stay in, you'd be happy, wouldn't you?'

'Yes, but there isn't a room.' Jenna studied Ellie's face. Definitely shifty. And then it dawned on her. She closed her eyes and sighed.

'Ellie, you know Mick's a bit of a gypsy. You're not getting any crazy ideas about him, are you? Please say you're not.'

203

Ellie opened her eyes and mouth wide. But she was no more an actor, than the cast of some of the daytime soaps. 'No!' She gasped.

Maybe some gypsy blood ran in the family. Jenna could become a fortune-teller, because she could see into the future...and she predicted heartache for Ellie.

'Jenna? I could share with you and Mick could have my room. It won't be for long. I don't mind, if it means you can have him around.'

I bet you don't!

'Oh, okay. If he wants to.'

Before Jenna could say any more, Ellie was halfway downstairs. She followed, wondering what she was getting into now.

'No, we don't mind sharing at all.'

'Well if you're sure? Jen?'

'It's fine, Mick.' She couldn't help smiling. 'But there are rules. Everything has to be kept clean and tidy.'

Mick tried but failed to smother a grin as his eyes swept the room and the pots and pans littering it. 'Of course. I'll help maintain your...usual standards.'

'Give us a hand to move some stuff out of my room, Mick,' said Ellie. 'I'll just get what I need for the next day or two, for now.'

Jenna knew even that much might take some time. When she and Ben were left alone, an awkward silence filled the room. He was obviously still upset with her. It was about time they cleared the air.

'Ben, are you still angry with me? I was only trying to help. I'm sorry.'

He hesitated before replying. 'Yeah, I suppose you were. But making stuff up like that isn't the way to do it, J.'

'Look, I know you don't believe in all that stuff. It's too weird. Isn't it easier to just believe that everything's black and white? That once you're dead you're dead? But Ben, there *is* a lot more to it than meets the eye. Literally.'

'Do you know what I think? You want to believe it, so you do. It's wishful thinking because of your parents.'

'Can you look me in the eye and tell me you haven't believed it, even for a second? After what we told you?'

He glanced at her then lowered his gaze. 'No, I can't. But I don't *want* to believe. It scares me.'

'But why would you be scared of Alesha?'

'You don't know her!'

'Oh, I do. I see your point.' They grinned and relief washed over her at having the old Ben back.

Alesha pouted and pulled a face. Jenna knew it wasn't the right time to tell Ben this.

'Can we just leave it, J?'

'Give me one more chance to make you see. Just one, that's all I ask.'

He rose from the chair. 'I've had enough of —'

'Hear me out. We opened up to each other a few weeks ago. In a way we've never done with anyone else. I thought we were friends and could trust each other.'

'So did I!'

'You *can* trust me. And I'm begging you to. I'd never hurt you, I lo…'

'Carry on.'

Jenna felt perspiration trickle down her back. What had come over her? What on earth had she been about to say?

Alesha clearly wondered the same thing. She gave the thumbs-up and winked. Jenna felt confused and uncomfortable. She turned her back on Alesha.

'I love having you around, and being friends with you.'

'Right,' he said, flatly.

'So you'll give me one more chance? Isn't it better to know rather than wonder? I didn't ask your ex to crash into my life, Ben. But she insists I make you see. I didn't want to be involved. But like it or not I am. And, to be honest, I really like her. Most of the time.'

He smiled. 'Okay, okay. But you'll never prove it to me, because no matter what you say, I'll always assume it was simply a good, if not great, guess.'

Jenna shrugged. 'We'll see.'

He continued. 'But if and when you *do* see her, tell her I know those shoes she passed off as being a tenner from the market cost eighty quid…No wonder she won't let me see her!'

Chapter Twenty

'So, girls, tell me what's been going on.' Mick sat at the kitchen table the next morning with Jenna and Ellie. It was Saturday, so Ellie wasn't at work. Ben had gone to see his parents.

'I'm not sure where to start.' Jenna grinned at Ellie.

'It's been a bit…eventful,' Ellie added.

'Start by telling me about Jake and the wedding.' Mick leaned back in his seat and blew on his steaming coffee. 'Your last email said the date's the twenty-third of April, right?'

'Yeah, that's right.'

'Is that it? Hopefully I'll get to meet him soon.'

'I'll ask him to come round,' said Jenna. 'He's really busy at work though, so I'm not sure when it'll be.'

'I see.'

'He doesn't come here much. He's not too happy about it being a bit crowded,' said Ellie. 'Is he, Jenna?'

'No, not really. But he's accepted that's the way it is, for now.'

'How's the wedding plans going?' he asked. 'You must be excited.'

Jenna squirmed. She wished he'd stop giving her that look. The one that said: I'm your uncle and I'm worried about you. She'd seen it plenty of times before. 'Mona, Jake's mum, is organising the wedding. It makes her happy and it's hard for me…without Mum.'

Mick nodded. 'I can understand that. She'd be thrilled to know how happy you are with Jake. You are…aren't you?'

'Yes!' Jenna nodded. 'Course.'

Ellie leaned forward. 'So she says. But Mick, I'm concerned that he's not —'

'So, what do you want to do today?' Jenna cut in. 'Stay in, go out?'

Mick's eyes narrowed as he looked from Jenna to Ellie. 'I'm sensing something's not right with this Jake. Does he treat you well, Jen?'

'Yes, he does. His mother's a bit of a problem, but nothing I can't handle.'

He gave a curt nod. 'Right. Any other news?'

Suddenly Jenna wanted to tell Mick everything. He'd know what to do. But would he believe her? She didn't want to risk him backing away from her too, as Ben initially had.

'Let's tell him, Jen.' Ellie grasped her hand. 'We've been thrown into the middle of it and we could do with some advice.'

Alesha's sudden appearance convinced Jenna that Ellie was right. He'd probably think they were on drugs or something, once they'd told him. But she had to know what he thought. Even if it wasn't what they wanted to hear.

They launched into all the events since the engagement. Mick said nothing as they elaborated on Alesha, Sabrina, Mabel

208

and Ben. Between them they hardly stopped for breath until they were finished. Mick twiddled a drink coaster round his fingers.

'So, do you think we're crazy? Making it up?' said Jenna. 'Well, it's true! Alesha's here now. She fancies you, actually.'

Ellie glared at Alesha, and then grinned. She'd clearly remembered that nothing could ever come of it, so could afford to be gracious.

'Does she? Well, she's got good taste then.' Mick laughed. 'Hi, Alesha.'

'But,' Jenna stuttered. 'Are you saying you believe us?'

'If you'd have said she *didn't* fancy me I might have been more sceptical.'

Jenna giggled. One of the things she admired about him was the ability to laugh at himself. But he still hadn't answered the question.

'Mick? Answer me.'

'Yes, I believe you,' he said. 'I've become much more spiritual during my travels. There isn't much that can surprise or shock me anymore.'

'That's fantastic!' said Ellie. 'I thought you'd laugh at us.'

'I knew a big tough bloke once. He turned to God overnight.'

'Did he? How come?' said Jenna.

'He won the lottery, and all we heard him saying for the next week was 'Thank you, God.' But joking aside, what's your next move?'

'Somehow,' said Jenna. 'We need to convince Ben we're not lying. Because if we don't, he'll always resent me for playing with his mind. Even if he doesn't say so.'

'Well, we can't have that.' Mick shook his head. 'But it's simple if you think about it. If you can't *tell* him something that will allay his doubts, you need to *show* him.'

'How do we do that?' Jenna frowned.

'It's down to you, Ellie. You'll have to draw something. Let him see something physical.'

'Like what?'

'Is Alesha still here?'

'Yes.' Ellie nodded.

'Okay, she needs to think of something. A scene that only the two of them would know. Get your paper and pens, Ellie.'

'Yes!' Alesha's eyes shone. 'That's it! Go on, Ellie. Get the paper.'

'Okay, think of something he can't question.' Jenna grinned. 'Any ideas, Alesha?'

'Hmm.' She tapped her nails on her chin. 'What about the first time we had sex?'

Ellie opened the pad and grimaced. 'No, I can't draw that!'

'You can!' said Alesha. 'Don't worry, you don't have to draw us naked. We weren't. It's the setting that's the key.'

'Erm, where was it?' Jenna wished Alesha had thought of something more appropriate.

'On the beach. We'd had a day out at the seaside. It was almost dark when we decided to take a stroll along the sand. The moon lit up the sky, but nobody else was around.' She smiled. 'We were play fighting and tripped up. We fell onto the sand and one thing led to another.'

'But what am I supposed to capture in this picture? His arse acting as the second moon? It's a bit much, Alesha.' Ellie closed the pad. 'I'm not doing that.'

'You don't have to. I was laid on a stick. It hurt. He thought my groans were passion. In the end I had to tell him, and we never stopped finding it funny. I was picking sand out from every orifice for days after.'

'Too much information.' Jenna blocked her ears.

'Oh, I dunno.' Mick winked. 'Sounds interesting to me.'

Ellie grinned. 'Okay, I'll try.'

Jenna, Alesha and Mick peered over Ellie's shoulder as her pencils skimmed the paper. Alesha said the dusky sky and moon were perfect, before moving onto the ground scene. Ellie chewed the end of the pencil and began drawing the sand. Next, she drew Alesha from behind. The stick was clearly visible at the base of her spine, just above her bum. Alesha was peering over her shoulder at it, while Ben was half on top of her with his eyes closed. She added a jacket to cover their middles and their modesty. After adding some extra colour, she held it out to Alesha.

'It's perfect!' Alesha hugged Ellie. 'He'll have to believe in me now.'

They waited on tenterhooks for Ben to return. A couple of hours later, they jumped when the front door opened and closed. He went into the kitchen.

'Come on, then,' said Jenna. 'Let's find out what he makes of this.'

The others followed Jenna down the hall. She hesitated before going into the room.

He was at the table with his laptop. He often worked, even on days off. They looked at each other in silence. Ben's expression became guarded. Jenna sensed the last thing he would welcome, was more talk of his dead ex. Still, they'd come this far and backing out now would help nobody.

'Can you spare five minutes?' Jenna smiled brightly.

'I hope this isn't what I think it is. I'm busy.'

'We have something to show you. It's important.'

'If you promise to then let it drop.' He pushed the laptop to one side with a sigh.

'I think I'll leave you to it.' Mick strode to the door.

'It was you who instigated this, Mick,' said Jenna. But he made a hasty retreat from the house without turning back.

'We will, Ben. We're just asking you to look at something. A last ditch attempt to convince you. Okay?' said Ellie.

When he didn't respond, Jenna continued, 'I hoped you knew me well enough by now to know you could trust me.'

'Look, you're itching to say something, so for God's sake spit it out.'

'Erm, this may sound weird, but —'

'As opposed to the kind of stuff you normally say?' He thrust out his chin. 'This better be good. I'm not in the mood for games, J.'

'Neither am I. So…the first time you and Alesha had sex, you remember it, right?'

He choked on the coffee he'd just taken a swig of. 'Pardon?'

'I'm not asking for a blow by blow account, don't worry.' A small smile played around his lips. 'I'll never forget it.'

'Alesha's told us what happened. Here, Ellie's drawn it.'

Ben took the paper, and just as Jenna thought he was going to rip it up, or refuse to look, he did. He stared transfixed at the image. His finger gently traced the outline of Alesha's face, and then his shoulders began to shake. Jenna wasn't sure if he was laughing or crying. She bent her head to get a closer look, and saw that it was a mixture of both.

He held his stomach as he laughed. And at the same time, tears splashed onto the table. Soon, the laughter ceased and he openly wept. It was the first time she'd ever seen a man cry. The reason, she suspected, was because she'd never known a real man before, until now. Apart from her dad of course. As she looked at Ben, she wondered if she'd ever know one again. But in that instant, it became clear that her future husband had a lot of growing up to do, to match up to the man in front of her now. The one who wasn't afraid to show his feelings. The one who encouraged her to talk about hers. Her tongue stuck to the roof of her mouth.

'Are you okay?' She squeezed his shoulder. 'I'm sorry if we've upset you further, but you do believe us now, don't you?'

She wasn't certain whether he'd heard her or not. He was still in a world of his own. But at least his lips were curling upwards once more.

'Tell her.' His eyes twinkled. 'She didn't know the meaning of the word pain. As she moved away from under me, I fell onto a large stone. A certain part of my anatomy took the brunt of it.' He threw back his head and laughed. 'She probably wondered why I didn't go near her for a fortnight. At one point I thought it was going to fall off. I'd tell her myself if I could see her.'

'You have told her, she's here,' said Ellie. 'She said ouch!'

Ben picked up the drawing and held it to his face. Alesha went to his side and draped her arms around him. 'We had some great times, didn't we, Ben?' she said.

'Yes, we did.' He smiled, and then froze. His eyes darted from left to right. He slumped back and rubbed his eyes.

'You heard her then,' said Jenna. 'You answered.'

'I was probably imagining it, as I have so often.' His eyes misted. 'But I can't deny what you've shown me is phenomenal. You couldn't possibly have made that up.'

'I have something else, too. It's a letter. Obviously I wrote the words, but Alesha dictated it to me.' Ellie held out a folded piece of paper. 'She said you know how much she hates being ignored. So here is the final proof.'

He reached out and took it with shaking fingers and began to read:

213

My Dearest Ben,

I'm so very sorry for what I've put you through since that fateful morning. None of it was your fault, so I beg you to stop blaming yourself. I was in a world of my own, not concentrating. The truth is, I wasn't even thinking about our silly argument at the time. I saw someone I knew and stepped in front of the car. The driver, Mabel, could do nothing to prevent it happening. It saddens me to know she is absorbed in guilt.

That poor old lady doesn't deserve to live the rest of her days this way. And neither do you, Ben. I need you both to look forward, not back.

I'm fine, don't worry, but I'll only be able to rest and be truly free, once I know you can do this. I don't want you to see me, Ben. The reason is because I want you to remember me as I was, and think of the good times.

I'm sure we would have remained the best of friends, like brother and sister. But we know there is one special person who can make you happy. I came to her for many reasons. I hope you can find a way to be together. Remember when we first met? She was there. I know she will be cringing as you are reading this. But not nearly as much as I did when I saw her trying to dance the Irish jig!

She needs to consider that just as I can't rest until I know everything is resolved, neither can her parents. I need your help with that one, Ben. And I think you are getting there.

Be happy, my darling Bumface
Alesha

Ps…Sorry about the shoes. I'm just thankful I got away with it at the time. Along with the five dresses, eight tops and three pairs of trousers, which also came from the 'market!' xxxx

Chapter Twenty-One

Ben, Jenna and Ellie sat, tears streaming down their faces. Alesha rolled her eyes and disappeared with a grin.

'Thank you.' Ben wiped his eyes. 'It's not often I'm lost for words, but I am.'

'I'm just glad you believe us now.' Jenna sniffed.

'How could I not?' said Ben. 'It's hard to get your head round though. I mean, souls living around us.'

'I know,' said Jenna. 'I still have odd moments where I think it can't be happening, even though I'm living with it every day now.'

'Alesha's lovely, Ben.' Ellie smiled. 'I didn't like her at first though. She was rude to me.'

Ben laughed. 'She said…some interesting things in the letter.'

Jenna lowered her gaze. It was one thing Alesha writing to Ben, but another entirely bringing her into it.

Ben filled the kettle. His eyes glowed in a way she'd never seen before. The closest they'd got was when they were singing. With a pang, she realised how much she'd missed that. Maybe now, he'd be happy to spend time in her company again.

He put mugs of tea on the table and Jenna was concerned to see his forehead crease and jaw clench.

'You okay?' she asked.

'I'm just thinking about Mabel. I didn't mean all the things I said.'

'I know,' said Jenna. 'I understand.'

'I feel as if a weight has been lifted off my shoulders. If only we could do the same for her.'

'Maybe we can.' Ellie drummed her fingers on the table edge. 'Maybe I can draw something?'

'I'm not sure.' Jenna grimaced. 'Like what? We can't go upsetting her further.'

'We need Alesha,' said Ellie. 'Maybe she can think of something.'

'Can you get her to come back now, J?' said Ben.

'ALESHA! Come here.' Jenna had a sinking feeling that Alesha would only come on one condition. The playful mood she'd been in probably meant one thing. She rose reluctantly, and did the jig. Aware of Ben's eyes on her, and the grin spreading across his face, she tripped over her foot and fell in a heap onto the floor.

'You okay?' Ben snorted and hauled her to her feet, as Ellie giggled.

She glared at Alesha, who appeared with a smirk. 'You called?'

'Yes. Can you think of anything Ellie can draw to convince Mabel? Something that won't upset her too much?'

'Well, I'm not sure it's appropriate in her case to be honest.'

'You're probably right.' Jenna sighed.

'Wait! There is something.' Alesha clicked her fingers. 'It may work.'

'What?' said Ellie.

'Just after it happened, in that split second, she reached for a cross hanging from the car mirror. She wrapped her hands round it.'

'Would anyone else know that?' said Jenna.

Alesha shook her head. 'No. But even Mabel might not remember doing it. The memories of those first few minutes might be a blur.'

Jenna wasn't convinced they should do anything, but it had worked for Ben.

'Can you have a go at drawing the cross dangling from the mirror, Ellie?' said Jenna. 'But nothing else. Just that.'

A few minutes later, Ellie put down the pencil. 'Is that right, Alesha?'

She nodded. 'Yes, but I'm with Jenna on this one. I can see by her face she's not sure it's a good idea either.'

They relayed what Alesha said back to Ben. 'Try it,' he said. 'And will you ask Mabel if I can go see her?'

'Hi, Mabel.' Jenna bent to give her a kiss.

'Hello, dear. Hello, Ellie.' She rose from her chair. 'I'll make some tea. It's nice to see you both.'

'Mabel, can you just sit down a minute?' said Jenna. 'We need to talk to you.'

'Alright.' She lowered herself back down. 'What's the matter, girls?'

Jenna glanced at Ellie and Alesha, who was sat on the arm of Mabel's chair.

'Go on.' Alesha urged.

Jenna told Mabel all about Ben and how the drawing had convinced him, missing out the actual scene of the drawing. There was only so much Mabel would be able to cope with.

'I see,' Mabel murmured. 'And do you have a drawing for me?'

'Yes.' Jenna stroked Mabel's hand. 'If you want to see it?'

'Show me.'

Ellie handed the piece of paper to her. 'Can you remember the first thing you did…after?'

Mabel didn't speak, but slowly held the drawing in front of her. She gave a low moan and the paper fluttered to the floor. A tear trickled down her cheek.

'I thought if I held the cross tight enough everything would be alright. I'd forgotten until now.'

Alesha hugged Mabel. 'Please don't cry. And please don't blame yourself. I can't bear it.'

'I can't help it, dear.' Mabel's upturned face turned to her left. 'I killed you!'

Jenna and Ellie exchanged confused looks. What was going on?

'You didn't! I killed myself. You're the victim, Mabel. Not me. I've inflicted so much grief on you. I put myself under the wheels of your car. You did NOT put me there!'

Alesha sobbed and buried her head on Mabel's shoulder. Jenna and Ellie looked on astonished, as Mabel stroked Alesha's hair.

'There, there, don't cry. Don't upset yourself, dear.'

'W-what's happening, Mabel? Who you talking to?' Jenna couldn't think straight. She could see Ellie was as perplexed as she was.

219

'I'm talking to the most beautiful girl I've ever seen.' Mabel gave a sad smile. 'I'm talking to Alesha, of course.'

'B-but.' Jenna was stunned. 'You mean you can see her?'

'Yes. I can. She's right here beside me.' Mabel reached up her sleeve for a hanky and turned back to Alesha. 'I don't know which one of us needs this more, dear.'

'Thank God! Thank God!' Alesha held her palms together in prayer. 'I'm so happy I've got through to you. I thought it would never happen.'

Jenna beckoned for Ellie to follow her into the hall. 'I don't know what to say, Ellie. I'm speechless.'

'Me too!' Ellie held onto the wall for support. 'Let's make the tea. Give them chance to talk.'

When they carried in trays fifteen minutes later, Jenna gasped and nearly dropped the tray. She stared open-mouthed, at Ben crouched by Mabel's feet.

'What you doing here, Ben?'

'I was hovering outside, desperate to knock on the door. I had to see Mabel. Apparently Alesha told her who I was and she beckoned me in.'

'And you're happy for him to be here?' Jenna asked.

'Of course, dear. And Alesha's delighted, aren't you? We've all had a good talk, although Ben can't see her, and rarely hears her, as you know.'

Alesha floated round the room, like a serene fairy. Jenna and Ellie watched her, mesmerised. Jenna had never seen such a picture of complete happiness before. It was beyond words. But as Jenna turned, the identical look was mirrored in Mabel and Ben too. They were positively glowing.

Mabel reached out to Jenna. 'Come here, dear.'

Ben moved to let her in. Somehow they both moved the same way, and they fell against each other. It was as though she'd had an electric shock. After they sprang apart, Jenna could still feel the imprint of his arm against hers.

Alesha giggled. 'Look at them! Their destiny is to be a couple, Mabel. I'm going to carry on haunting them until they agree and thank me for bringing them together.'

Mabel smiled, and Jenna was thankful that at least Ben couldn't hear Alesha. She was cringing enough as it was. But she was startled when he muttered behind her. 'If only it was that simple.'

Surely he hadn't heard Alesha? All the times she'd willed him to and he hadn't. The one time she didn't want him to, it seemed like he had. What had he meant: 'If only it was that simple?''

Mabel pulled Jenna towards her in a bear hug. 'I can never thank you enough, dear. I really can't. I'll never get over what happened, of course. But I can live out the rest of my days at peace with myself now, because of you. And I know for sure I'll see my Bert again, one day. He'll have to be patient for a while yet, though. I've got some living to do first.'

'I'm so glad, Mabel.' Jenna whispered. 'I love you as much as if you were family. Maybe you're ready to start going out again, now? An all night rave? A casino? Or maybe just a change of scenery by visiting us in the mad house next door, for now? We'll break you in gently.'

Mabel chuckled. 'I'll stick to the latter. And maybe you'll start living a bit yourself too? Old age comes quick enough, so grab life with both hands while you can, dear.'

Jenna's phone bleeped, indicating a text from Mick: *Jen, where are you? I'm in the house and I'm injured. Can you come?*

'What's happened?' Jenna shrieked as she opened the door to find Mick sprawled in the hallway. Ellie and Ben gasped from behind her. 'Have we been burgled?'

'No.' Mick winced as he tried to lift himself up. 'I'd just got back when I heard a key in the door. I went to greet whichever one of you it was.'

'Who was it?' Jenna crouched beside him.

'Well…we didn't get as far as formal introductions. But I think it was your fiancé.'

'Oh, no! What did he do?'

'He asked who the hell I was and threatened to call the police. I tried to explain, but he wasn't listening and hit me. He knocked me straight down.'

Jenna put a hand to her mouth and gasped. 'He must've been mortified once he realised who you were?'

'In hindsight I should've told him I was your uncle and had a key, before telling him I wasn't a burglar.'

'And?'

'When I mentioned the word key, he frothed at the mouth and his eyes glazed over. I thought he was having a fit. He was moaning a lot.'

Jenna put her head in her hands. 'Go on.'

'I asked him what medication he was on. I suspected him of being a druggie.'

'Did you say that in words?'

'Yes. I said I didn't know how he'd got the key, but he was getting nothing out of this house to sell for his next fix.'

'Christ.'

'He told me you'd given him it. That he was your boyfriend. But I was taking no chances.'

'What did you do?' Jenna whispered.

'I reached up to try to grab the key off him, but I couldn't get it. Then he dropped it on the floor. I said: 'As far as I'm aware, the people with keys are: Jenna, Ellie, Ben and now me.' Then he asked who I was.'

'And you told him you were my uncle, right?'

'No, I didn't get chance. I got as far as saying I was your new lodger.'

'Nooo. Please tell me you didn't!'

'Yes, and he frothed a bit more, gurgled incoherently and lunged forwards. But he had a little mishap and slipped, landing on top of me. He's heavy. Has he always been a bit of a porker?'

'Then what, Mick?' Jenna squeezed her eyes closed.

'Well, his face was touching mine. I told him I was fine and that mouth–to-mouth resuscitation wasn't necessary.'

'And?'

'He frothed a bit more for good measure and then left. I think he's in a worse state than I am. He was limping.'

'What did he slip on?'

'Here's the thing, Jen. It's a bit ironic really…but he slipped on the key.'

Chapter Twenty-Two

Needless to say, Jake was less than thrilled by his meeting with Mick, and was in no rush to repeat the experience. Jenna suspected Mick of deliberately winding him up, but of course he denied it.

She was astounded that after six weeks of being in the country, he showed no signs of leaving. He'd got a job on a construction site. Some nights were spent with various mates, during which time Ellie got her room back, but more often than not Mick was at the house. Jenna was increasingly concerned that Ellie was the main attraction. The biggest fear was that Ellie had fallen for his charm and attentions, only to be left with a broken heart once he grew restless and headed back for the airport. Since Mick had arrived, they'd spent more and more time together.

Jenna had been doing a lot of extra shifts at work, to cover staff holidays. It was depressing to hear of sun, sand and sea. But still, she and Jake would be jetting off somewhere nice for their honeymoon. This thought cheered her up. Slightly. That and the fact that it was her turn to have a week off from work. Although she wasn't going anywhere, spring had turned into summer and she was anticipating lazy days and evenings in the garden. Maybe jungle would be a better description, but Mick and Ben had offered to tidy it.

She changed into frayed denim shorts and gaped in the mirror. They hung off her. When had she lost so much weight? Now, her proportions were the same as when she'd been at uni. She looped a belt through the waistband of the shorts. She, Ellie, Ben and Mick had taken to cooking up delicious meals. Many of the recipes came from Mick, which he'd picked up on his travels. When Jenna thought about it, she realised the food they'd been eating was far healthier than the takeaways and junk food she'd been living on.

She dashed out onto the landing when she heard Mick calling upstairs.

'Jen? Look what I've got. Shall we test it out this evening?' He held up a barbeque with a grin. 'I'll take it into the garden. The weather's lovely, it's a shame to waste it.'

'Cool! Hopefully Ellie and Ben won't be late back from work,' said Jenna. 'Shall I ask Mabel if she wants to come?'

'Yes, good idea.' Mick nodded. 'Do you want to invite Jake and his mum? I promise I'll behave.'

'No.' She hesitated. 'Erm, let's test it out first, shall we? And maybe get the garden a bit more presentable. I don't want Mona having another heart attack.'

'Very wise,' said Mick. 'Another time. I'll, erm, look forward to it.'

They spent the rest of the day cleaning the garden furniture and hunting out the plastic plates and cutlery which hadn't been used for years. Once the garden was as ready as it could be, they went to stock up on burgers, sausages, and some vegetarian alternatives for Ellie.

'We're home,' Ben called a couple of hours later. Jenna's stomach lurched. They'd been spending as much time as possible together, since Ben had accepted the truth about Alesha. He still felt uncomfortable when Jenna and Ellie had a conversation with her, though that was to be expected. But the easy-going friendship between Jenna and Ben had been restored. They'd started singing again, which Mick enthused about. And also, they engineered as much time away from the others as they could. Jenna knew she wasn't the only one, Ben constantly sought her out too. The lingering looks that passed between them had become more frequent. But Jenna refused to analyse what this all meant. She was content to just enjoy the time with Ben, Alesha, Ellie, Mick and Mabel. While she still could. Everything would change once she was married. But for now, she was happier than she'd been for years and she didn't want it to end. That time would come soon enough; there was no point in dwelling on it now.

'Come and look at the garden.' Jenna beckoned to Ben and Ellie. 'Hope you're hungry.'

'Wow!' Ellie beamed. 'This is fab, guys.'

'It is,' agreed Ben. 'Here's to a long hot summer. Cheers.' He clinked glasses with Mick as Ellie opened a bottle of wine.

'So,' said Jenna casually, 'are you sticking around for the summer then, Mick?'

Ellie took a sharp intake of breath beside her.

'Yeah, I'm planning to, if that's okay with you?'

Ellie heaved a sigh of obvious relief.

'It's fine by me,' said Jenna. 'It's nice to have you around.'

'All that travelling sounds so exciting, Mick,' breathed Ellie. 'I wish I could do it.'

'There's nothing stopping you now, is there?' Mick raised his eyebrows.

'I'd never be able to afford it,' said Ellie. 'It must cost you a fortune.'

Mick laughed. 'Not at all. I've been doing it for years. The first time, I had the flight money and enough to pay for a couple of month's accommodation. And just a bit to spend. I saved up for a while, obviously. But think about it, if you go on holiday you pay for a flight, accommodation and spending money. I just needed a bit extra, that's all. Enough to get by until I found work.'

'What kind of work do you do?' said Ben.

'A bit of everything,' said Mick. 'I've worked in bars, boat trips, boat hire, restaurants and even cleaning beaches. I always go to places where I'm most likely to find work.'

'It sounds amazing.' Jenna smiled. 'But for now, your job is to get that barbeque going while I go and fetch Mabel. She's keen to come.'

'I'll go.' Ben jumped up. 'We won't be long.'

Alesha appeared and sat on the grass. She was almost hidden by the weeds.

'It's so lovely to see Ben with Mabel. He goes round there quite a lot now, doesn't he?'

'Yes,' said Jenna. 'He's been doing some odd jobs for her. She loves him to bits.'

'I know.' Alesha grinned. 'It makes me happy to see the two of *them* so much happier. There's only you to work on now, Jenna. Then my work here's done.'

A lump lodged in the back of Jenna's throat. She couldn't envision a time where Alesha would disappear, never to be seen again. As if she'd never existed. It didn't bear thinking about.

227

'Hello, dears. Thank you for inviting me.' Mabel hobbled down the garden, her arm in Ben's. 'And being escorted by such a handsome young man, too.'

'Hi, Mabel, sit down.' Jenna pulled out a chair. She helped Ben lower her into it. 'A glass of wine?'

'Why not?' said Mabel. 'Though you may have problems getting me home in one piece.'

'We'll worry about that later.' Ben laughed. 'Enjoy yourself.'

Ellie turned up the volume of the stereo which they'd taken outside, and pulled Jenna onto her feet. 'Let's dance.'

By this time they'd had a few glasses of wine, so, after a moment's hesitation Jenna began swaying to the music, and started singing along. Ben soon joined in. The conversations around them ground to a halt as everyone watched and listened.

'You've both got incredible voices,' murmured Mabel. 'How truly wonderful you sound together.'

'They do,' agreed Ellie. 'Hey, Mick, they're talking about singing at a place in town. We'll go and watch them, shall we?'

'Definitely,' said Mick. 'Let's do it.'

'Okay.' Jenna was buoyed up by the praise, the wine and Ben's eyes upon her. 'Soon, Ben. We're gonna be on the stage. What do you say, partner?'

She couldn't fathom the penetrating look he gave her. Flustered, she stumbled, and found herself in his arms. The feel and smell of him was more intoxicating than the alcohol. His lips moved against her hair. 'Oh, Jenna, I wish we'd met before.'

'We did,' she whispered. 'But we lost our chance.'

She stepped back from him when Mick gave a loud cough. He winked at Jenna. 'Okay?' He grinned.

She became aware of Mabel, Alesha and Ellie staring intently in their direction. They gave each other knowing looks.

Jenna wiped a bead of sweat from her forehead, and it wasn't there because of the sun.

'The food smells wicked, Mick. I'm starving. Hey, I love this song.' She knew she was garbling, but couldn't seem to stop. Something had happened in that moment. She wasn't sure what, but whatever it was, everyone else had seen it too. And were clearly much happier about it than Jenna.

Once Mabel was safely home, Ben went up to his room. Jenna had kept her distance from him, for the past few hours. Ellie and Mick offered to clear up the garden and kitchen. Jenna curled on the sofa where Alesha soon joined her.

'Hey,' said Alesha. 'What's wrong?'

'I don't know. Nothing. Everything.' Jenna shrugged. 'I'm…confused, but I'm not sure what about.'

Alesha smiled and snuggled into Jenna's side. 'You think you know where you're headed and then bam, something comes along to throw things. But you know, you've been so much happier lately. I can't *make* you say or do something, Jen. I can only tell you what you already know, deep down.'

'What?'

'You're still heading down the wrong path. You know what you need to do to be on the right one, but you're scared. I get that. I can't say anymore, there's no point, but I'm still here for you.' She brushed Jenna's cheek with her mouth and vanished.

Jenna hauled herself off the sofa. She may as well go to bed. When she reached the top stair, she heard the strum of

229

Ben's guitar. Creeping closer, she realised he was singing. She made no attempt to wipe the falling tears as she listened:

> *'I saw a girl in front of me, with hair of copper and gold,*
> *I wanted to approach her, but wasn't feeling bold.*
> *The way she held her body, had me so mesmerised,*
> *But then she left - and I wasn't surprised.*
>
> *Now all these years later, I see her everyday,*
> *But she belongs to someone else, there's nothing I can say.*
> *I long to kiss and hold her so very close to me*
> *Yet I have to accept – that it can never be.*
>
> *Oh, J, it hurts to –'*

Jenna couldn't bear to hear any more. She went to her room and flung herself facedown on the bed, and sobbed in a way she hadn't done for years. It was a relief to let go completely.

It was as though she had one foot in one life with Jake, and the other foot in another life with her friends…and Ben. The two worlds were becoming increasingly distant. To the point where she was doing the splits. And she was in danger of being badly hurt…in more ways than one.

Chapter Twenty-Three

'I don't know if I can do this, Ben.' Jenna glanced round the packed pub in apprehension. She was bitterly regretting her alcohol fuelled confidence about performing in public.

'You'll be fine,' said Ben. 'It's only an informal thing. We'll just do one song and see how you feel.'

'You'll be amazing,' said Ellie, and Mick nodded in agreement.

Jenna had tried her best to focus only on the music, since the barbeque. But it had been impossible to shake off the image of Ben's eyes burning into hers, and the feel of him against her. The restlessness that had been building slowly, had now reached crisis levels. Her sleep was more disturbed than ever. The only time she managed to drift off easily was when Mona talked about the wedding. Catching up on sleep was the only plus point to visiting Jake and Mona.

He hadn't been back to the house since the fracas with Mick. When he picked her up he waited in the car. He'd declined to go with them to the pub, and Jenna knew he was far from happy about it. When she'd stood her ground, and said she wanted to do it, he'd said nothing. But she sensed he thought it would just be a flash in the pan, and the singing would soon be forgotten. Maybe he'd be right about the pan, but the forgetting part was another matter.

They watched some other musicians do their set and then it was their turn. Jenna wiped sticky palms down her jeans. Her stomach was doing somersaults worthy of an Olympic medal. She followed Ben to the stage on shaky legs. As her eyes strayed to the denim-clad thighs in front of her, she knew she was also on shaky ground.

The music started and Jenna took a deep breath. She focused on a high-back stool in front of her. The first note was off-key, but soon the music overtook her, and she was lost in a world of her own. The sound of rapturous applause brought her back to reality. Glancing at Ben, her stomach flipped. He smiled and winked before starting to play another song.

Jenna was vaguely aware of loud whistles coming from Ellie and Mick, and cheering from the crowd. This buoyed her up into doing another four songs, by which time her throat felt like sandpaper.

She slumped onto a chair next to Ellie and took a huge gulp of ice cold beer. Strangers nodded and smiled in their direction. She jumped when somebody tapped her on the shoulder from behind.

'You were great!' A burly bald-headed man held out his hand. 'I'm the manager here. Do you fancy a regular spot once a week? I can't pay much, but it'll get you good exposure.' He turned to look at Ben. 'The crowd loved you.'

Jenna and Ben exchanged looks. They both nodded and grinned.

'Yes.' They spoke at the same time. Jenna was elated, and even the sight of Mick's arm snaking round the back of Ellie's seat didn't bring her down from the ceiling. It was clear there was something going on between them. Ellie wasn't likely to listen to Jenna's warnings now. It was too late. But, really, it had been too late from the moment Ellie saw Mick walk into the house all those weeks ago. Jenna worried for her friend, though they were both adults. She couldn't be responsible for what they may or may not do. But she suspected 'not do' wasn't relevant anymore.

'It was fabulous, Jake.' Jenna told him a couple of days later. 'I can't believe we're going to get paid to do what we love doing.' He clearly was of the same opinion. The silence dragged on until she could bear it no longer. 'Jake?' She nudged his arm.

He regarded her with narrowed eyes. 'Look, I can see how much it means to you. But it can't possibly be taken seriously.'

'Oh, why's that?'

'Because it's not a real job, is it? It's not —'

'What? Respectable enough for you? Is that it?' Jenna's nostrils flared. 'I'm still going to be working full-time. I don't see the problem.'

'But when we're married you can't be gallivanting off to some dingy pub to sing, Jenna.'

No, course I can't. I'll be too busy putting your dinner on the table at whatever time you roll in from work. And keeping your mother company, won't I?

'I'll still be my own person, as you will,' said Jenna. 'We won't be joined at the hip! Christ, Jake, we don't even see much of each other now, do we?'

'No,' said Jake. 'You're right, we don't. And who's fault's that?'

Jenna opened her mouth to argue, then closed it swiftly. She *had* been withdrawing from him. After spending much of their relationship waiting around for Jake to dictate when they'd see each other, the tables had turned. But it was partly his fault. He refused to spend much time at the house since Ben, and then Mick had moved in. Mona wouldn't let them share a room at her house, so where did that leave them? They were reduced to holding a conversation in his parked car outside Mona's house.

'Look, Jake, I know we haven't had any time to ourselves recently, and I miss that too.' She nestled against his shoulder. 'We're planning a last barbeque on Friday. The weather's already starting to turn. Please come? And stay over?'

He hesitated and then nodded. 'Oh, okay. But where will Ellie sleep now Mick has her room? It's ridiculous, Jenna.'

'Don't worry, I'll sort it.' She placed a placating hand on his arm. It wouldn't be a problem. Ellie would sleep in her own bed. With Mick. Jenna suspected it wouldn't be the first time. Or last.

'I'm sure Mum would enjoy getting out. Maybe you could invite her to the barbeque?'

Jenna sighed. 'I thought you were going to stay over? How will she get home?'

'I'll put her in a taxi,' said Jake firmly. 'I want some quality time with my future wife. And I don't give a damn who it suits or doesn't suit.'

'Cool.' Jenna grinned. It would be nice to have time with him, to reconnect. She'd almost forgotten what it was like to actually share a bed with him. She needed reminding. Friday couldn't come soon enough. It had been too easy to let other things take over, but Jake was her future. Everything else was here and now. It couldn't last. Although she'd keep in touch with Ellie, Mick and Ben, for the most part they'd be living separate lives. But for the time remaining, she wanted to enjoy it. While she still could.

Mick and Ben were pulling out weeds when Jake arrived with Mona. Jenna, Ellie and Mabel were sat around the table chatting. They budged up to make room for Mona.

Ben and Mick wiped their hands down their sides and strode over.

'Nice to see you, Mrs Mansfield.' Ben held out his hand. Mona eyed it with distaste, but took it briefly.

'Yes, nice to meet you.' Mick smiled at Mona, then turned to Jake. 'Hello…again.'

'Yes, hello,' Jake muttered. 'Erm, you've been busy. The garden looks much tidier.'

Jenna heaved a sigh of relief. They were never going to be best friends, but at least they were making an effort to be polite.

'Yeah, it does.' Mick nodded. 'You wouldn't believe the crap people have been throwing over the fence. Disgusting, isn't it, Ben?'

'Yep. Broken furniture, household rubbish, you name it.' Ben grimaced. 'We just want to get this corner cleared and then we'll be with you.'

Jenna swallowed as she watched him work. Her face flamed when Jake clicked his fingers in front of her face. 'Hello?' His jaw clenched.

'Erm, sorry,' said Jenna. 'I was just thinking how much better it is out here now. The garden looks so much bigger.'

Jake made no comment, but threw her a hard look. What was the matter with her? Why was she suddenly thinking about the last barbeque, when she'd fallen into Ben's arms? Although it had been accidental, it had felt …right. But her emotions had been all over the place lately. Alesha's arrival had stirred up a lot of things. Soon things would settle down. Including the fizzing in her stomach when she looked at Ben.

'Everything for the wedding is booked now.' Mona told Mabel. 'It's costing a fortune, of course. Jakey says it's worth it though.'

Jenna froze. Everything booked? The words swam round in her head. Why wouldn't it be though, with Mona in charge? Still, she'd wasted no time. And then it hit her. In a few months' time she'd be the new Mrs Mansfield. Suddenly it felt real. Getting carried along with events of the last four months or so had pushed it to the back of her mind. Much as she told herself that this was what she wanted, she couldn't shake off the feeling that her life was going in the wrong direction. Just as Alesha had warned her. Why hadn't she listened sooner? Now it was too late. She could call it all off now, of course, but no way would she do that to Jake. It was her mess and her fault.

Jenna - the biggest idiot I know! How could I have been so stupid and so blind? I'll have to make the best of it, it'll be okay. Once I'm not seeing Ben every day…

'What on earth's that?' Mona pointed at something hopping about on the grass like a demented frog. 'It's making a strange sound. Is it some kind of kitchen utensil? A whisk?'

Jenna's blood curdled. The buzzing and the phallic shape told her it was definitely no kitchen utensil. Well, not unless you preferred to use it in there than the bedroom. It hopped nearer. Ellie gasped and covered her mouth. Jenna turned away in horror. What in heaven's sake was it doing here, in this garden? Obviously someone had tired of it and thrown it over the fence. But how could she prove that?

Smothered laughter echoed around the garden from everyone barring Mabel and Mona, who got out of her chair to peer closer. 'I wonder where you buy them,' she said. 'It would whip up my puddings in no time.'

Ellie gurgled and turned a deep shade of purple. Mick, Ben and even Jake snorted into their glasses. Jenna spotted Alesha laughing uncontrollably, nearby.

'Though I'm not sure about the colour' Mona continued. 'Black would be better suited, I think. Mind you, it looks on the big side. I'd need a smaller one. My wrists wouldn't take the weight of that going off in my hand.'

Jenna put her head on the table and laughed until the tears poured down her cheeks. She lifted her head, but collapsed again when she caught Ben's eye.

'For goodness' sake, what's so funny about that?' Mona crossed her arms across her bony chest. 'I don't know what to make of you young ones, these days.'

Mabel looked equally perplexed. 'It looks quite upmarket. I'm not sure what those knobbly bits are for. Maybe they help with your peaks. Would you like one for a wedding present, dear?' She smiled at Jenna. 'Jenna? What's the matter, dear? You've gone a funny colour.'

The more Jenna forced down her giggle, the worse it became. But on the plus side, Mona decided to leave earlier than expected.

'I'll call you a taxi, Mum.' Jake pulled the phone from his pocket.

'So, you're staying here then?' Mona sniffed. 'I'll see you tomorrow. But I don't approve.' She tossed back her head and disappeared up the garden.

Shortly after, Ben left too. Jenna couldn't fathom the look he'd given her when Jake said he wanted Jenna alone. But the mood had changed. The atmosphere made her feel uneasy. But this was her house, and she was determined that no visitors or lodgers would make her feel this way. How dare they? She and Jake were to be married, and even if they hadn't been, it was no business of theirs what they did. It was hardly the Victorian times. Deep down though, Jenna knew it wasn't *what* she was doing, it was *who* she was doing they had the problem with.

She'd told Ellie calmly, that it was up to her and Mick who would be sleeping where. Although Ellie was paying rent, it had been her idea to have Mick stay. She was the one who had pushed it. Tonight was about her and Jake, and to hell with the rest of them.

She climbed into bed beside Jake. He'd dimmed the lights and was propped on his elbow smiling softly at her.

'At last I have you to myself.' He pulled her to him. 'God, I've missed you, Jenna.'

His lips found hers. They felt familiar. Comforting. She wrapped her arms round his back. He gave a low moan and kissed her harder. Jenna tried to get into the moment…but it wasn't happening. The loose plaster on the ceiling had got worse and a coat of paint wouldn't go amiss. A nice bright colour. Maybe Jake could put a couple of shelves up too. As he slid into her and banged away, she found she was more excited by the prospect of him hammering shelves rather than her.

'Wow! That was great, Jen. How was it for you?'

Amazing! I've just mentally re-decorated the bedroom.

Chapter Twenty-Four

Jenna stared mouth agape at the kitchen window. She watched the family from a few doors down struggle into the house with a boxed Christmas tree and decorations.

What on earth are they thinking? It's only...What date is it, Jenna?

She strode to the calendar on the wall. Tears burned her eyes when she saw it hadn't been turned over since May. Ben had clearly avoided looking at it as much as she had, and Ellie walked around in a daze much of the time, especially as her romance with Mick had gone to another level. They were open in their relationship now, and spent most nights together. Jenna had tried to warn Ellie not to get too involved, but it had fallen on deaf ears. But who was she to talk? She and Ben were spending more time alone, and this was when Jenna felt truly happy. They'd been practising new songs, and Thursday nights performing at the pub was the highlight of her week. Luckily her boss was accommodating and let her do the early shift on Thursday, or gave her that day off.

She scooped up her phone to check the date and gasped. The first of November? Where had the time gone? Since the end of the summer each day had blurred into one. Work, singing and making time to see Jake. He was busier than ever at work, so they were lucky to see each other three times a week just lately. He'd stopped complaining about 'the lodgers,' which was a bonus.

Jenna jumped when Alesha appeared beside her. Even after all this time she hadn't got used to her turning up out of the blue.

'Hi.' Alesha grinned. 'What's up with you?'

'I was just thinking how quickly this year's gone. I mean, Christmas next month. Where have I been living these past few months?'

'With your head in the clouds.' Alesha gave her a mischievous look. 'Haven't you?'

Jenna lowered her gaze. 'Yeah, it's been a bit…hectic.'

'Hmm.' Alesha drummed her chin with her forefinger. 'The wedding will be here before you know it.'

Jenna's heart pounded against her chest. 'Oh, God, Alesha.' Panic welled up and she lunged for the light switch. Nothing. She still felt as though everything was closing in on her. The walls seemed narrower, the ceiling seemed lower and the floor felt as if it moving towards her. 'I've been mega stupid. Unbelievably bloody stupid! It seemed so far away, kind of like it wasn't real.'

Alesha stood in front of Jenna. 'Look at me.'

Jenna's eyes met Alesha's penetrating ones. 'What?' she whispered.

'You've been a fool. And you know it. The question is what are you going to do now?'

Jenna shrugged and slumped forwards against Alesha's shoulder. 'Nothing. It's too late.'

'You're pathetic!' Alesha held her at arm's length, nostrils flaring. 'You've had months to talk to Jake. But you take the easy way out and bury your head in the sand. Well I've got news for you: the wedding countdown's really on now. And you're with the wrong man.'

'I'm not!' Jenna bristled. 'I'm…you're right.' She put her hands over her face. 'But I can't let Jake down. I should've done it before. I was going to, but then Mona had the heart attack.'

'That was months ago! You've been so wrapped up in the singing and Ben, you haven't stopped to think clearly.'

Jenna felt the heat creep over her cheeks. 'I, erm, love the singing. It always made me happy, and I've discovered it still does.'

Alesha placed her arm on Jenna's. 'It's not the only thing you love, is it? And I'm not talking about Jake.'

Oh, God, she's right! I've been denying it to myself. What a mess.

'Erm,' began Jenna. 'I erm —'

'Love Ben.' Alesha's surprisingly painful nails dug into Jenna's arm. 'Face it!'

Jenna nodded slowly. 'Okay…I do. I've had feelings for him…for a while now.'

'I know.' Alesha's face softened. 'I told you it was meant to be.'

'But even if I wasn't marrying Jake, Ben probably wouldn't be interested in me that way.' Jenna threw up her hands. 'He thinks of me as a friend.'

Alesha sighed. 'That's not true, and you know it. There's been something between you both all along. I'm amazed he hasn't said something to you, to be honest.'

'See? You're imagining it.'

'No, I'm not.' Alesha shook her head. 'You heard the song he wrote about you, and the way he watches you says it all. Surely even you can see that.'

Jenna hesitated. 'Maybe…but what can I do?'

'Talk to him? Talk to Jake? And failing that, stick your microphone where the sun don't shine. It'll hurt less than continuing with this ridiculous charade.'

'And say what? I can't do it, Alesha.'

'Please yourself.' Alesha shrugged. 'It's your life. But think ahead, one year, two. It's not too late now, but before long it will be. That's all I'm saying.'

'Okay, I'll talk to Jake. But I need to think about what to say and when to say it first.' Jenna's heart thudded at the thought. 'Even if Ben and I just stay friends, I still shouldn't marry Jake. It's not fair on either of us.'

'Good girl.' Alesha nodded. 'Don't waste your life any more. Grab it with both hands. While you can.'

Jenna hugged Alesha to her. 'Thank you. You're a pain sometimes but I kind of love you too.'

Alesha's eyes shone. 'Soppy cow! I'm going before you set me off. See you later.' She waved and disappeared with a grin.

Suddenly Jenna needed to see Mabel. As she shrugged on her coat her phone rang. She jabbed the screen to answer.

'Hi Jake, you okay? I was just going to see Mabel.'

'Jenna.' Jake sounded out of breath and agitated. 'Mum's put the house on the market. I got home to see a 'For Sale' board outside. It may take ages to sell, but you need to warn the others. I've let it go for months, but it's time they found somewhere else to live.'

Her hands felt clammy around the phone. 'Jake —'

'I need to go. I'll talk to you later. Bye.'

Jenna stood rooted to the spot. How could she have let things go this far? Digging the cold metal of the phone into her palm, she watched distractedly as it indented into her skin. She tossed the phone onto the table and sprinted to the door, banging it shut behind her. She strode up the path, then turned back locking and unlocking the door a number of times until finally satisfied it really was locked.

Jenna flung herself into a chair. 'What on earth's wrong, dear?' Mabel's eyes widened seeing Jenna's consternation. 'I'll put the kettle on. A nice cup of tea will make you feel better.'

'Even tea won't help with this one, Mabel.' Jenna ran her hands through her hair. As she spilled everything out in a garbled hurry, Mabel hobbled over and placed an arm around her shoulders.

'So, it's my fault entirely I'm in this mess.'

Mabel patted Jenna's hand. 'I agree it's a little complicated, dear. But nothing that can't be solved. What's your main worry?'

'Hurting Jake,' said Jenna. 'Letting him down. Especially as he's paid for a lot of the wedding now.'

'Forget the money. For now. You'll be hurting him a whole lot more by going through with it. You both deserve more than that. You're denying him the chance to find somebody who *does* want to spend the rest of their life with him.'

'I know!' Jenna nodded. 'To start with I thought we could be happy. And I admit I was being selfish too. I was thinking about the house…and keeping it for my parents.'

244

'Jenna.' Mabel faltered. 'Your parents don't need the house. I don't mean to be harsh. I understand your way of thinking, but it's wrong, dear.'

A tear ran down Jenna's cheek, landing with a plop on her hand. 'I *do* love Jake, Mabel…just not…enough.'

Mabel wiped Jenna's eyes with her thumb. 'I can see that. Your heart belongs to another young man. And he feels the same. Don't throw away your chance of happiness. That's the last thing your parents would want.'

'Alesha keeps saying that, ever since she arrived.'

'Yes, Alesha and I have regular chats,' said Mabel. 'Between you girls, you've given me my life back.' She smiled. 'I don't want to waste what time I have left. My Bert wouldn't want that. I know he'll be waiting for me when the time comes. But until then, life goes on.'

She glanced into the far corner of the room and Jenna followed her gaze.

'Mabel!' She gasped. 'You've got a computer!'

'Yes, dear. Ben gave me it. He's been teaching me how to use it and send computer letters.'

'Emails?'

'Yes, dear, that's right.'

'Blimey.' Jenna's jaw dropped. 'I'm impressed.'

Mabel laughed. 'So am I! It's all so complicated. But I managed to send an e letter to my previous neighbour I haven't seen for ages. She sends Christmas and birthday cards with all her contact details.'

'Well done!'

'But that media stuff is beyond me. Facepage and that other thing.'

'You mean Facebook and Twitter?'

'Yes, dear, I think that's what Ben said.'

Jenna had a sudden urge to go back into her own Facebook profile. Shutting herself off from her previous life and friends had seemed easier, but now she wasn't so sure.

'But I know how to look up things on Goggle.' Mabel beamed.

'You mean Google.' Jenna grinned.

'No, my eyes definitely goggle when I see some things.'

Jenna laughed. 'Yeah, me too. Right, I'm going to leave you to your goggling and writing, chatting, or whatever. I have some of that to do myself...but something tells me it's not going to be pleasant.'

'Maybe not, but life wasn't meant to be easy. Don't beat yourself up, dear. You're kind and thoughtful and don't like upsetting people. But it's time to think of yourself now.'

'See you later.' Jenna headed to the door.

'Ben's going to be delighted if you call off the wedding,' Mabel called after her. 'He's smitten, dear. Just like you are.'

Smitten sounds so sweet and innocent, like a kitten. But this is no fairy story. Having said that, Jake will probably play the part of the big bad wolf from 'Three little pigs' once he hears what I have to say. I just hope he doesn't threaten to 'Huff and puff and blow the house in.' I fear that's all it would take!

246

Chapter Twenty-Five

'She's got a viewing?' Jenna spluttered into the phone. 'But she can't have! Not already!'

'She has,' said Jake. 'Can you be there, Jen? Two o'clock? I can't get away from the office and I'd feel better if someone was there. Mum'll get stressed about it.'

'Okay.' Too right she would be there. No way could anybody buy Mona's house. She hadn't had chance to speak to Jake, and in the meantime it was imperative to put the viewers off. 'The estate agent will be there though, won't he?'

'Yes,' said Jake. 'But make sure you follow him round. Do what you can.'

Oh, I will! Don't worry about that!

'I'll do my best. See you later.' The board had only been up five minutes. She had to get round there, and fast.

Ben came up behind her. 'You okay, J? You seem a bit stressed.'

'Yeah.' Jenna wondered how much to say to Ben. But it would be wrong to tell anyone else about her change of heart towards the wedding, before she told the expectant groom. 'Erm, I'm just going to Mona's. See you later.' She gave him a quick smile. How she wished she could stay there with him. But she couldn't. It was time to tell these people about the rough neighbourhood they'd be moving to.

'Have I missed anything?' Mona's beady eyes scanned the room for a lurking speck of dust. 'I could've done with more warning.' She sniffed.

'It all looks fine.' Jenna was dismayed to see that it did. 'Try to relax, Mona.'

When the doorbell rang, Mona sprang out of her chair with a final glance around.

A young, bespectacled man followed Mona into the room. He looked like he should be in the school playground. A young couple stepped around him and stood in the middle of the room.

'It's a decent size.' The woman nodded. 'We'd get everything in here, no problem.'

'It's light.' The man went to the window and peered outside. 'Seems nice and quiet.'

This is going too well. I need to get them on their own.

'Do you want me to show you upstairs?' Jenna inclined her head to the door. 'It's okay, I'll take them.' She told the estate agent, firmly. 'Is there anything you need to be, erm, going over with Mona?'

'Right.' He sat and opened his briefcase.

Jenna led the way upstairs, taking care to appear enthusiastic as she peered over her shoulder at the couple. She led them into the smallest bedroom first.

'This will be an ideal nursery.' The man winked. 'For when we need it, of course.'

'Oh.' Jenna grimaced.

'What?' The woman's eyebrows furrowed.

'Well…it can get a bit noisy. Not every night, but the local gang are here more often than not.'

'Local gang?'

'Yes.' Jenna nodded. 'But as long as you keep your head down they won't bother you.'

'I see.' The man exchanged looks with his wife. 'Let's see the other bedrooms.'

They went into Mona's room and opened the wardrobe door. 'Loads of space.' The woman smiled. 'I like this.'

Oh, no you don't!

'It's lovely.' Jenna agreed. 'I have no idea why Mona insists it's haunted.' She laughed.

'Haunted?' The woman's eyes widened.

'Oh, don't be silly.' The man tutted.

'It's probably just the neighbours she can hear.' Jenna lowered her voice. 'Throwing furniture around.'

'What?' The man spun round.

'Yes,' said Jenna. 'The son was let out of prison recently. He gets into a rage if he can't have his fix.'

'You mean he's on drugs?' The woman twiddled a ring around her finger.

'Well, yes,' said Jenna with a shrug. 'But that has nothing to do with why he was in prison.'

'Why was he?' The man's eyes narrowed.

'Oh, taking an iron bar to someone who crossed him.' Jenna lifted the curtain and thought about the lovely family who really lived next door. She smothered a giggle. 'But I'm sure he's fine once you get to know him.'

'I think I've seen enough now.' The woman stumbled to the doorway. 'Let's go.'

Jenna painted on a smile when they entered the sitting room. Jenna was struck immediately by the sad look on Mona's face.

'Are you okay?' She bent over Mona's chair. 'You look tired. Didn't you sleep well?'

She looked at the couple and grimaced once more. That should do it. The board wouldn't be coming down anytime soon. At least not to be replaced by a 'sold' one at any rate.

'We'll be in touch.' The man put his hand on the woman's back and ushered her to the door. 'Thank you.'

'Wait!' The estate agent trotted after them. 'I'll call you.' He threw over his shoulder in Mona's direction. 'Goodbye.'

Silence hung in the air after they'd left. Jenna wasn't used to Mona being quiet.

'Mona? They, erm, seemed to like it.'

'Yes,' said Mona. 'That's what I'm frightened of.'

'What do you mean?' Jenna was confused.

'Seeing strangers poking through my things.' Mona took a hanky from her sleeve. 'I've lived here for forty years, Jenna. It…won't be as easy as I thought to pack up and leave.'

Jenna was torn. One part of her felt elated. But another part wanted to comfort her. She hated seeing anyone so distraught. She clasped Mona's hand.

'Don't put yourself through it, Mona. There's no need really. Is there?'

'But I wanted to be with you and Jakey. My family.' Her voice cracked. 'And I'll be lonely here on my own.'

Jenna traced her finger over the veins on Mona's hand. 'But you'll still see Jake all the time…and I'll come and visit you.' Jenna wondered if Mona would want to see her at all once she called off the wedding. She suspected not. She clamped her lips shut. Much as she wanted to tell her Jake would be going nowhere, she had to tell him first.

'I have to go now, Mona. But will you tell Jake I need to see him?'

Mona nodded. 'Of course.'

'Call the estate agent. Tell them to stick their sign up their erm…'

Mona gave a watery smile. She wasn't all bad. It was just a shame Jenna was only realising it now.

The others were sitting round the kitchen table when Jenna got home. Alesha sat on the worktop kicking her legs. It seemed ages since they were all together at the same time. She'd missed it.

'Hi, Jenna.' Ellie scraped back her chair. 'I'll get you a glass of wine.'

'Thanks.' Jenna slumped into a chair and kicked off her shoes.

'You okay, girl?' Mick gave her a hard look. 'What's up?'

Nothing.' Jenna took the glass off Ellie and toyed with the stem. 'I'm…okay.'

Ben said nothing but she felt his eyes burning into her. She raised her gaze level with the cleft in his chin.

I'd love to pour my wine into it and drink from there.

'Jenna?' Ellie nudged her. 'Are you listening to a word we're saying?'

She gave herself a mental shake. 'Erm, what? Sorry!'

'Ellie and I have seen a poster advertising a talent contest, and we think you and Ben should enter it,' said Mick. 'It's at the theatre in town at the end of the month.'

'Oh, I dunno.' Jenna couldn't concentrate on anything until she'd spoken to Jake. 'Maybe.'

Ben leaned back in his chair and took a swig of beer. His eyes were brooding and his mouth set in a tight line. 'If you don't want to, it's fine.' His voice was clipped. 'No worries.'

'But I do…I think.' She sighed. 'I've just got other things on my mind at the moment, that's all.'

'Anything we can help with?' asked Mick.

'Not really, but thanks. Anyway, can we change the subject for now? Please?'

The others exchanged looks but simply nodded.

'Hey, I've been hearing all about you teaching Mabel how to send e-letters, Ben.' Jenna grinned. She needed to fill the silence. 'And she even knows how to goggle stuff.'

The mood lightened instantly. This was what she needed.

'Oh, I know!' Ellie snorted. 'She's so happy lately.' She turned to look at Alesha. 'And it's mainly down to you.'

Ben and Mick turned in the direction Ellie was looking in. Mick took it all in his stride. Although Ben believed everything now, he still felt uncomfortable knowing Alesha was there, but not being able to see or hear her.

'And you!' said Jenna. 'Your drawings have helped so much, Ellie. Haven't they, Ben?'

'Yep.' He nodded. 'They sure have. It's still weird though.' He coughed. 'Sorry, er, Alesha. But you must understand how crazy it is to be in the same room as you, and not hearing your incessant chatter.'

Alesha giggled. 'Tell him his mate's got some new dressing up outfits. He adores the slinky Lycra dress. Shame about the chicken legs though.'

Ellie repeated this to Ben. He covered his ears. 'Tell her to stop it! I'm seeing him tomorrow! I'm not listening.'

Jenna was only vaguely aware of the collective laughter. She picked up her phone, willing Jake to call.

'Excuse me.' Jenna scraped back her chair. The sound of the legs squeaking over the wooden floor went through her. 'I'll be back down shortly.'

She went to her room and left a message for Jake, then flopped onto the bed. A few seconds later she hauled herself back off and went to her bedside cupboard. A cloud of dust floated around her as she took out her laptop. After wiping it with the cuff of her sweater she turned it on. It hadn't been used for ages. There wasn't much reason, everything was on her phone. But some things were easier to see on a bigger screen. Like Facebook.

Her heart thudded as she brought up her account. Would it be still active after so long? Did she even want it to be? The familiar blue branding popped up on her screen. She gasped at the amount of notifications and messages. There was hundreds. With shaking fingers she read slowly:

'Jen, you okay?'

'Message me, tell me you're alright.'

'So sorry to hear about your parents. Always there for you.'

'Sending massive hugs, babe.'

'Contact me. Miss you!'

And on it went. Most from her uni friends. She looked through their profiles and photos. She was shocked by what she saw. Some of the most promising careers had been halted by nappies and prams. And on the flip side of it, some people had gone on to do well, despite struggling through their various courses. But the common factor with all of them was that they

253

remained in contact. They hadn't forgotten old friends and the good times they'd shared.

Her fingers hovered over the laptop. Could she? The attention it would bring was likely to be huge and she didn't know if she could handle it.

After hesitating, fingers poised, she typed: 'Hey! How's it going? Sorry I disappeared off the face of the earth, guys…but I'm back now!'

She hit Post and immediately wondered whether to delete it. Instead she closed the laptop and jabbed at her phone. Her stomach fluttered when Jake answered. 'Hi, Jenna. I was just going to call you. Mum's in a bit of a state. It seems she's having second thoughts.'

She's not the only one!

'Yes, I know. It's for the best. Jake, I need to talk to you. It's urgent. Can you come over?'

'Okay. Any chance we'll have the place to ourselves?'

'Yes. The others are about to go out.'

I'll bribe them if I have to.

'Right. Give me half an hour.'

She sprinted downstairs and strode into the kitchen. All eyes turned to look at her and the room fell silent.

'What's wrong?' Ellie jumped from the table and raced round to hug Jenna. 'Are you ill? You look terrible.'

'Look, I need you to do me a massive favour. Can you all go out please? I need to speak to Jake. Alone.'

'Okay.' Mick nodded. 'Come on, we'll go to the pub up the road.'

They hurried to put on coats and headed for the door. Mick ushered Ellie out but Ben turned to face Jenna, his hand on the door handle. 'J, I don't know what's wrong…but you know you can talk to me anytime. You know…how I feel about you.' He closed the door quietly behind him.

Jenna paced up and down the hallway. She jumped a few minutes later, when Jake opened the door. She spun round on shaky legs to greet him.

'Jenna, has something happened?' His brow furrowed in concern. He took her in his arms and stroked her hair.

Why can't he be horrible? Then it would be easier.

She pulled back from his grasp. 'Come and sit down, Jake. We need to talk.'

'You've got me worried now. I've brought a bottle of wine. Something tells me I'm going to need it.' He went to get glasses from the kitchen and then sat next to her on the sofa.

Jenna took the glass from his outstretched hand. 'I don't know how to say this.' Her knuckles were white against the glass. She tipped the contents down her throat and spluttered.

'Steady on.' Jake patted her back. 'Spit it out.'

'I c-cant m-marry you, Jake. I'm so sorry.' She swiped at the tears rolling down her cheeks. 'I love you, but I'm not ready to settle down.'

Jake's face turned ashen. He put down his glass and ran his hands through his hair.

'What? Why?' His eyes narrowed into slits. 'Is this to do with Ben? Has something been going on between you?'

'No!' She shook her head. 'It's got nothing to do with anyone else. I feel as if I've missed out on being young, I guess. Because of what happened.'

'But twenty-six isn't too young to be married.'

'I know.' Jenna agreed. 'Not for some people. But my life has been on hold for five and a half years. I want to make up for some of that, Jake. Can you understand?'

'No, not really.' His shoulders slumped. 'What is it you need to do that's more important than marrying me?'

Jenna hesitated. 'I've been living as if I'm middle-aged. I've realised life's too short to waste and getting married isn't where I want to be. You're a good man, and I know you'd look after me and be a good husband. But you deserve more than having a wife who will end up resenting being tied down.'

'Tied down? Like a prisoner?' Jake spat. 'Thanks for that!'

Jenna clasped his hand. He looked as though he was going to snatch his away, but he didn't. 'Honestly, Jake, do you think we're meant to spend the rest of our life together? We're so different. Neither of us are wrong, but we're not right together. I'll save up and pay back every penny you've spent on the wedding.'

'You think it's about the money?' Jake's jaw clenched.

'No, but I feel as though I should cover the cost…somehow.'

Jake grasped her shoulders. His eyes misted over, much to Jenna's dismay.

'I can't believe you've left it until now to tell me this. Will you agree to keep it quiet until I get my head round it, before we tell Mum and everybody else?'

We? Oh, shit!

'How long?'

'Until after Christmas,' said Jake. 'That's the least you can do. It's so close now and I don't see why her Christmas should be spoiled. It could be her last one.'

Jenna's heart sank. Christmas may only be a few weeks away, but it was going to seem like an eternity, keeping this to herself. She felt a spike of anger go through her at the emotional blackmail. If only she wasn't such a wimp! But maybe he was right: it *was* the least she could do.

'Okay.' She sighed. 'But it's not going to be easy.'

'Well poor you! Can you imagine how *I* feel?' he muttered.

God, he's devastated! This is far worse than I could've imagined.

256

'Yes, course I can. I'm so sorry, Jake.'

'I mean, it's a bloody disaster.' His voice broke. 'My poor mother…all her plans gone to waste. Not having the wedding to look forward to could destroy her!'

What? He's more bothered about Mona than losing a wife! Jenna Croft, you may be stupid at times…okay, many times, but you've just done the most sensible thing of your life. It's time to get your act together starting with the one at the theatre. 'New Attitude' in more ways than one.

'Well, all is not lost Jake.' She picked up a notebook and pen from the coffee table. 'I'll design some new wedding invitations.' She scribbled on the paper furiously:

'You are invited to the wedding of Jake Mansfield and Mona Mansfield

Jake is marrying his mother!'

Chapter Twenty-Six

'I'm happy with that.' Ben put down his guitar with a grin. 'What about you, J?'

'Yeah, I'm mega excited.' Jenna clasped her hands together. 'It doesn't matter if we don't win, but it'll be cool to perform in a proper theatre.'

'You'll walk it!' Ellie jumped up and down. 'I can't wait! Can you, Mick?'

The smile died on Jenna's face. Ellie and Mick had become like a double act. The trouble was, Jenna didn't find it funny. Mick may be her uncle, but Ellie was her best friend. He seemed besotted with Ellie in a way Jenna had never seen before with anyone else, but what would happen when his feet became decidedly itchy once more? There'd be women all over the world only too happy to scratch them.

'I don't think you know how good you really are.' Mick looked from Jenna to Ben. 'I'm getting the tickets today. I was thinking of getting Mabel one. Do you think she'd like to go?'

'Course she would.' Ellie's eyes shone. 'She'll love it!'

Jenna glanced at Ben. Her stomach flipped as he smiled at her. His mouth looked happy, yet his eyes looked sad. He reached out his arm to Jenna, but dropped it quickly.

Jenna wondered what Ben would say when he found out about the cancelled wedding. Would it matter to him?

She and Jake hadn't spoken for nearly a week, since that night. He'd texted to say that they needed to put up a front over Christmas, but that was it.

Ben switched off all the sound equipment while Ellie and Mick wandered off into the kitchen. They'd bought a ton of Christmas decorations and the room was littered with bags and boxes. Jenna swallowed down the lump in her throat. The festive season had been hard over the last few years. She wiped her eyes as she recalled the smell of mince pies and turkey being cooked, while her mother sang carols. She smiled at the memory of her dad taking hundreds of photos. Most of which would never be looked at, except by him. A hundred times over. Maybe the camera was in the loft? Ellie had helped sort most of her parents stuff out, a few months after the accident. Most went to a charity shop, but a couple of boxes went into the loft to be dealt with at a future date. Maybe that future date had arrived.

'J, you okay?' Ben placed a hand on her shoulder. Her skin scorched from his touch.

'I was thinking about Christmas...before.' She gave a watery smile. 'My dad used to ring a bell on Christmas Eve. I got so excited as it got nearer to my bedroom. I squeezed my eyes closed so that Santa would leave me presents.'

'But you knew it was your dad?'

'In later years. One time I couldn't resist a tiny peek. That was the moment I knew Santa didn't exist.'

'How?'

'He was supposed to be wearing a red suit, not a button-down cardy.'

Ben laughed. 'He sounds lovely.'

Jenna nodded. 'Yes. They both were.' Tears streamed down her cheeks.

Ben took her in his arms. She smelled the citrus in his hair and inhaled deeply. Her arms snaked around his back. Ben gave a low groan as he pulled her closer to him. They sprang apart when the others clattered back into the room.

'Hey, we've been —' Mick hesitated and looked at Ellie. Her mouth turned upwards and she winked at Alesha who had just appeared.

'What?' Ben raised his eyebrows.

'We've been thinking it would be fun to go to the Christmas market in town.' Mick continued. 'Do you fancy it?'

Ben looked at Jenna and nodded. 'Yeah, you up for it, J? Unless you're busy?'

'I don't want to spoil anyone else's fun,' said Jenna. 'You go ahead. Christmas is…difficult.'

'Hey, come on, girl,' said Mick. 'You may enjoy it. It's what…they'd want you to do.'

The tears jabbed Jenna's eyes, but she nodded. If it made the others happy, she'd make an effort to convince them she was okay. 'Alright, but can you get me a couple of boxes out of the loft first, please?' She looked from Mick to Ben. They both nodded and left the room.

The smell of sausages and doughnuts wafted through the air. Music played from a speaker in the centre of the market.

Crowds of people jostled to see the wares on offer at the craft stalls, and couples ambled along, arms entwined, caught up in the festive atmosphere. Jenna wanted to run. She didn't belong there, when all she wanted was for Christmas to be over. Yet another date on the calendar to be endured.

'Look.' Ben pointed to an open-air café. 'Let's get a hot drink, shall we?'

Jenna blew on her hot chocolate and sipped it slowly. The cream on top went up her nose.

'Here, let me see.' Ben reached over and wiped it gently. She found herself swaying closer to him. He wrapped his arm around her. 'You're freezing. Take my scarf.' He placed it around her neck and tied it loosely. She gulped. What would it feel like to rub her face against the faint stubble on his chin? As they both moved to take a drink at the same time, their hands brushed together. A jolt of electricity ran through her. Very briefly, his hand curled around hers discreetly. In that moment something else inside her changed. She wasn't sure what, but an unfamiliar emotion engulfed her. Hope.

Jenna opened her laptop in apprehension. Her eyes widened as she logged on to Facebook. Seventy-eight likes and the same amount of comments on her post. Thirty-five private messages were in her inbox. Every single one was from her uni and school friends, all astounded but delighted to have her back. She tapped eagerly to update her status:

'Fab to hear from you all! If anyone's around on the twenty-ninth, my new singing duo 'New Attitude' are entering

the talent contest at the theatre in town. You'll probably guess
where that name came from…'

Comments pinged through immediately. It seemed some
of her local friends were around for Christmas and would be
there. Jenna was elated. In a way, chatting to them all now felt
as if they'd spoken yesterday. But that's what true friends did:
pick up years later.

Alesha appeared and glanced over Jenna's shoulder.
'They've all missed you.'

'I know!' Jenna jabbed the screen. 'And they're coming to
the contest, the ones who can get there. Can you believe it?'

'Yes.' Alesha nodded. 'They love you, Jenna. Time
doesn't change that, does it?'

Jenna turned from the screen. 'Are you talking about my
friends or my parents?'

'Both. It's hard to not love you. I know I do.'

'Alesha, that's lovely. I love you too. Can I tell you
something? Will you keep it to yourself for now?'

'Yeah, what?'

'Do you promise not to tell Ellie or Mabel yet? Until the
time's right?'

'I promise.'

'The wedding's off. I've told Jake, but he's asked me to
wait until after Christmas before announcing it.'

'That's great news, but why's he want to keep it quiet?'

'So it doesn't spoil Mona's Christmas.' Jenna grimaced. 'I
don't want to upset her either, but she needs to know.'

'Well, why can't you tell the others? They aren't likely to
mention it to Mona, are they?'

'No.' Jenna agreed. 'But I made a promise and I intend to
keep it.'

'You promised to marry Jake, but you didn't keep that.'

Jenna's fists curled into balls. 'How can you say that? You're the one who's been telling me not to go through with it.'

'Don't blame me,' said Alesha. 'I was guiding you, not forcing you into doing anything. You would be marrying him if you wanted to, regardless of what I say. But anyway, I'm trying to help you here.'

'How?'

'I can see you're feeling guilty yet again. There's no need. Jake's happy to let you take the blame publically, but in private he's relieved.'

'What?'

'He's been busy on Facebook himself.'

'Jake? On *Facebook*?' Jenna threw back her head and laughed. 'Yeah, right.'

'Okay.' Alesha shrugged. 'I'll leave you to it.'

'Hang on. You're not serious, surely?'

'I am, search for him now.'

Jenna rolled her eyes and typed in his name. A list came up on screen. Just as she was about to toss the laptop aside, a profile photo caught her eye. She scrolled down and peered closer. It *was* Jake. She clicked on it and there he was, smiling into the camera. He wore a shirt and loosened tie. But that's all that was visible because his profile was set to private. She hovered over 'send friend request,' then pulled her hand away.

'I didn't know,' Jenna gasped. 'He's never mentioned it.'

Alesha ran her hand over the screen. 'Well, he wouldn't. He's only on there because his ex asked him to.'

'Amber? But how, why, when?' Jenna was stunned. Alesha must've got it wrong.

'They've been emailing. She said she missed him and thought about him a lot. He said he felt the same, but that he was marrying you now. That's his saving grace, he was determined to remain loyal to you.'

'How's that being loyal if he's saying how much he misses her?'

'She's coming back to the UK next week and wants to see him. He's refused because it'll stir up feelings he has to try and forget. Because of you.'

'I don't believe this. How would you know anyway?'

'When he was here towards the end of the summer, you took some dinner round to Mabel. As soon as you left, he got his laptop. He looked shifty so I decided to investigate. I saw the emails and spied on him. I was there when he set up the Facebook profile.'

'But why Facebook?' Jenna shrugged.

'Amber wanted him to see the area where she lived in Italy,' said Alesha. 'But I think it was more to do with him seeing how gorgeous she looked in pictures than anything else.'

'Christ.' Jenna took a deep breath. 'And they've been private messaging, I suppose?'

'Yeah. But he hasn't told her the wedding's off yet, which I'm a bit surprised about.'

'Hmm, that's strange,' said Jenna. 'If you're telling the truth about all this, why wouldn't he tell her immediately?'

'No idea,' said Alesha. 'But he's got no right to pin all the blame on you for breaking off the engagement. He should've admitted how he felt then. His mother clearly does come first. I suppose we can't knock him for that, under the circumstances.'

'Why didn't you tell me before?'

'I didn't want to influence your decision about the wedding, Jenna. He wasn't going to meet her, or anything. I've blown your mind enough as it is already, haven't I?'

'Yeah, you could say that.' Jenna grinned. 'I need to talk to him, but how do I tell him I know?'

'I don't know,' said Alesha. 'But it's not worth stressing over. Give him a call.'

Jake opened the car door and Jenna climbed in. He drove off in silence, and didn't utter a word until they pulled up in a quiet layby. He undid his seatbelt and turned to face her.

'Have you changed your mind about the wedding?' he asked.

'No.' She shook her head. 'And neither do I think you want me to.'

'What's that supposed to mean?'

'Cut the crap, Jake. It's not me you want, not really. I was always second best. Oh, I know you'd have tried to make me happy.' She held up her hand when he opened his mouth to speak. 'But you're still in love with Amber, aren't you?'

The blood drained from Jake's face. 'N-n-no, don't be ridiculous. Where have you got that idea from?'

'Emails and Facebook. Don't deny it.' Jenna held her breath. Had Alesha got it right?

Jake gaped. 'How dare you! You've been hacking into my private correspondence!' He thumped his hand on the steering wheel.

'How would I know your passwords, even if I'd wanted to? Which I didn't.'

'Then…how else could you know?'

'So it's true?' Jenna folded her arms over her chest. 'Oh, it doesn't matter how I know. The important thing is that I do.'

Jake's face turned scarlet. 'Tell me how, Jenna!'

She hesitated. 'Oh, Ellie's psychic. She told me.'

'Don't be ridiculous,' Jake spat.

'If you prefer to think I hacked into your files, well okay. But what happens now? I think it's down to you to speak to your mum. And soon.'

Jake's face crumpled. He threw back his head. 'I'm sorry. I should've told you. I think we've both been guilty of keeping quiet for far too long. But I did love you. I hope you believe that.'

'I do.' She nodded. 'And likewise. But it wasn't enough, was it?'

'No.' He sighed. 'I guess not.'

'See Amber. Tell her the wedding's off.' Jenna lightly touched his arm. 'I want you to be happy, you know.'

'Are you going to be with Ben? I've seen the way you look at each other.'

'I don't know. We've not spoken about it, but there is an…attraction. My priority is sorting out my life though, Jake. Deciding what it is I really want. I'm not rushing anything, even if he wanted to. I'm not sure if he does. It's probably wise for us to just be friends. Especially as I love singing with him. I don't want anything to spoil that.'

Jake considered her words. 'I can see how much it means to you. I'm sorry I didn't take it seriously before.' He smiled. 'Jenna, I'd love us to be friends. Is that possible? You know, like brother and sister?'

'I'd like that too. Some friends of mine ended up in a similar situation. I think they'd have managed to do it.'

'What do you mean?'

'She died.'

'Oh…I'm sorry.'

'Me too.'

'I know you think I'm too soft with Mum, but I saw what it did to her when Dad died.' Jake sighed. 'I couldn't help her.

I've tried to make up for it since, but I know I've gone about it the wrong way.'

Jenna laughed. 'Well, stand your ground with her as far as Amber goes. You've lost her once, so don't make the same mistake again.'

'I won't.' Jake's eyes shone. 'Thank you.' He pulled her to him.

'We'll tell her together. Say it's a joint decision. And if you still want to, we can wait until after Christmas. But in the meantime, see Amber. Okay?'

'Okay.' He kissed the top of her head. 'Let's get moving. I'll take you home.'

'Jake,' said Jenna, as they pulled up outside the house. 'Just a thought…but we're entering a talent contest on the twenty-ninth. I'd love it if you were there.'

Jake nodded. 'You know what? So would I. I *will* be there.'

'Maybe you could bring…someone.' She raised her eyebrows with a grin.

'Won't that raise awkward questions as to who she is?'

'Does it really matter, Jake?' Jenna opened the car door. 'As long as we're happy with the situation.'

'Maybe.' He winked. 'I'd still love to know how you found out about the messages though.'

'Do you believe in ghosts?' she asked.

'Yes, one's just appeared back into my life, when I thought she was firmly in the past.' He smiled.

'There you go, then. Anything's possible.' She stepped from the car and closed the door softly behind her.

Chapter Twenty-Seven

Jenna stood backstage, her anxiety levels nearly hitting the extremely high ceiling. Her whole body felt clammy against her clothes and her stomach muscles clenched. If Ben was nervous it wasn't evident, instead he showed concern for her.

'You'll be fine, J. Listen to that crowd out there. I'd forgotten how big this place is.'

'Thanks for that, Ben. You've put my mind at rest.' She wiped her hands down her top. 'I think I'm going to throw up.'

'No, you're not.' He laughed. 'Look, you're fab. I'm your biggest fan, and I think you'll wow the lot of them. Try and enjoy it.'

Her heart raced as the compere's voice echoed round the room.

'Good evening, ladies and gentlemen,' he boomed. 'And what a show we have lined up for you. First up, give a round of applause for 'Juggling Jed.''

A middle-aged man dressed in a green and yellow all-in-one stepped out onto the stage. Jenna and Ben watched from the side as he began juggling balls. They flew in every direction except his hands. The crowd clapped and cheered, clearly thinking it was part of the act. Once they realised it wasn't, they began booing. Jenna couldn't bear to watch.

'Shit, Ben, I can't do this.' She wrung her hands together.

'We've got no competition from him,' said Ben. 'I wonder who's up next.'

They soon got the answer.

'Give it up for New Attitude.' They were beckoned onto the stage. Jenna thought her legs would give way. She heard whistling from the crowd, but couldn't pick out faces. Everything was a blur. She clutched the microphone in both hands and took a few deep breaths, which echoed down the microphone. Loud clapping and shouts of 'Go Jenna' followed, until the compere told the audience to be quiet. The backing track started playing.

A movement caught her eye. She blinked and looked again. She saw her dad ducking and diving in the front row, his camera round his neck. Then her mum came into focus. She stood in the aisle, alternating between dabbing her eyes and clapping. A flashback of that night appeared in front of her. She desperately remembered Mabel's words: 'Don't let the image get too close. Make it stay a distance away, hold it there and place it in a box. Put the lid on.' She did. Instead of focusing on what had happened later that evening, she remembered how proud and happy her parents had been watching her, just as they appeared now. Jenna knew it was only her imagination, but it felt comforting. She needed them there, and wanted to re-live the happy moment once more. She began singing. The room fell silent, other than the imaginary clicking of her dad's camera.

When the song finished, Jenna saw that the front two rows were taken up by her friends. Even Jake was there as promised, with a girl who could only be Amber.

The beams from all their faces could easily light up the vast space, without the need for electricity. She could still see her parents. They looked happier than she'd ever seen them before. Tears welled in her eyes as she blew them both a kiss and mouthed, 'I love you.' They called back they loved her too, and then she couldn't see them anymore.

She turned to Ben as he led her off stage. 'That was amazing. I don't know what to say.'

'I know,' he agreed. 'I couldn't believe how confident you sounded, J. You were awesome.'

'I imagined my parents watching, Ben. They spurred me on. I did it for them…and you.'

Ben moved towards her, but then stopped in his tracks. He smiled, but his eyes moistened and he turned away.

Another ten acts performed. Jenna longed to be with her friends, but they had to wait where they were. Finally, an interval was called and they were free to head to the bar where they'd arranged to meet everybody.

Ellie and Mick rushed over to them, holding hands.

'I'm so proud of you both.' Ellie gushed. 'Mick is too, aren't you, Mick?'

'Yep.' He nodded. 'I sure am. Mabel's at that table there. She wants to see you.'

Jenna bent to kiss her upturned cheek. 'Hi, Mabel, what did you think?'

'The best evening I've had for years and years.' She choked on her words. 'You two should be so proud of yourselves.'

'You were fab!' Alesha grinned. 'Totally brilliant!'

'Jenna!' a voice called from behind. She spun round. 'Kerry! Oh. My. God!' Then a group of friends from uni rushed towards her behind Kerry. She squealed and flung herself on them. They all ended up sprawled across a table, sending glasses crashing to the floor. They looked at each other and giggled. It was déjà vu. How many times had this scene happened in the past? They hauled each other upright. Jenna turned to apologise to the people sitting at the doomed table.

'Hello, Jenna.' Jake was attempting to mop red wine from his trousers. 'Nice of you to, erm, drop by to see us.' He grinned. 'This is, erm, Amber.'

A petite pretty girl smiled uncertainly. 'Hi,' she whispered, looking to Jake for support.

'Hi, Amber, nice to meet you.' Jenna pulled out a chair next to her.

'You were really good,' said Amber.

'Thanks. You're okay about being here? About Jake and I being friends?'

'Yes,' said Amber. 'I wanted to meet you, to check —'

'That the relationship is definitely over?' Jenna finished. 'It is. But as you've probably gathered, Mona doesn't know yet.'

Amber grimaced. 'She won't be happy. About the non-existent wedding, or me being back on the scene.'

'She made out the two of you had been the best of friends.' Jenna laughed.

Jake coughed. 'Erm —'

'Chill, Jake,' said Jenna. 'Hey, I've had an idea! You two should get married instead. That way, all the bookings needn't be cancelled and Mona will be slightly happier.'

Amber's eyes widened. 'Oh, no, we —'

'Think about it.' Jenna cut in. 'It's not as if I planned the wedding myself, Amber. That was all down to Mona. The only thing I had anything to do with was the dress.'

Jake loosened his collar, and wiped a bead of perspiration from his brow.

Jenna jumped up from the table. 'I'll shut up now.' She grinned. 'I need to get back anyway. Wish us luck.'

Mabel beckoned her over. 'Fingers crossed, dear. If there's any justice you'll win. If you do, you'll get to perform again. Oh, I do hope so. I missed half of it, because a man was blocking my view. He was all over the place taking photos.'

Jenna froze. 'What did he look like, Mabel?'

'Well, I think he was wearing a button-up cardigan, dear. And the camera was round his neck. He kept saying he'd never been prouder in his life. Is he related to Ben?'

'No, Mabel,' Jenna whispered. 'He's related to me.'

'Are you okay, dear?' Mabel's brow furrowed.

'Yes, I'm more than okay, Mabel. I'm over the moon, I'm —'

'We need to go back, J.' Ben took her arm.

Chances are you're going to miss more yet, Mabel. Dad will be taking at least a couple of hundred more photos. And Mum will start blowing her nose. They'll think it's another act...she sounds like a trumpet when she starts.

Chapter Twenty-Eight

Jenna rubbed the sleep from her eyes and realised with a start it was Christmas Day. The run-up to it had been okay. They were all still on a high from 'New Attitude' winning the contest. The prize had been five hundred pounds, which Jenna and Ben had agreed to use for some new equipment. There'd be a bit over, which they wanted to use to make Christmas extra special for everyone. What had made winning so special for Jenna though, was knowing that her parents really had been there. Alesha had been right: they would always be close when she needed them even if they weren't visible. And they were proud of her. That gave her the strength to live her life to the full, knowing it was what they wanted, safe in the knowledge that they'd see each other again one day.

Against her will she'd promised to have lunch with Jake and Mona. Ben was having lunch with his parents, and Ellie and Mick were staying at the house. Ellie's family was travelling to visit relatives and she'd preferred to stay with Mick. But they'd all agreed to have a big Christmas dinner together that evening, which Ellie and Mick would prepare.

'Merry Christmas, J,' said Ben when she walked into the kitchen half an hour later.

'Merry Christmas.' She stood on tiptoe to peck his cheek. Before she had time to consider what she was doing, she moved her lips to his mouth. As soon as their lips touched, Jenna sprang back, horrified. What was she thinking? And more to the point what would Ben think of her?

'Erm…sorry,' she mumbled. 'I guess the festive spirit has got to me for the first time since…'

Ben regarded her in silence. She hopped from one foot to another, mortified. 'Hey, how we gonna manage to eat two Christmas dinners?' She tried to fill the silence. 'How greedy are we?'

'One of us more so than the other,' said Ben flatly. 'One's never going to be enough.'

Jenna's face flamed. Now he thought she was a cheating slut. She wasn't having that.

'Look, I've said I'm sorry.' She raised her palms. 'What's the big deal anyway?' But the truth was, she could still feel the imprint of his lips. And she hadn't imagined the split second where his mouth had pressed harder against hers. But now his jaw was clenched, plus the pulse in his neck throbbed. That one second had changed everything. A part of her had wanted to take his head in her hands and pull him against her, the other part though, wanted to consider her every move carefully. Not just with him. The last thing she wanted was to do anything that would prevent her from keeping a clear head about where her future lay. Things had been confused and emotional enough as it was, the last few months. Her life was going to change, that much was definite. It already had as far as Jake went. But one thing Alesha had taught her was not to waste a moment.

Although she had no idea what life had in store, Jenna knew without a doubt it was not going to involve constantly worrying about bills and house repairs. It also wasn't going to involve caring for adults who'd reverted back to childhood for much longer either. That was too depressing and upsetting. She'd had her fair share of that, and was the first person to say if it got to the point of hating doing it, it was time to get out.

'What's the big deal?' Ben sneered. 'Try asking your fiancé what he thinks. It might be nothing to you, but it is to me. It seems I've got you wrong, J.'

'That night, when we won the competition,' said Jenna, hands on hips. 'You all wanted to know who Amber was. I said a friend, but the truth is —'

'Merry Christmas.' Ellie and Mick chorused. 'Any coffee on the go?' Mick added.

'You know where the kettle is.' Jenna pointed to it. 'I'm popping to see Mabel before I go to Jake's. See you later...and Merry Christmas.'

She stomped through the hallway, ignoring Ellie and Mick calling after her. She needed to get out, as far away from Ben as possible.

Jenna mellowed as soon as she saw Mabel. The calming atmosphere soothed her.

'One of us will be round to escort you later, Mabel.' Jenna sat on the arm of her chair. 'Sorry dinner's going to be so late, but Ben and I have to get through two today.'

Mabel turned Jenna to face her. 'What's the matter, dear? I suppose you're missing family. It must be hard for you.'

'It has been.' Jenna agreed. 'And it still is. But it's seemed slightly easier this year. Alesha and the others have helped me come to terms with things. Also, I know Mum and Dad want me to be happy, whatever that takes. I know it and I feel it. Trouble is, I'm not sure what that is exactly yet.'

'Time will tell, dear.' Mabel patted her hand. 'But I thought it was going to involve a certain young man. I was wrong. We all were. You're going to be married soon. Isn't that enough to make you happy?'

Jenna slumped over Mabel's shoulder and it all came out in a jumbled rush. Jake, Amber, and what had just happened with Ben. Mabel listened without interrupting until Jenna finally stopped for breath.

'Hmm, well, I can't say I'm too surprised about Jake,' she mused. 'Nothing wrong with him, he's a family man. But not quite suited to you, dear.'

'I've made up my mind, Mabel, I'm going to tell Mona. Today.'

'Are you sure that's wise?' said Mabel. 'Without telling Jake first?'

'Oh, you don't know it all,' Jenna scoffed. 'I joked, well half-joked, that Amber takes my place at the wedding. Guess what? She is! He rang me a couple of days ago, checking I was genuinely alright with it. They've waited long enough apparently and want to go ahead.'

'But,' Mabel spluttered. 'But that's outrageous! They can't do that!'

'I think they should, actually!' Jenna laughed. 'At least I don't feel as though I need to pay for a non-existent wedding now. But do you see why I've made up my mind to force the issue with Mona today? I think she has a right to know the name of the bride has changed, don't you?'

They looked at each other and burst out laughing. But Jenna knew it wouldn't be quite as funny once faced with the wrath of Mona.

'Mabel, do you have any alcohol? I need some dutch courage.'

'I'll join you.' Mabel chuckled. 'Get the brandy out of the sideboard, dear.'

Jenna coughed as the burning liquid hit the back of her throat. 'Bloody hell, that should do it!' she gasped.

Mabel took a tiny sip and stared into the glass thoughtfully. 'You know, I wouldn't fret too much about Ben. He's hurting because he wants you, while thinking you belong to someone else.'

'I don't know about that.' Jenna shrugged. 'But anyway, I'm not getting involved with anyone else just yet. I need to decide for myself where I'm going, literally in life. It's been on hold for over five and a half years. I have to figure out where to go from here.'

Mabel reached onto the floor for her bag. 'Maybe this will help you figure it all out, dear.' She handed an envelope to Jenna. 'This is for you to do with as you see fit.'

Jenna's forehead creased as she opened the envelope. Her jaw dropped open as she took out the cheque. The numbers blurred together. She squinted and looked again.

'A hundred thousand pounds?' She gasped. 'Mabel, don't be silly. Here.'

Mabel waved Jenna's hand away. 'Listen to me. You've given me something that's priceless: my life back. I never thought I could be happy again after the accident, and then losing my Bert. But you've given me that, dear. And more. You treat me like family and include me in everything you're doing. You all do. And I can't put into words how that's made me feel. So I've put it into numbers instead.'

'No way am I taking this! I —'

'It's important to me that you do. Money's no use to me. I regret the years me and my Bert scrimped to pay off a mortgage. And for what? We had no family to pass it down to. We should've enjoyed ourselves more when we had chance. You'll make good use of it, dear. I know you will. And before you say anything else, it would've all been going to charity. Some still will. So, I'd rather see you have it now, than leave it for when I've gone.'

'I-I don't know what to say. It doesn't feel right, Mabel.'

'Please?' Mabel looked at her with pleading eyes.

'But…what should I do with it?' Jenna stared at the cheque. 'I'm not used to this amount of money.'

'It'll give you more options. Either you can pay off the mortgage on your house and get it all fixed. Or you can sell it and buy somewhere nice. Less maintenance. Or you can buy somewhere smaller and probably have enough left when you put all the money together, to go back to college. Do some kind of course or training, maybe. But whatever you decide, it's going to make life a bit easier, isn't it? You won't have to rely on anybody else.'

Tears streamed down Jenna's face. This was unreal. She stumbled to Mabel and caught her in a bear hug.

'Careful, dear.' Mabel laughed. 'Now, let's finish that drink to celebrate, shall we?'

'I'll make you proud of me.' Jenna's chin jutted out. 'I promise.'

'I already am, dear,' said Mabel. 'But when you're proud of yourself I'll be properly happy.'

'Oh, Jake's parked outside.' Jenna lifted the curtain and waved. 'Wish me luck! See you later.'

'I can't wait to hear all about it,' said Mabel. 'See you later.'

'So, you're getting married…still.' Jenna laughed. 'Wow! Aren't you going to thank me for giving you both the idea?'

'Yes.' Jake pulled away from the kerb. 'It's all a bit weird though. I mean, here we both are going to Mum's together. She thinks we're getting married, but *we* know I'm marrying someone else. It's crazy.'

She'll know the truth soon enough.

'You're completely sure about Amber, aren't you?'

Jake nodded. 'I am, but I still feel uncomfortable saying that to you.'

'Don't be. For what it's worth, I think she's lovely and you seem right together.'

'You're lovely too, Jenna. Your friendship means a lot to me. I don't ever want to lose that.'

'You won't. Having someone care about you, in whatever way, is precious. I hope we can always be there for each other, Jake.'

He took one hand off the steering wheel and groped for her hand, squeezing it.

'Ouch!' She snatched it out of his grasp. 'I get the message.' She laughed. 'Right, let's quit being soppy gits. Come on, it's time to give your mum a Christmas she won't forget.'

'Merry Christmas, dear.' Mona patted the sofa. 'Come and sit down. Jakey, pour us a sherry please. The turkey will be ready shortly.'

'It smells delicious.' Jenna's nostrils twitched.

Jenna screwed up her face at the sickly sweet taste of the sherry, but she swallowed it in one gulp. Mona watched in obvious distaste, sipping hers slowly, with her little finger pointing upwards.

Drink up, Mona, you're going to need it!

Jenna perched on the edge of the seat, unable to relax. Mona droned on about the queen's speech and the amount of repeats on TV. She was only vaguely aware of what Mona intended to put into the letter she planned to send to the TV licensing people.

An hour later they sat at the table. Jenna's stomach rumbled at the sight of the golden turkey and steaming vegetables but when she picked up her knife and fork her appetite disappeared. It was just as well she'd be having the same that evening. By then the conversation with Mona would be over.

'Aren't you hungry?' Jake pushed his empty plate away and held his stomach. 'I couldn't eat another thing.'

'It's absolutely perfect,' said Jenna. 'But there's something I need to say, Mona.'

'What? You think the potatoes are undercooked?' Mona narrowed her eyes. 'They were —'

'Everything's fine.' Jenna took a deep breath. 'Just as the wedding will be.'

Jenna saw Jake's warning glance but it had gone far enough now.

'Yes, it will be.' Mona's eyes brightened.

'Jake's very happy.' Jenna continued. 'Aren't you, Jake?'

He swallowed and closed his eyes. 'Yes,' he muttered.

'The cake's going to be perfect,' said Mona. 'It's going to have your names entwined in red and silver.'

'Has it been iced yet?'

'I don't know.' Mona looked at her in surprise, as well she might. Jenna had shown little interest in the wedding so far. 'Don't you like the sound of it, dear?'

'Yesss…with one teeny adjustment.' Jenna grimaced. 'One of the names will need icing over, and replaced with a different one.'

Mona looked from Jenna to Jake in confusion. 'I don't understand.'

'Jenna, leave it,' Jake pleaded. 'Now's not the time.'

'Well, when is? She needs to know.'

'Know what?' Mona whispered.

'Jake's getting married as planned…only not to me.'

Mona's knife and fork slipped from her fingers and clattered onto the plate. Her mouth gaped but she couldn't speak.

'Jake's marrying Amber, Mona. They want to be together and should have been all along. I'm cool with that and I've met her. Jake would have gone through with marrying me because he's that sort of man. But I called it off. It's one of those things. Nobody's fault.'

'No!' Mona stared wild-eyed at Jake. 'This isn't happening.'

'It is.' Jake nodded. 'I'm sorry, Mum, but I've made up my mind. I know it's a shock, but you need to get used to the idea…because I'm doing it whether you like it or not.'

'B-but…'

'You love Amber, Mona. You've told me that loads of times.' Jenna smiled brightly.

Mona's face reddened. 'Yes, well, I've got used to *you* now.'

'I don't want to settle down yet, but Jake and Amber do. And.' She winked at Mona. 'You know what that means? Grandchildren will be on the scene a lot sooner than if it was me marrying him.'

'Jenna!' Jake gasped.

'What?' She threw him an innocent look.

'Grandchildren? Babies?' Mona suddenly beamed. 'I've got a pile of knitting patterns in the loft. Can you get me them, Jakey? I'm sure I've got ones for bootees and baby cardigans. I need some wool. Maybe white and lemon. I've got all the needles. I'll —'

'Mum, stop it!' Jake held up his hand. 'Let's not get carried away.' He shook his head in fury at Jenna. She smothered a giggle.

'Tell you what, Mona.' Jenna stood. 'Jake and I will wash up while you go over your lists. There's a lot for you to think about.'

'Alright.' Mona left the room, still muttering about wool.

'What do you think you're playing at?' Jake hissed. 'Why did you tell her then? And babies? For God's sake!'

Jenna rounded on him. 'Aren't you relieved to have it out in the open? If it had been left to you, she'd have found out on the wedding day. As for mentioning babies, it softened the blow, Jake.'

He let out a sigh. 'Okay, sorry. And thank you…I think!'

Jenna filled the bowl with hot soapy water. 'You're welcome…daddy.' She ducked as he dived towards her with a handful of bubbles.

They made a pot of coffee and carried it through to Mona. She looked up from scribbling in a notebook.

'Just one thing, Jakey.' Her eyes darkened. 'I'm not having any Grandchild of mine having one of these new-fangled names. It seems to be all the rage to call children after fruit, like apple or peach. I've even read about a girl called lettuce. How ridiculous! Don't you dare come to me and announce the arrival of 'Cucumber Mansfield!'

'That's hilarious!' Jenna snorted. 'And on that note I'm going to call a taxi and leave you both to it.'

'I'll drive you, I haven't had a drink.'

'No, thanks. I think you need to make a phone call, don't you? I'm sure your mum would be happy to continue this conversation with Amber. I wonder what her views are on names. Personally I like Tomato. Don't worry, Mona…it could be shortened to Tommy!'

Jenna shuffled down the hallway to the kitchen. The sound of laughter and the smell of delicious food was enticing, but the prospect of facing Ben wasn't.

She hesitated with her hand on the handle, before entering, with a painted-on smile.

Ellie, Mick, Mabel and Alesha greeted her in excitement.

'Thank God you're back!' Ellie beamed.

'Why?' Jenna's brow furrowed.

'Because we've missed you,' said Mick simply.

'It's not the same without you here,' Alesha added.

'Are you okay, dear?' Mabel threw her a look of concern.

'Yeah.' Jenna nodded. 'Erm…where's Ben?'

'I'm here.' He came up behind her and strode to the fridge. He poured her a glass of wine. 'Did you have a nice time?'

His expression was blank. She took the glass from him, in apprehension. Was he still angry with her?

'Define nice.' She ran a finger round the rim of the glass.

'As in, a nice Christmas day with your *fiance* and future mother-in-law.' The room fell silent as everybody exchanged looks.

'No.' She shook her head. 'But I had an okay time with my ex-fiancé and non-prospective mother-in-law.'

Ben's head shot up. A collective gasp ran round the room as all eyes swivelled in her direction.

'So, you did it then, dear?' Mabel was the first to find her voice. 'How did she take it?'

'Jen? What's going on?' asked Ellie. 'Is the wedding off?'

'No, it's on,' said Jenna. 'But he's marrying Amber, the girl he was with at the contest. Not me.'

'The fucking bastard!' Ellie raced round the table and hugged Jenna. 'What an arsehole.'

Jenna eased her away. 'He's not. I called it off, but it's all worked out well for Jake. He's with the right person.'

She related the whole story while Ben's eyes bore into her. 'So, there you go,' she finished. 'I'm young-ish, free and single.'

'I'm glad,' said Mick. 'Luckily you both spoke up in time.'

'Yeah.' Ellie nodded. 'I never thought Jake was right for you. There's somebody out there who is though!'

Jenna stared at the table as everyone turned to Ben. She could feel his gaze still on her, but she was unwilling to meet it yet.

'I take it this was decided long before today?' He said quietly. 'You knew the wedding was off…this morning?'

'Of course.' She lifted her face to meet his. 'It happened weeks ago, but I kept quiet because Jake asked me to. I don't like breaking promises,' she added pointedly.

'Right.' He scraped back his chair. 'Can I have a word with you…in private, J?'

She followed him into the other room. He raked a hand through his hair. It stood on end as if he'd had an electric shock. Fighting the urge to flatten it down she raised her eyebrows.

'You wanted to talk to me?'

'I'm sorry for judging you, J. I should've known you wouldn't mess around behind anyone's back.' He moved towards her. 'I wanted to take you in my arms this morning and carry you upstairs when you kissed me. In fact, the truth is, I've wanted to do that since I first set eyes on you.' His eyes twinkled. 'But I've kept quiet because you were with Jake.'

Jenna took a step back. 'Ben, I guess you know —'

'That came out wrong.' Ben cut in. 'I don't just want you for sex. I've, well, I've fallen for you. I can't stop thinking about you and hate it when you're not there.'

She studied him in silence. It was hard to put the thoughts that had been going round her head into cohesive sentences.

'I've made you feel uncomfortable.' Ben put his head in his hands. 'Of course you don't feel the same. Can we forget I said anything?'

'Ben.' She took his hands from his face. 'I love you, like, mega love you, idiot.'

He gaped and moved to grab hold of her. She held her hands in front of her to stop him.

'But,' she continued. 'My head's been such a mess. You know it has with…everything. I don't want to rush into anything. Especially not with you. I need to make sure it's the right thing before we take it any further.'

'But you've just said you love me.' He frowned. 'I love you too. What's the problem?'

'Me.' She sighed. 'This is going to sound weird, I know, but I need to find myself again. I've kind of got lost along the way. I love what we've been doing with the music and don't want anything to spoil that, or our friendship. And, most of all, I need to figure out what I want from life. All these years my only goal was to somehow keep the house. I thought it was what my parents would want but I couldn't have been more wrong.'

Ben caught the tear trickling down her cheek with his forefinger. 'Go on,' he said, softly.

'I love the house and what it stood for.' Jenna sniffed. 'But I don't know whether a fresh start is the way forward. Selling it will be horrendous, yet part of me thinks it's the right thing to do.'

'You don't need to rush a decision like that.' Ben cupped her chin with his hand.

Jenna continued 'And seeing all my old friends again made me realise it's not too late to continue with some form of studying. Not going back to uni, that part of my life is definitely gone, and that's the way I want it.' She wiped her eyes. 'But there's loads of other things I can do. Study from home, do a course at the local college. I don't know, but I need time to work out what's best for me. Can you understand that?'

'Yes,' he whispered in her hair. 'And I think you're right. I want the best for you too. Even if that doesn't include me.'

'Oh, but I have a feeling it will.' She smiled. 'Can I ask you a question?'

'Yeah.'

'How would you feel if I poured wine in here?' She traced the cleft in his chin with her finger. 'And drank from it? With you lying down, obviously. I mean, hypothetically, in the future.'

'Would it turn you on?'

'Yes.'

286

'Then no.'

No?

'No?'

'No. Not now. As you say, maybe in the future. If and when the time's right. For you.'

She nodded. 'Okay.'

'Can I ask you a question now?'

'Yeah.'

'How would you feel if I kissed you? You know, just because it's Christmas, like you said this morning.'

'Would it turn you on?'

'Is this a trick question?'

'Yes.'

'In that case, it wouldn't turn me on at all.'

'Okay, do it!'

Their lips met and moved together slowly. Jenna's legs buckled under her. She held onto him tighter for support. He groaned, and kissed her harder, before dragging his mouth from hers and holding her at arm's length.

'Wow! Merry Christmas.' He grinned. 'Santa's been good to me this year. I must've been a good boy.' He picked up her hand and kissed it. 'And I promise to continue to be...unless you tell me otherwise.'

'Come on.' She smiled. 'I didn't eat my first dinner of the day. I'm starving.'

They walked into the kitchen hand in hand. Jenna saw the delighted expressions in front of her.

'We're taking it slowly,' she said. 'We understand each other. So, leave it for now guys. If and when anything changes you'll all be the first to know.'

'It already has.' Alesha clapped her hands. 'My work here is done.'

'No!' Jenna's eyes widened. 'No, Alesha, you can't go yet. I don't want you to!'

'I'll have to go soon.' Alesha wrapped her arms round Jenna. 'I can't stay forever.'

'But, wait to see…what happens.' Jenna buried her face in Alesha's hair. 'Please!'

'I'll give you until the date,' Alesha whispered. 'The seventh of May. That's my cut-off point.'

'Okay. Maybe that's a good timescale for me.' It would give her plenty of breathing space to think. And she knew that whatever path she was on at that point would be the right one. Out of the corner of her eye, she saw the smiling faces of her parents shining from the Christmas tree baubles. Just as she'd seen the face of Alesha all those months ago from the crystal on the curtain pole. 'I don't think I'll be lost anymore by then, Alesha. It's going to hurt, but that's when I'll let you go.'

Jenna looked around at the happy faces, as she ate. It felt as if a weight had been lifted from her shoulders. Being surrounded by her favourite people in the world was all she needed. But she accepted that things would change. Life had a way of moving constantly. Like a chapter of a book. Nothing stayed the same, but that didn't mean she couldn't find her happy ending.

Right on cue, Mabel spoke, 'Can I give some gifts out now? I know we said we'd wait until later, but I can't!'

'Okay,' said Jenna with a smile. 'I can't thank you enough for mine. Just as you said I'd given you your life back, well, you've done the same for me, and opened so many doors.'

'Good.' Mabel handed Ellie an envelope. 'It's for Mick too. Open it.'

'A voucher for an airline.' Ellie waved it in the air. 'Wow! Thanks, Mabel!'

'Blimey, I don't know what to say,' said Mick gruffly. 'A round the world ticket. That's so generous of you.'

'It's open-ended, so you can take off when you like. Show Ellie some of the wonderful places you've been to, Mick. She deserves it. She's a good girl.'

'Yes, she is.' Mick pulled her to him. 'And I don't mind saying in front of you all, she's the one for me.'

'That's great, I'm happy for both of you.' Jenna smiled. 'I know you'll look after her, Mick.'

'This is for you, Ben.' Mabel dug deep into her bag. 'And Jenna, too.'

Ben's eyes widened. 'Look, J, it's a recording voucher. We can record our own album in a proper studio.'

'Cool! That's amazing, Mabel. Thank you so much.'

'Oh, it's for me really.' Mabel chuckled. 'I want a copy. Hearing Ben's husky voice singing to me every night, well, what can I say? I'm being totally selfish.'

They all laughed. Mabel held up her hand. 'One more thing. For you, Ellie. I've paid for you to do an online writing course. And before you thank me, I'm being selfish there too.'

'How do you mean?' asked Ellie.

'Well, dear, with due respect, I'm tired of hearing about Elizabeth turning off her bloody alarm clock in paragraph one…I'd love you to progress beyond the first page before I finally croak it!'

Chapter Twenty-Nine

Jenna linked arms with Ben as they turned to watch Amber make her grand entrance. She wore a dress in complete contrast to the one Jenna had chosen. As Amber got closer, a bubble of laughter rose from the pit of Jenna's stomach, until finally erupting from her mouth. She bent double as people turned and tutted, then wiped the tears from her eyes.

'Are you okay, J?' whispered Ben in concern. 'Is it harder than though thought it would be, seeing Jake marry someone else?'

'No.' She grinned. 'It's the dress. All I'll say is that Mona will be happy. She was determined to get her way on that one.'

At least Amber looks like a pretty snowman!

Jenna had given being there a lot of thought. But there was no reason not to witness Jake's happiness. The room was festooned in the red Mona had decided on. It did look pretty, Jenna conceded.

As the guests congregated in the bar, prior to the meal, Jenna took the opportunity to speak to the bride and groom.

'Congratulations both of you.' She grinned. 'The service was lovely.'

'Thanks.' Amber beamed. 'And thank you for coming.'

'Yes, it means a lot.' Jake bent to kiss Jenna's cheek. 'I hope you can be as happy as I am, Jenna.'

She looked up at Ben. 'I'm getting there.'

Since Christmas day, Ben had stuck to his word. He seemed to sense when Jenna wanted to be alone and when she needed company. But he'd refrained from mentioning their relationship since then. Yet each time they locked eyes, something unspoken passed between them. Even when they were cooking together, which they'd been doing more and more, they found a sensual element to simple things like reaching for a spoon. As their hands brushed, the volt of electricity got stronger.

Ben held out his hand to Jake. 'Congratulations, mate.' Jake took it without hesitation.

'You too. You've got a wonderful girl there. Look after her.'

'I will,' said Ben. 'If that's what she wants.'

'We're going now, Jake.' Jenna smiled. 'There's things we need to discuss. But we'll catch up after you get back from honeymoon, okay?'

'You sure you want to leave?' said Ben.

'Yes.' She nodded. 'But I need to speak to Mona first.'

'Hello, dear.' Mona looked elegant and in her element. 'It's nice that you came.'

'I wouldn't have missed it,' said Jenna. 'And for what it's worth, Mona, you've done a fabulous job. Everything's perfect...and if it had been my wedding, I'd have been delighted.'

291

They exchanged smiles and promised to see each other soon. Jenna was surprised to realise that she did in fact want to keep in touch. It was different now that they weren't going to be related and in each other's pockets.

As they strolled through the maze-like cobbled streets of York, Jenna not only saw, but felt too, what she loved about the city. The majestic minster, the unique little boutique shops, the street entertainers and open-air cafes, perfect for watching the world go by.

But it would all be here when she returned. She pointed to a bench. 'Come and sit down, Ben. There's something I need to say.'

'Am I going to like it?'

'Depends whether you still want me. I've kept you waiting. Have I left it too late?'

He turned to look at her, a huge smile lighting up his face. 'I'd have waited for ever for you, J.'

She rested her head against his shoulder. 'I didn't mention this before, because I wasn't sure. But Mick knows a guy who owns a club in Spain. He's looking for new acts for the summer season. Apparently Mick sent some videos from his phone of us performing. The guy is keen to book us.'

'You're kidding!' Ben looked incredulous. 'That's fantastic!'

'I didn't know what you'd think. You'd have to give up your job. I wasn't staying in mine anyway.'

'That's fine. It's time for us to live a bit, J. Take a few chances. I can always get another job doing what I do, when we come back. *If* we do.' He laughed.

'I hope you don't mind me speaking to Mick about it, Ben, but he says if we do go, he and Ellie will look after the house while we're gone. When we return, the two of them will use Mabel's ticket and do a bit of travelling. Ellie's going to ask if she can take a month off work apparently.'

'It shouldn't be too much of a problem, if she saves up her annual leave,' said Ben. 'The boss is okay.'

'I can't believe we're actually doing it.' Jenna gasped. 'Blimey. I've already decided about other stuff too, Ben.' She lifted her head to face him. 'I'm going to sell the house. Maybe next year, once all of us are sorted. Ellie's husband is buying her out of their house, and the divorce is going ahead. I think she and Mick will end up getting somewhere of their own.'

'You sure about the house?' His forehead creased.

'Yes. A fresh start all round. I'm going to buy somewhere smaller and more modern. And do a college course.' She smiled. 'But first, I want to spend summer in Spain. Sun, sangria, sea…and you.'

'Hey, I can think of another S word to add to your list.' He winked.

'I knew I'd forgotten one.' She tapped her head. 'But can I ask you to wait just two more weeks? We've waited this long. I want to —'

Ben held his finger over her lips. 'I know, J. Me too. What better time to start our new life together, than…then. You know you said that you couldn't imagine wearing your wedding dress in front of Jake?'

'Yes.' Jenna nodded.

'Could you imagine wearing it in front of me? You know, hypothetically.'

'Yes, Ben, I could. Hypothetically.'

They ambled back along the river, stopping every few steps to kiss. Jenna halted at a row of daffodils dancing in the breeze. She took out her phone and set the video to record them.

'Symbolic?' Ben bent to touch them gently.

'Yes. I didn't think it was possible to be this happy,' said Jenna. 'I hope it's not going to be snatched away.'

'Hey, don't talk like that!' Ben gripped her shoulders. 'This is our time now, and nothing's going to stop us. Right?'

'Right.' She stood on tiptoe and kissed his chin. 'Come on, I'm ready to tell the others our plans now.'

'Are you sure you're going to be alright, Mabel?' Jenna crouched by her feet. 'I'm really going to miss you.'

'I'll miss you too, dear, but we can send e-letters. The time will soon go, and you'll be back.'

'Ellie and Mick will be keeping a close eye on you until then, madam, so behave.' Jenna grinned. 'You are happy about all the stuff I've decided, aren't you? You're not just saying that?'

'I'm delighted, dear. Stop fretting. Now, leave me in peace to listen to my wonderful CD again. That was the best money I've ever spent. I still can't believe you both wrote a song about me and recorded it!'

'I'm really going to miss you, Ellie,' said Jenna. 'You're sure about the divorce and Mick, aren't you? I want you to be happy.'

'Yes. I love Mick.' Her eyes shone. 'And I told you I needed someone with eyes far apart, cheekbones not too high, fairly long ears and medium to long lips. That's Mick, Jen!'

Jenna thought back to the grotesque picture Ellie had drawn the previous year. That Frankenstein lookalike bore no resemblance to the handsome Mick. But if Ellie was happy then so was she. 'Hey, if you got married you'd be my auntie.' She giggled.

'Yeah, I'd get to boss you about.'

'And buy me presents and spoil me.'

'Whatever! Mick and I will fly out to see you for a long weekend soon. We're so excited for you.'

'Everything's worked out fine.' Jenna smiled. 'Against all the odds. We couldn't have wished for better.'

Two weeks later, Jenna lay with her eyes squeezed shut. She waited for the familiar pain to engulf her. Six years. Her eyes began to sting. Then a strange thing happened. A smile tugged at her lips. If they were to get on that plane tomorrow, she needed to finish packing. But the main things were already in her case: photos she'd found on her dad's camera, which had luckily been in the loft. It would be impossible to take them all, of course. She wanted the plane to leave the ground. But she had a pile, all showing her and her parents smiling and laughing. She heard the faint voice of her mother instructing her in what else needed to go in the case. Then she heard the clicking of her dad's camera. They'd be going with her. She felt sure they wouldn't be far away, wherever she was, or whatever she was doing.

Alesha appeared and sat on the bed. 'Come here.' She beckoned to Jenna.

'No!' She shook her head. 'Because if I do, you're going to tell me I won't see you again. I can't bear it, Alesha.'

'Jenna.' She held out her hand. Jenna reluctantly took it. 'I do have to go today. But you'll be fine. You're off on an exciting new adventure.'

'I know,' said Jenna. 'But I'll still miss you.'

'I won't be disappearing from your life forever.' Alesha smiled. 'I'll come back one day, to see how you and Ben are getting on.'

'When?'

'This date next year,' Alesha promised. 'Now, go and make sure Ben has packed everything he needs. 'Don't worry, I'll see you before you go.'

Jenna nodded, and dived under the shower. Her body had healed and was smooth and soft. She smiled to herself and tied her robe around her waist then made her way to Ben's room. She tapped on the door.

'Can I come in?'

He opened the door and stood aside to let her through. 'How are you feeling, J? You okay?'

'Strangely enough, I am. We've come such a long way from this time last year, haven't we?' She perched on the end of the bed. 'Although I'll always be sad on this date, I'm going to see it as a positive time too. It's the start of our new life, Ben. We'll never forget the old one, but it's time for us to move on.' She pulled him down beside her. 'And you know what? I don't feel guilty anymore. I know it wasn't my fault. The only thing I was guilty of was wanting Mum and Dad there for an important time in my life. I'd be feeling a lot guiltier if I hadn't wanted them there, and shut them out. They knew how much I loved them, and still do. I'm going to look forwards, not back, for them.'

'You're so right. I'm not to blame for anything either. Alesha wasn't concentrating it's as simple as that. She'll always be special, and I'm sad she died, but I'm not to blame. Here, I've got something for you. I wanted you to have it today.'

Jenna took the bag from Ben and gasped. She took out the pot daffodil and held it against her chest. 'I love it.'

'Look.' He pressed a switch on the base. It began dancing. 'I know it's not the real thing, but when you're sad look at it, and remember how happy you were when you stopped to take that video.'

'Come here.' Jenna pulled him closer. 'We've waited long enough.'

'I'm afraid we'll have to wait another couple of minutes.' Ben grimaced. 'Not romantic, I know, but I need to empty my bladder.'

She laughed, then jumped when Alesha appeared. 'I have to —'

'Don't say it,' Jenna whispered. 'I know. Alesha, Mum and Dad will know I'm in Spain, won't they? I don't want them looking for me and not knowing where I am.'

'They know, don't worry. Right, be happy and look after each other.' Alesha hugged her. The electric shock feeling of touching Alesha had become normal. But this time it was different. More powerful, and Alesha was slowly fading from sight.

'See you next year. The seventh day of May.'

Ben came back into the room. Jenna could just make out Alesha's outline, which glowed. She watched as Alesha kissed Ben on the cheek and whispered something in his ear. He turned his face slightly and a smile lit up his face. He turned back to Jenna, and took her into his arms, pushing her gently back onto the bed.

'Where were we?'

Over Ben's shoulder she caught a final glimpse of Alesha walking from the room backwards, hands covering her eyes. She heard a faint, 'I'm off before you go any further!'

'Don't forget to come,' Jenna whispered.

'Thanks for reminding me, J,' said Ben, a smile in his voice, 'but I think I'll remember.'

10723875R00180

Printed in Great Britain
by Amazon.co.uk, Ltd.,
Marston Gate.